The Boat That Brings You Home

Set in the Sultry Caribbean Sea

BONNIE KOGOS

authorHOUSE®

AuthorHouse™
1663 Liberty Drive
Bloomington, IN 47403
www.authorhouse.com
Phone: 1 (800) 839-8640

Published by AuthorHouse 06/17/2019

ISBN: 978-1-7283-0840-1 (sc)
ISBN: 978-1-7283-0838-8 (e)

Library of Congress Control Number: 2019904557

Print information available on the last page.

The Boat That Brings You Home

Adventure, Daring, Romance,
Resiliency, and Survival…at Sea

A full-blooded, salty, sinuous Caribbean sailing
adventure begins with an idyllic atmosphere of
beauty and delight. Rainbows and sunsets steadily
darken, approaching daring challenges through
incidents of brutal, murderous fury. This well-
conceived tale of sailing offers action and observation
that only a seasoned sailor can provide. Settle in for
disbelief, for more than a rollicking adventure.

Living upon the sea.

NOTE WELL, YEE WHO EMBARK

Also by Bonnie Kogos

Manitoulin Adventures: *I was Mistaken for a Rich, Red, Ripe Tomato* (2001)

Manhattan, Manitoulin (2012)

Dedication

For Alan Phillips

Scattered by the wind, in different
ports, are all my teachers,
from writing, to sailing, to love. The
ocean has been good to me.
Upon it, I found a loving home
on a graceful sailing ship.
I surely know that on the sea, home is only temporary,
those vast forces pulling and shaping human
destiny, and those of my loved ones.
What a bracing, wind-stung time it was.
Starlight, silence and love.
When the ocean was heaven, I was a rider on the tide.

***

While wistfully wondering what would await me
in the weird, wonderful williwaws of the West Indies,
I wearily wandered my way, while the
world whispered a weighty warning,
in the wild, woolly Western wind.

George Baumgarten, Barbados 1988

Welcome Aboard

In St. Croix, the U.S. Virgin Islands, three sailors sat aboard their own beloved boats, sharing a sensuous, romantic dream of plying the magical islands of the Caribbean. Their beautiful boats, anchored next to each other, gently rocked on the rolling swells, dazzling in the tropical sun.

What a glamourous new world to be in. What could go wrong?

Aboard Yacht *Quadriga*, Amy, the daughter of a Harvard professor, originally came to New York City to develop her life's dream of finding a singing career. Yet she has found Captain Quentin "Dutch" Teerstrat, on his forty-foot Hinckley B40 yawl. Far more love and adventure than she's ever planned…

Yacht *Bravo's* Captain Beth, a Harvard Business School scholar, with her First Mate and husband Brad, have chucked their business suits and Wall Street, and are at the beginning of their sail around the world. Their unsinkable, well-stocked sloop was originally constructed for a rich couple with no expense spared. It was sold to a Captain Poole, then to Beth and Brad. Built on a long keel, it had sturdy teak decks with mahogany on oak. Brass scuttle gimbaled oil lamps hung throughout. A bright and rigorous young couple, ready for any ocean.

Aboard Yacht *Zephyr*, Zoe, laughing, has trained herself to sit still and learn how to sew. In New York City, at the peak of her career, she paid people to sew for her. By exquisite chance, she met Captain Zebeder, from Manitoulin Island in Northern Ontario, on a friendly dock in the Caribbean. Invited aboard to sail on his fifty-foot Germain Frers' designed ketch, she's fearful, having taken such a daring physical and emotional plunge at middle age, to change her entire life. For love. Her mother declared Zoe has been rescued; oh please. Zoe wonders if he's too good to be true. He is private, and hates going ashore. She has always dealt with many people. Does she have the courage, strength, and smarts to begin such a new adventure? Afloat, she is.

The beautiful boats, docked side-by-side-by-side, offer adventure of life aboard in the Caribbean. Who knows what awaits? Which boat may sail to destruction, which may be boarded and which will be troubled in a different way, all in Paradise?

Will events and intrigue alter and
enmesh their lives forever?

Dare to venture aboard?

Permission Granted.

Prologue

Many Years later....

"Amy darling, why'd you call me and Beth to get here so fast?"

"It's thirty years. Not all truths need to be told," Beth whispered.

"Look what's printed in the New York Post!"

"We've been dealing with this for years," Zoe grouched. "Hasn't success been the greatest place to hide? We're way past any danger..."

"It's resurfaced again. Another goddamn story about the disappearance of two well-known island men from Antigua and Montserrat," Amy said, showing them the page in the newspaper. "Drug smuggling, and again, the legend of a red sailboat carrying cocaine, with people pretending to be touring sailors, charterers..."

"Current news is so boring. Don't they have anything else to write about?"

"We deserve to be alive, but I still can't cut a piece of steak."

Amy's lovely Fifth Avenue apartment overlooked Central Park's green vistas. Beth poured the wine, while Zoe stuck to her glass of water and lemon. Amy and Beth were in their fifties, Zoe in her late seventies; each one, vigorous, beautiful and healthy. Worried.

"There's more," Amy said. "An exhausted wreck, a small boat, turned up off the cost of Belize. An ancient Oldport 26 foot yacht club launch. They found a partial identification number, which, they believe, has led them to an ancient ownership. There was the mystery of three ropes trailing off the back of this boat. Authorities are examining the boat to see if there's any clues or DNA."

"It's only the boat. Nothing else."

"Those terrifying demands on us, "Amy sighed. "We couldn't have done it any other way."

"Remember how your instinct and cunning saved us."

"We deny we're animals, until we become prey," Zoe said, with unashamed frankness. "But I'll never fail to recall the terror!"

"I wish my father's psychiatrist hadn't died. He was so helpful, and we can't talk to him," Amy wailed. "Or my dad's lawyers."

"Hey, they're all dead. We got nothing."

The three smiled bleakly, completely absorbed that they could only relax when they were together.

"We had such precious times," Zoe said, "Great sailing and for me, romance..." All our adventure, loving, sailing..."

"We can never tell the truth."

"We can't change the past. We've been working on changing our interpretation of what it all meant. You know there's no truth," Beth declared. "We're all accidents, even our accidents. We're a mixture of hope, fantasy, illusion...."

"People think we thrived aboard our sailboats."

"We did," Amy said. "We became warriors."

"We were efficient. Our weapons came from our men and our hearts."

"Corny, Amy. I still can't believe we got away with it."

"Sure you can. Courage. Stupidity! Luck! Stop being saturated by the past, you two," Beth demanded. "We're so far away from this. Sailing's different today. Have you read my latest report on mini-subs! They're towed by sonar rays with long cables, covered with underwater microphones and dragged behind a ship, mini-submarines can be detected in deep water. Carrying large dope shipments."

"The paradox is that we're alive," Zoe said.

"Zoe darling," Beth commanded. "As Shakespeare said to Hamlet, and I demand of you, dearest friend, do not pluck out the heart of our mystery!"

"We've gone beyond this: Zoe, you're a well-known Canadian music critic!"

"How'd we get away with all of it?"

"Jimmy always knew I kept something from him."

"There's got to be a statute of limitations? Pour me another glass!"

"Please, Zoe, all the strength and radiance in our sailing lives were brought to bear on us, Amy cajoled,

"And we made it though. We were three willing riders on the tide…"

"Amy," Zoe snorted, "You're writing another hit song, aren't you!"

Chapter One

**Logbook: of *Yacht Quadriga*: Dock
B in Stamford, CT. May, 1980**

Name	Location	Latitude	Longitude
Quadriga	Yacht Haven, Stamford, CT	41° 2.144'	73° 32.003'
	Cedar Town Beach Cove, Mt. Sinai, NY	40° 57.729	73° 01.575
	Yacht Haven, Stamford, CT	41° 2.144'	73° 32.003'

The boat slip was empty. She stood on the dock, feeling empty, herself, her shoulders. Drooping. Stepping back, her 24-year-old sized-ten foot, slammed a piece of metal off the dock.

Splash.

"That's one hundred bucks!" Who shouted at her? Watching from his boat in the next slip, a large fellow, handsome, muscular, totally amused, wearing only his red speedo, jumped off his deck and quickly stood on the dock, towering over her. Forced to retreat, Amy Sandler's foot hit another piece of gear.

Splash! Off the dock. Into the water.

"One clumsy broad," the deckhand snorted. "Three strikes against you! Two machines, and you couldn't be here on time? Crane's my pal. Anyone who disturbs him, has to deal with me. The day's so breezy, I wouldn't have waited for you either."

While soft winds blew along Dock 11 did not buoy her up, Amy pushed long brown hair out of her sweating face. How dare this giant swear at her? Of course, she respected Bert Crane, her boss at the Tiny Tot Book Club. His was the first interview she'd been sent on when she came to New York City from Cambridge two years earlier. Happily, he hired her immediately, approving of her English major degree from Radcliffe, which enabled her to direct the sale of children's books, and to deal with authors. She loved her job, selecting books, and even put on jeans to pack 3,000 books each month for delivery to subscribers. Mr. Crane acknowledged Amy often, her diligence. Membership kept growing; soon, they were able to pay others to pack the books.

Quentin gazed down at the tall, slim, silent young woman, looking away from him, into the harbor. He smelled, oddly an old perfume, Bellodgia. His mother had worn that, and he breathed in the memory, compelling him to take a closer look at this strikingly beautiful girl. As she turned toward him, her angelic face looked up. He took another a deep breath, and a step back. Framed by long brown hair, her head was well placed on a graceful neck. Struck was the word that came to his mind. He looked down to behold long well-shaped legs in the shorts she wore. Damn. He didn't need this. Those long eyelashes, her smooth cheeks of youth.

The guitar case, still in her hand, was lowered carefully on the dock, her thoughts on her boss, how she had waited over a year to share with Mr. Crane, her self-produced album, titled *Seaside Dreams*. When he did hear her songs, he was delighted, insistent he introduce her to his friend, Sam Miller, a prominent record producer in New York. This afternoon, Sam Miller was aboard *Yellow Cat* with Bert Crane, sailing somewhere on Long Island Sound. At twenty-four, Amy had smartly sold four of her original songs to aspiring singers, which were recorded and published. Maybe this was too old to begin any singing career. She was more of a songwriter than performer.

"Forget the wood sanders. Crane's so rich, he'll never miss 'em." Demanding again, "Why are you so damn late?"

"Is this your business?" She shot back, deflated to be standing in front of the empty slip. Her guitar was safe. It hadn't gone off into the water. Her handbag was on her shoulder. Looking out beyond the harbor, all that water, she realized how thirsty she was. Raised as a kind, privileged young woman with good manners, she turned and spoke calmly to the rude, but handsome fellow, towering over her.

"Would you believe it was running water that kept me? As I was leaving, a pipe in my bathroom burst. It was bad. Luckily, Joe, my super, was home. Fixed it. I took a chance to get here. When I arrived at the Stamford train station, I found a taxi to Yacht Haven. But it didn't matter."

"Running water?" He said, stepping back, and laughed. She was interesting. "That kept you from sailing?" He had watched her lope down Dock B to find the slip where *Yellow Cat* was docked. "Please forgive my rude manners," he said, standing back, straightening up. He swallowed. "I'm Quentin, but please call me Dutch. That's my boat in the next slip."

"Who cares," she said under her breath. Her musical head working full time, around all these boats, she said aloud, "Sailor, seasoned, seaside, sailing."

Her music album, *"Seaside Dreams"* that she'd written, sung, played, and produced in Cambridge, was to be given to Mr. Miller. Ten original songs, copyrighted. She had worked steadily on Martha's Vineyard for many summers as a reliable waitress and good performer.

"Young lady, you all right?" She was far away; was this broad crazy? He knew she was in her own dream. She thought of Mario, her exacting, often obnoxious, but caring techie pal, in his Cambridge recording studio. "Amy, your songs are nice enough, but where will you sell them?"

"On the Vineyard," she declared. "Where I work."

"People buy your album to be nice to you," he smirked. "Be realistic. Thousands of singers and writers' creativity keeps a-rolling along."

"Mario, I've got to get to New York!"

"And leave me in Cambridge?"

"That's easy."

***

Her thoughts came back to Dock 11; this dangerously good looking fellow hovered over her. She blinked, looking up, pushing her hair out of her eyes.

"I apologize for my rudeness," Quentin said, strangely enamoured. "It'll be six 'til they dock. Come aboard my boat. Have some water."

She took an unsteady step back.

"Don't go wobbly on me," Quentin said, reaching out a muscular arm and wrapping it around her, bringing forth an erotic sensation, sensually from his skin to her skin. She wondered how this idiot, attractive in an overpowering way, could have such a beautiful boat. Did men have to have brains, smarts and good manners to earn and afford such a big boat in the next slip? Shyly, she looked up into his angular face, blue eyes, and a big nose accentuating his profile. The Indian on the old American nickel peered down at her. Well-built, well-made, good looking with blond hair, sure of himself.

However, Amy was glad to be steadied. She straightened up, and nodded thanks. She gazed beyond to the big sailboat behind him, the hull painted a bright tomato red, the boat's wood and polished stainless steel gleaming in the afternoon sun. The name, *Quadriga*, was painted on a horseshoe-shaped life preserver, the old fashioned way.

'Dutch' smiled at her, his blue eyes deep into hers. Stillness between them for a moment.

She stepped further back, away from him, seeing busy sailors on the dock talking, carrying equipment, all happy to be beside their sailboats. "All sailboats have radios. Would you mind calling Mr. Crane for me?"

"No can do. Radio's being repaired," Dutch said. "I've known Bert twenty years. As we got richer, our boats got bigger. Please come aboard and have a drink." Unsettled, she stood mute. "I'll be sailing soon and you're welcome to come. My friends will be here any minute. We're off to Port Jefferson where Bert usually anchors." He paused. "Hey, you don't have to be afraid of me," he said casually picking up her guitar. She stepped further away, this time losing her balance at the edge of the dock. Again, he caught her. "Lady, you're definitely safer on my boat than you are on any dock."

"Don't be so sure," she responded.

"I'll take excellent care of your guitar," he said gently, amused. "And you."

Mr. Crane had never mentioned a boat neighbor; was this a con? This hypnotically handsome fellow who was rude. But maybe he'd take her to the producer; she'd gotten this far. Why resist a warm May afternoon? Without waiting for a nod from her, Dutch took her guitar case and carefully put it aboard. He helped her grab onto *Quadriga's* rails. She gingerly stepped aboard the deck, solid beneath her feet.

"Look at these large decks!" His mood was joyful: "She's one of the first fiberglass-hulled yawls made by Hinckley in Maine. I was lucky to get her second-hand. Fixed every part of her myself. I live for weekends, for winds that change in a minute, and the contentment after a good day's sail. A quiet cove to put the anchor down." With sudden childish delight, "I was told you write songs, say, maybe you'll write one about *Quadriga*."

"Unlikely," she thought. Who was this narcissist? She looked past him to watch a large powerboat pass behind his boat heading out of the marina. It held a big cockpit and two fishing chairs. The wake bounced them. "I hate powerboats," he declared.

"Dutch, traffic's the usual Sunday stink, sorry we're late!" His friends, Harry and Jackie Sloan, stood on the dock, looking up at Amy. Who was this gorgeous, young thing? Was she the latest in the long line of Dutch's dates? He'd been divorced for four years, still often grieving, defensive, edgy, and always outspoken. Amy looked at the couple standing on the dock, looking normal, ordinary. Safe.

"Hurry aboard, the wind's up and I've got to get this girl a cold glass of water!" She took it gratefully, and then sat in the cockpit. "Meet Amy, who missed one boat, and doesn't know yet — that she's found me!"

Amy nearly spit out the water. The Sloans hopped aboard with familiarity, bringing bags of food, stowing ice and drinks. Amy smiled wanly, longing to be part of something breezy. As they motored out of the slip, she sat in the cockpit, out of everyone's way. She looked down at the tranquil stir of the water. It was musical. What a lovely boat he had.

***

Out of the harbor, *Quadriga's* three sails went up. As breezes flowed continuously, Amy felt her burden of self-defeat lift, signalling contentment in the unexpected freedom of sailing in the warm May afternoon. She knew Dutch had taken to her, hadn't let her fall off the dock. She'd never been aboard a beautiful boat this size; the polished wood, the white sails, the comfortable cushions in the cockpit that invited you in. An hour later, sailing in the middle of Long Island Sound, her opinion of him shifted. Handling the wheel effortlessly, he looked at her, and there it was, a stillness and inquiry between them.

Harry kept talking about the mysterious forty-footer docked next to *Quadriga* some months ago. Scuttlebutt on the dock filtering from other sailboats that had been in St. Thomas, told of the boat captain being killed, the deckhands arrested for cocaine trafficking. The boat had been impounded, stripped, refitted, and resold oh so cheaply. It had been next to them for two months.

"You coulda, woulda, shouda," cajoled Dutch.

"Why, when I have your boat, Dutch, and you to sail it for me?"

"You wear a suit at the bank, and hate your job. I've got Paradise, right here."

"You're some bull shitter," Harry said affectionately.

***

Amy sat quietly in the cockpit, half-listening, watching Dutch move, easing a line here, adjusting a sail there, secure in his domain. He often smiled at her. Now more comfortable, she thought, okay, this is one day and I'm here. How glad she was to be in New York. She thought of her former life in Cambridge: vocal lessons, playing piano and guitar, her abiding childhood dream to be heard; to sing her stories, her songs. The CD, *Seaside Dreams*, had, respectfully, sold two hundred copies. And bought not out of pity. She had the voice, focus, and skills to produce it and nobody who heard it told her it was bad. She'd been written up in the Martha's Vineyard's newspaper. She remembered her mother saying, "Amy, you're a sweet, well-bred girl," when she informed her parents she was moving to New York City. "Take that teaching job in Belmont."

"Mom, it's 1980," Amy declared. "I'm already there."

***

Long Island Sound shimmered with flecks of bright afternoon sunlight. *Quadriga* sailed under gentle winds and easy seas. Why had she, with all her privileges, never been aboard such a sailboat as this? She came from a wealthy family, with education the main goal. Her life now... New York City, and today, Connecticut and Long Island Sound.

Dutch gave the wheel to Harry as they approached the Cedar Town Beach cove of Port Jefferson. After they anchored, he challenged, "Anyone for a swim? Who's not chicken?"

Her red bathing suit was in her duffel. Ready! The fancy Hinckley ladder, able to fold six ways, was lowered over the side. Dutch was first in, treading water by the ladder. Amy changed into her bathing suit and plunged in, immediately swimming a lap around the boat in long, practiced strokes, around back to him. Her long wet hair floated in tendrils around her bare shoulders.

"Hey, you're not a hot house flower," he gasped.

"Who said I was?" she said, happily splashing him. They swam together around the boat, Dutch's teeth chattering while he keenly observed the young lady swimming with sure strokes in front of him. She was something new, feline. A mermaid to this old guy? It shocked him that he wanted to earn her trust. And his eyes on her, electrifying him.

***

Back aboard, Dutch offered her a fresh hot-water shower on deck, specially made for the Hinckley. "These towels are Porthault in Paris," he informed her, as he wrapped the plush towel slowly around her shoulders. Drying off, she went below to the head, to change back into her clothes. Alone in the main cabin, she observed the polished teak table, bright red sailcloth cushions, piped in white, and four sleeping bunks on each side of the main cabin. Reading lights, with faded fluted shades from a bygone era, gave the salon an old sense of elegance. What a delight it must be to live aboard this miniature heaven, a sculpture on water. His time, love, and money put into *Quadriga*. Obviously elegant.

Amy peered into a corner of the salon to see a small black stove big enough to warm a dollhouse. Words engraved on it: "*Tiny Tot Stove*." She laughed; her job title was Director of the Tiny Tot Book Club; books for kids ages 3 to 7. The ship's clock chimed. She noted the key of C. She gazed at the navigation desk, with stacks of charts and an engine manual. She looked up at small, exquisite oil paintings hung on the bulkhead. Too bad Captain Dutch had no class.

Dutch stepped slowly down through the companionway and stood behind her. He saw that she lingered, clearly appreciating the decor and nuances of his boat. Amy turned and their eyes met. Feeling her cheeks flush, she quickly turned to dry her hair with the towel. He moved past her, opening cupboards to show her pots and pans in order. He held up a Limoges dinner plate with a red schooner motif. "My Aunt Bea has that pattern in her home in Cambridge!"

"Hey, a gal who knows Limoges!" He took down a Waterford crystal glass from the built-in rack. What a show-off, she thought, but admitted, "Your boat is lovely."

"I like only the best," he said, taking her hand lightly and leading her to the forward cabin. Opening the door, she saw a large, well-made triangular bed with pillows. Freshly made. This looked like a photograph in a design magazine. He turned to open a brass handle on a door to the head, showing a clean mirror on each wall, marble counter and basin, with fluted gold faucets. He then slid back a panel to display folded red towels. The boat was full of elegance.

***

"Come up, you two! Lunch," Jackie yelled from the cockpit, putting out turkey sandwiches, coleslaw, and pickles. Dutch came above and set dishes on a small, varnished table that lifted up into the cockpit. "I made this table and varnished it. Want to know the secret of perfect varnishing?"

"Stop showing off," Jackie said, winking at Amy. "It's lunch time!"

"I use a dozen pieces of sandpaper for every quart of varnish. I gave the cabin sole twenty coats, maybe thirty. That's the floor inside the boat, Amy."

"He's obsessed with *Quadriga*; we never hear the end of it," Jackie told Amy. "When we're finished with lunch, would you sing for us?"

"I'd be delighted." Dutch brought her guitar up. She tuned it and easily sang the sea shanty, *The Keeper of the Eddystone Light,* to applause. She moved into a blues tune she was working on, and saw Dutch take a big bite out of his sandwich, a slug of white wine and then close his eyes. She sang two more, and put the guitar away. They raised sails again to idyllic breezes.

She heard the ship's radio loud and clear: "*Quadriga, Quadriga*, Bert here. Back at the dock."

"Dutch, you creep, you lied! Your radio's not broken!"

"I'd have said anything to get you aboard."

***

Dutch expertly slid *Quadriga* back into her slip. *Yellow Cat* was berthed, her guests waiting. Mr. Crane greeted Amy happily, heard her excuse and introduced her to Sam Miller. "Would you please get your guitar?"

As his other guests talked while she sang, Amy thanked those summers that enabled her to sing amid drinking patrons in the restaurants. But Mr. Miller was polite, focused on her, and graciously took her album, saying he'd get back to her.

Dutch sat quietly, watching her. What was it about her? Even with people chatting around her songs, he loved that she was focused, powerful, and savored her phrases and notes. He heard her ambition through her potent communication as a musician. People stopped talking to listen now, as if they were all tasting her notes, her inner core of charming naïveté, and then, the next song, bitterly cynical. Who was she?

***

In the warm May evening, the thought of driving back to New York City in Sunday night traffic was untenable. "I've got steaks for dinner. Why don't you three stay for dinner and overnight?" He turned to Amy. "I'll drive you back in the morning. I promise not to come on to you! Just enjoy the boat. And sing again for us."

"Stay overnight? I don't even know you."

"Lady, I'm not jumping your bones," Dutch said, enjoying her prim face. "You're clearly from Boston. I purely want to share my boat with you."

***

The steak, cooked over the grill, was delicious. The potatoes and onions were done perfectly. The evening was breezy and warm while they ate, talked, and drank wine. Beautiful under the stars. Dutch had softened, becoming more interesting. Almost gentle. Not just a good looking older man with stories and a nice boat; how old was he, anyway? It didn't matter. He became more attractive. And funny. What is this, she thought, feeling comfortable and lighter; she never drank this much wine. She looked above to twinkling stars and lulled by the plink-plink-plink of the halyards, realized she had to get off this boat.

"Thank you," she said. "May I have my guitar? I work tomorrow. I'll take a taxi to the train."

"You're not taking a train home."

"Oh, but I am."

"Nope, I'll walk you down the dock, and hire a car for you," he said, reaching for his wallet. He certainly wasn't going to fight her. She gathered up her things, and they walked up the dock, this time, slowly. Dutch found a cab, gave the taxi driver a $100 bill, and closed the back door for her, smiling, as they drove away. Walking back to his boat, he said aloud, perhaps to *Quadriga*, "Who sent you into my life? You're already dangerous to my well-being."

***

Dutch phoned her office. "Amy, I don't wear suits. I produce colors of the rainbow. Currently, I have no significant other because nobody can stand me. Tonight, at seven, I'll pick you up for dinner."

As she listened, again, he became a pushy jerk.

"Amy, I like your voice, your songs. You're good for my forty-two-year-old, sarcastic, world-weary heart.

Yesterday, with all of us, was wonderful. You owe me one dinner. That's the least you can do for this old guy."

"I'm twenty-four and you're forty two. Doesn't that bother you?"

"Not at all. It's poetic," he said. "Pick you up at seven."

***

At seven, she buzzed Dutch up to the fifth floor and opened the door. He wore jeans and a clean shirt, gawking at her; "What's with the white pants and a navy blazer? You're dressed like a power boater going to a cocktail party?"

"What about your fancy linens from Paris?"

"Oh, please. Why not have the best! I stopped dressing like that twenty years ago. Here, take these," he said, handing her a bunch of fresh pink peonies. He walked past her to regard the high ceilings, her minimal furnishings, and the wide windows that overlooked Eighth Street. His presence filled the loft. "You already know what's going to happen! Any woman interested in a man knows within two minutes."

She turned, sharply; "Why did I let you come upstairs?"

"Is it your Boston accent, your lovely voice, your innocence or that you're tall and beautiful and don't seem to know it. It's been awhile since I've been interested in anyone." He smiled. "I confess, while I'm an acutely imperfect man, I do have a hypnotic effect on women."

"Dutch, it was fun yesterday aboard your boat. I'm willing to overlook your vanity. And your shit. I'll put on jeans. There's a nice Italian restaurant down the block."

***

"I've given up reading hard-copy newspapers," Dutch told her at dinner. "Newspapers are owned by conglomerated national media. There's minimal local content, too many political-alliance opinion pieces, and more conjecture and crystal-ball-gazing than 'news'. Sports take up an inordinate amount of page space, the cartoons are not funny, and the editorials are hardly thought provoking. Someday, I'll let you know what I really think."

He told her about his parents, immigrants from Holland who settled in New Jersey, worked hard in the clothing industry, and bought the factory. "I played basketball at Dartmouth. After my stint in the Army, I took over dad's business. Learned to sail on Greenwood Lake on my first Sunfish. I moved up to chartering sailboats in the Caribbean. My first serious sailboat, twenty feet, became too small. Now I'm forty-two and I have forty-foot *Quadriga*, the dream of my life. I can make any boat move!"

"I'm sure you can. With our huge age gap, why are you interested in me?"

"It's your charm, Amy. You're naïve and adorable," he said smiling. "There's definitely something of value between us. I need to tell you more. My dear ex-wife, Naomi, all we'd built together, we had to take apart. She's a terrific woman who hated sailing. She was patient in our divorce. She remarried, and thankfully, our son Nels, who's fifteen, is in great shape. Life's to be lived, not wasted. I do have quiet moods, however. I'm also extremely modest, an excellent sailor and provider," he said, taking a breath. "I pray you won't think I'm too old for you.'

"Is that prey or pray?"

"Come sailing with me next Saturday?"

"No, thanks. I perform at Freddy's Pub."

"Hey, I'm only asking for a day, not your life. I've work to do aboard. Bring your guitar, your music, and practice. There's serenity aboard. You might become an anchor woman."

"Unlikely," she said. "Be careful when you say that! Anchor woman, indeed!"

"By the way, I know Freddy," he said.

Engaged by his unexpected humor, his blunt observations and then, his own self-deprecation, Amy laughed.

"Yah, I might not want to go sailing with myself either,' Dutch said. "Sailboats without sailors have no dimension. A boat is a box, but not this one. *Quadriga* definitely took a huge liking to you. She's got a soul. She wants you to come and sing on Saturday. Fresh lobster will be waiting. Come on, you're a New England girlie," he said, smiling, as he took her hand for a moment across the table. "Take a chance!"

***

Odd, wasn't it, that Freddy had her perform Friday and didn't need her Saturday night.

"I'll pick you up at 9 a.m."

"By any chance, did you phone Freddy?"

"None of your business," he said.

***

While he sanded the toe rail, Amy sat in the cockpit, under the red and white awning, practicing scales and chord changes on her guitar. Aboard the spacious sailboat, there was an amiable flow between them, with his silence, her songs, and later with jokes. He often looked at her, as if with a secret caress. Since the weather turned, no wind, he suggested, "We're ready for the lobsters. Would you please consider staying over? You'll have the fore cabin and head. Complete privacy. A shame to drive back to the city."

Twinkling stars in the beautiful night beguiled her. He set up the forward cabin for her, yet thinking her ingenuousness was hard to believe. Was he too old, too seasoned, brash and arrogant for this young woman? Well, he earned every part of his life, a thriving business and time to sail. His kid was healthy. He had no patience for stupid, whiny people. How he adored his sailboat, his soul boat. This young lady, what could he offer her? This prim, prissy woman from Cambridge, Mass, with enormous musical talent, who thought she was becoming a New Yorker. This was too interesting to rush. He put on Beethoven's Seventh Symphony. If he took his time and wasn't sarcastic, he might share an abundance of joy with her. Maybe love her. He'd get a haircut. Maybe she'd love him back.

***

All afternoon, her songs permeated the boat. At dinner, they dug into the lobsters, bibs on, and drank Chardonnay, talking easily. She told him about her parents and her sister. After a while, he took the dishes, washed them, put a movie on and returned to her. "May I put my arm around you, Amy?"

"What's happened to you? You're getting polite?" she said, allowing herself to subtlety nestle against him. Aware of the sensation of his skin next to hers. Not so fast. Why would she want him? How old was too old? While waiting for news from the record producer, Dutch and *Quadriga* could be pleasant diversions.

***

Wednesday brought the returned music cassette to Amy's office with a letter and a respectful thought-provoking decline. His assessment: you have a sweet voice, excellent musical skills, but you require more *edge*. And, because she worked for Bert Crane, she was, indeed, welcome to send him her next music collection.

Edge? What the hell was that? Amy studied the word; authority, the brink or brim, power, ability. Okay, each knock was a step forward. She kept mulling, couldn't get at it, and then became grateful for his assessment of her skills. And lack of them. She performed at Freddy's Pub regularly; a sweet storyteller. No edge. Gratefully, at her performances, though she felt deflated, she received satisfactory applause. How was she going to get at and develop edge?

Chapter Two

Name	Location	Latitude	Longitude
Quadriga	Yacht Haven, Stamford, CT	41° 02.144'	73° 32.003'
	Long Island Sound vicinity, NY and CT	41° 04.937'	72° 51.268'

Clearly, Dutch had a pull on her with his sweet, foolish grin. He was funny, bright, and knowledgeable, a voracious reader. He gave her books to read, told her stories about sailing, about business, and charmed her. In a series of spirited conversations, she was ready to believe his stories and opinions, and at other times, to set his beliefs aside. Life, she told her sister Charlotte on the phone, now felt in Technicolor.

"Bluntly, Charlotte," she reported, "Dutch's a strong, beautiful man with a boat. He makes me laugh and teases me about being a polite naïve New Englander."

Dutch felt crafty, smitten, ultra-careful, not to tip her by any comments, or suggestiveness, into any rejection. By now, she had sailed with him for three full weekends, polite, staying aboard in her own cabin. No rush. He forced himself to be patient.

This weekend, the beginning of June, had more exquisite weather. All sails were up as they made eight to ten knots, *Quadriga* reaching. The mizzen, mainsail and genoa were full. By now, she'd learned to tie a square knot, a double-stopped, a bowline, and a square knot. When they were under sail, and the sails made a loud flap or the boom hammered, it meant that the wind had changed direction. She learned to varnish, how to take an instant shower, and to make her way around the boat under sail. She smiled often, realizing her buttocks became the seat of her stability. She learned to stand at the bow, hold a line, and jump off, praying to reach the dock. All of this unaccountably absorbed her. She loved the smell and constant movement of the sea.

"Great, you are holding our course in a close reach," Dutch said, "You're a born sailor."

"Don't puff me up!"

Yet, she felt exulted and enveloped by the wind, and Dutch's gaze. Musical Amy heard for herself, a new harmony in sailing, the wind, the majesty of the waves. Were sailboats animated, feeling this strong and breezy along with their masters? *Quadriga* heeled to starboard, wind coming over forward of the port beam. At the helm, he counseled, "The boat's only obstinate if you struggle with her. Let *Quadriga* be and she'll take care of you. Trust her. This boat of mine sails beautifully on the water she was made for. She's a pure-bred champion of the seas. She's in my soul. You keep seeing this, don't you?"

Amy looked up at him with happy, affectionate eyes, her spirit breathless as the wind surged, holding the wheel in constant discovery.

***

They were sailing on weekends, now one month. She didn't feel he was too old, or she too young. They made a joke of twenty-four and forty-two, meeting in the middle.

By dusk, they entered a small cove. He was glad to be the only boat at anchor. She stood at the wheel, complying absentmindedly with his directions for setting the anchor. At his signal, she put the boat in reverse to dig in the anchor. He signalled for neutral and checked the line. Cut the engine.

Silence. Lovely.

"Bring up the chilled Chablis and two glasses," he directed. "Let's celebrate how well you handled the helm," he said quietly. "It's one lovely month that we've been sailing. I pray you have a sense of me that I'll never hurt you or take away any of your dreams."

Flushed with the success in their cooperation of sailing well together, she nodded happily. He poured the wine and toasted her. "To what we love the most!" He smiled, put down his wine glass, and hers, and softly allowed his fingers to trace the line of her cheek. He kissed her slowly. She sighed, her arms reaching around him.

"May I," he asked carefully.

She nodded, allowing him to unhook her bathing suit top.

"I love the wisps of your hair at the nape of your neck," he whispered, as he kissed her shoulder. "I love everything about you." He moved his hand slowly to her right small breast and caressed it. She breathed. Finally, this was happening. She felt desire, a wetness, anticipating… breathing… waiting… as his hand moved down to her waist. She loved his touch.

He helped her take off her bathing suit bottom. He took his bathing suit off. How beautiful his erection was. She caught her breath, hoping she'd be able to handle this with ease. How she wanted him inside her. She'd known two young men before, who helped relieve her of her virginity. Good, she thought, the act done for this late bloomer. Then each broke up with her.

She felt herself become wet, breathing deeply and allowing his hand to move to open her up. As dusk darkened and the wind flowed over them, he slowly, carefully, lay her down on the cockpit cushions. She looked up into his blue eyes, saying yes with her own.

"Amy, how I've waited for this. Please be ready for me? Do I need protection?"

"No, I'm okay and why are you so polite," she gasped, breathless.

"Now you don't want me to be polite? This is everything, Amy. Sharing, winning, accepting, giving, having, and learning...loving..."

"Stop talking."

He lay over her, holding his weight with his arms, and guiding his hard penis slowly and deep within her. They stayed still for a moment, and then rode together, seeming to sail above the anchored boat, and she gasped with ecstasy. Her cries of orgasm filled the air and went into the woods by the pond. Their boat, impossibly alone in the cove.

"Dutch, another one!" He slowed down. He could hold his strength for another minute or two, restraining his desire. This was too important, their first and unforgettable time. He was getting older. She was so young. He wanted this; he wanted everything. He wanted to give her everything. Her ardent sounds consumed his passion.

Her body raised, open, racing to another exquisite orgasm. She cried out with a beautiful sob, reaching above to the dark sky. As if her bow was plunging and rocking to a height she'd never experienced before.

Dutch had her, and as she fell limp underneath him, he drove into her, throbbing, feeling the rush of his own incredible orgasm. He was sovereign of the night, these precious, divine moments, pumping into her hunger and the beginning of love. She felt his strong cock caressing her inside, his arms around her, face near her, his smell.

As the heart rate of each slowed, they lay together on the cockpit cushions, holding each other silently. Fresh breezes blew over them. Aboard *Quadriga*.

Chapter Three

Name	Location	Latitude	Longitude
Quadriga	Yacht Haven, Stamford, CT	41° 2.144'	73° 32.003'
	Long Island Sound vicinity, NY and CT	41° 04.937'	72° 51.268'
	Block Island, NY	41° 10.945'	71° 34.495'
	Edgartown, Martha's Vineyard	41° 23.505'	70° 29.961'

Amy enrolled in a Celestial Navigation course at the New York Planetarium, wanting to learn how to take a reliable sight. In the auditorium, she sat next to friendly Beth Turner, a tall, solidly built redhead with her hair pulled back in a no-nonsense ponytail.

"My husband and I have a 30-foot sloop. We're living for the time we can leave for our circumnavigation. *Bravo*'s on the hard at Minneford's Boat Yard on City Island."

"What does it mean that the boat's on the hard?"

"A sailing term, meaning she is not on the water."

"Beth, aren't you afraid to sail around the world?"

"Are you kidding? Been waiting my entire life! I grew up aboard boats in Oyster Bay. I'm the only daughter with three smart-ass sailing brothers. My Wall Street father likes to play sea captain on weekends. To this day I out-sail my brothers. I can feel the wind. With my cheeks. I earned both my electrical and structural engineering degree from M.I.T. and a Master's Degree from Harvard Business School."

"Wow, Beth, you must know so much!"

"No one knows everything on the sea. I'm a humble, constant learner. I've researched waves and wave action, made conclusions and formulas about the wind and the tides that determine the force of waves. For fun, I make mathematical equations and formulas about the water and study the shipping routes of the freighters in our major oceans," Beth said matter-of-factly.

Amy laughed with delight, liking this young woman. "You're a genius!"

She giggled. "An egghead, Amy. Attending the Business School, I was a nerd. All I did was study and eat. The only way I met men was to tutor them. One day, I was sitting on a park bench, eating an ice cream cone from Brigham's, chocolate, and Brad sat next to me. His was vanilla. He had that elegant Kennedy, New England look, with a charming down-east accent from Maine. He was in one of my classes, the one he hated. He knew I got A's. Everyone knew I got A's. As he licked that ice cream cone, I stared at that mouth, that face. He was soft spoken. It was spring, the air sweet, the ice cream rich; I fell in love with him that afternoon."

Beth took a breath. "As a Radcliffe grad, you know how stuck up these good-looking smarties from the rich families that attend the B. School can be! Inflated with themselves. He wasn't. Adding to this, he told me his sturdy New England family sailed along fog-bound shores. I told him about our boats. We had four. It took me less than twenty minutes to offer to tutor him. He coughed for three minutes. What had I done? Then he blew his nose, cleared his throat, and told me he had asthma. So what! He was real, authentic from the start."

"More," Amy begged.

Beth smiled. "Brad was not only indebted to me for getting him through school, he fell in love with me. Oh, was I was surprised. I was being my natural egg-headed self, though I often kept my mouth shut and became girly. You can see I'm not girly. I got the courage to bring him home to Oyster Bay. My brothers wanted to take him sailing. Haze him. I warned I'd cut off their dicks, slowly. They know I'm tough and can out-sail them in any condition. Since Brad was my only suitor, everyone hoped he'd rescue me. Well, that's the way it was. My dream came true. We graduated, got married, moved to New York, and found jobs on Wall Street. When *Bravo's* ready, we'll sail around the world. She's a classic sloop in mint condition. I bought her from Captain Poole who was, first, unconvinced a woman could buy a sailboat, that I might be serious about buying his boat, then actually and smartly negotiate for it."

"'Where's your husband?' Captain Poole asked bluntly. I said Brad was in Maine visiting his family. He trusts me. I'm the captain. He peered up at me; his face grizzled, and slapped his knee. 'You might want to sail my *Bravo* around the world?'"

"This sloop was built for a rich couple. Sturdy. Mahogany on oak. With teak decks. The rig is staysail, jib, main, topsail and mizzen. No expense spared. She has brass port lights, and below, a bright cabin with gimballed oil lamps, brass scuttles and a long keel. We wanted a timber boat in great shape. Captain Poole wasn't anxious to let *Bravo* go easily. He allowed me to have it surveyed. His wife, Mary, died a year ago. She was a redhead, too. That's why they painted the boat Nantucket red. You could see when Mary was sailing home."

"'She's a boat that brought us home,' Captain Poole told me. They conceived three children aboard. He took me for a sea trial," Beth said, "and she handled beautifully. I made an offer. The money's always been mine. No issue with Brad. Captain Poole even gave us his new Avon dinghy with the motor. He made me promise to send him a postcard from every single port. Why don't you and Quentin visit us and come to Minneford's Boatyard?"

***

Logbook: Minneford's Boat Yard, City Island, *Bravo* up on a cradle, June, 1980

Name	Location	Latitude	Longitude
Bravo	Minneford's Boat Yard, City Island, NY	40° 50.563'	73° 47.040'

At the boatyard, on the hard, Brad Turner invited them from the ladder he stood on: "Climb up and see our boat properly." Tall and skinny, Brad owned features that were model-Maine-coast perfection; sandy-haired, an aquiline nose set in a handsome face. Amy was smitten right away by his charming Maine accent. He told them, "You can't believe how much work we're doing to go sailing!" Amy and Dutch nodded eagerly.

In *Bravo*'s cockpit, Amy felt cramped. *Quadriga* had ten feet over her in length and one foot more in beam. Why did Beth and Brad choose this boat to make a 25,000-mile sea voyage, even if it was sturdy and beautifully built?

In *Bravo*'s galley, Brad seemed to hear her unspoken thought; "She's as solid as a brick shit house. We like a small, sturdy boat. Less to maintain." He opened a bottle of champagne and poured servings into paper cups.

"After we sail through the Chesapeake, we're taking the Intracoastal, then out at Morehead City. Maybe you'll go along with us?"

Beth looked at Amy, who secretly shuddered, mouthing "Nooooooooooo…."

***

Aboard *Quadriga*, summer unfolded into August as Amy absorbed sailing terminology, becoming sure-footed aboard. She was told by friends that she was lit with a new radiance. She felt strong and fit. "Ah, ha, *Quadriga*," they teased? No, it was Dutch, and so what if he was older. Twenty-four minus forty-two equals eighteen. Together, they were each eighteen. Amy did not tell her mother about Dutch, or *Quadriga*. What was there to tell?

"Are you dating anyone," her mother asked on the phone. "You're kind of quiet."

"Nope, performing at Freddy's and going to my job."

"You sound awfully happy."

"It's being in New York, mom."

***

When Dutch snored, she slept in the main salon, starboard, upper berth. Busy practising her music, she'd stop and half-listen to Dutch's rambling views about most women afloat, impossibly involved with their hair and nails, shouting back, not listening to commands. An equal opportunity criticizer, he also accused men of being sarcastic and harsh, not giving the correct sailing terms, nor praise for a job well done. Not at all like him.

"I'm forty-two. *Quadriga* and I are in peak working order. Amy, I'm selling my business. Sailing to the Caribbean," he said. "A boat is just a box without loving sailors. You know you love me. You love this boat. And sailing. You've learned to raise sails, crank a winch, and put the handle back properly and not to drop it overboard! You stay confined in a small space for long times, close to me, and I don't want to kill you. You're able to concentrate, be separate from me and still stay connected."

"While I like spending time with you on *Quadriga*..." her voice trailed off.

"Didn't the producer say you had no edge?"

"That's not nice, Dutch. I'm working on it."

"Sorry." He turned away, embarrassed.

***

At the end of steamy August, Amy took vacation time aboard *Quadriga*. They sailed from Stamford to Block Island, up the coast and across to Edgartown on Martha's Vineyard.

Amy took the midnight-to-four watch, confident at the wheel, easily holding a compass course. Dutch had spent a considerable sum buying her foul weather gear, a red jacket and pants, top-of-the-line and warm. She liked wearing them. With bare feet.

While it was rainy at the helm, steering became exhilarating, keeping her heading as cold spray assaulted her face, running down her nose and neck. After three hours, she beamed the flashlight down onto the big clock in the main salon. No stars tonight. Not even the moon could find an opening in the heavy, rain-laden clouds above them. Of course, her safety line was attached. She looked down into the dimly lit cabin.

He appeared below, making hot coffee. He brought up a cup for her, and sat, watching her from the dodger where he was dry.

"You take the damn helm," she yelled in the wind at him. "I'm exhausted!"

"No whining!" He yelled back. They changed places, his steady hand holding the wheel. Climbing down the companionway, she took off her foul-weather gear, changed into warmer clothes, and came back up to sit under the dodger. Yup, a trooper, she thought.

Quadriga sailed up and down troughs, intermittent spray flying across the deck that almost drowned out his voice. Over the wind, he shouted, "When we make mistakes, we learn. The story of human history is one long effort to exert control over everything. Here it's wind and sea. We'll always fail. When we fail, we learn. You were good on the helm tonight." He paused. "Amy, I need to tell you I'll be leaving to sail in the Caribbean, before the Christmas winds of November. It's a ten-day voyage. By the way, my manager, Angelo, has bought my company."

Her eyes opened wide. "What?"

He stood up, as if defying Poseidon, and yelled gloriously into the dank night; "I'm ready to take on the Atlantic! My life's dream with *Quadriga*. I began with twelve years sailing on small lakes, around Long Island Sound and New England waters. I keep reading about endless horizons, like all my sailing heroes. Now it's my turn!" He blew his nose and stuffed the hanky back in his pocket.

He yelled above the wind and spray; "*Quadriga* yearns to be anchored in palm-fringed coves. Tortola, Virgin Gorda, Anegada, and down the island chain to the Grenadines!" He shouted, "How many people spend their time dreaming away their lives? I have excellent trust accounts in the Caymans. I know I'm a moody son-of-a-bitch. I can design you an entirely different life, aboard, sailing the Caribbean with me." He stopped, blew his nose. "And you've learned how to pay no attention to me. More coffee, please!"

Speechless, Amy nimbly brought up two cups of coffee, handing one to Dutch. He cupped his hands around his mug, holding the wheel steady with his knee as he sat on the high side of the boat.

"Amy, don't be offended; competition's cut-throat. While you've got a sweet voice, good skills, you aren't hungry enough. You're from well-educated, wealthy parents who love you. Spend the winter aboard with me loving and sailing. You love this boat, you can keep singing, and see where that takes you. We'll sail and make love…."

"Can you wait a year?"

"Nope. Got health, dough, the perfect yawl. Your baby-club bookwork is boring!"

"It's not, and I sing at Freddy's." She yelled. "Do you feel competent to handle hurricanes, sharks, sail rips, accidents, being swept off the boat, drowning…. sinking the boat?"

"I can handle anything on this boat," he provoked, "Except you!"

**

She needed to confide in her elder sister, Charlotte, feeling serious about Dutch. They talked several times a week by phone, trusting each other.

"The future is unknown, "Charlotte said, "You've known him since May, a few months, although you've spent much time together. I can't believe you haven't told mom and dad. What do you know about real sailing? We were brought up to be normal, thrive on land, do what our parents want, what everybody else wants for you. I'm worried, Amy. This could be dangerous."

"He's smart and funny, an expert sailor, he treats me well, and we laugh," Amy implored. "Who thought I'd love sailing, and love being on the water. What a stupid problem!"

Charlotte laughed. "On the other hand, you've an invitation to escape ordinary life! I'm housebound up to my ears, with Daryl, always working, and I'm stuck with two nose-blowers. I'd say, for God's sake, go sailing!"

"I don't know!"

"You've sailed to the Vineyard, Nantucket, and Block Island without telling any of us? How mean you are! For God's sake, tell mom and dad."

"It's 1980. They'll say stay home, stay safe. Follow my New York dreams!"

"Stop whining! Look at the adventure you might have! I'm close by Mom and Dad. If you don' tell them, I will."

***

The following weekend, *Quadriga* entered the harbor at Edgartown, slicing through the water at six knots, Dutch stretched to reach for the chart. A clobbering, scraping, screeching sound along the port side of the hull echoed harrowingly throughout the boat. Amy sprang to see a huge steel robot, a buoy marked "13".

"The flashing beacon lights are out! That could have split us in two," Dutch exhaled.

That instant, Amy learned the importance of being on constant watch at sea, or approaching a harbor, no matter what life-changing subject was being discussed.

***

The tiny streets of Edgartown, the quaint old New England buildings and the ivy-covered red-brick library, were more than familiar to Amy, due to her summers working there. The Edgartown Yacht Club launch motored by. "Two persons on the dock. Waiting for you."

***

Shyly, Dutch greeted Amy's parents on the dock. He saw the elder, elegant Professors Evelyn and Elliot Sandler, informally dressed, standing tall and straight, sizing him up. He, the too-much-older, handsome stranger who seemed to hold their young daughter's heart. "We thought we'd better get a look at you, Quentin," her mother said, with an arched smile.

"Please, call me Dutch."

"We're staying at The Harborside. I urged Elliot to leave his writing for a few days. Anytime he does that, it's a real celebration."

"She forces me to enjoy life, in spite of myself," her dad said, grinning. "Please join us for dinner."

"With pleasure, sir," Dutch said, bending to shake Dr. Sandler's hand.

Dutch was tongue-tied at first; Dr. Sandler was a world-famous scholar, and professor, but soon they were drinking wine, enjoying dinner and good-natured joking. During their seeming acceptance, Amy was the topic of conversation, which resulted in laughter and a twinkle in each man's eye.

The twinkle was not there when Amy glanced at her mother. With a slight sideways lift of her head, Evelyn signalled Amy to follow her. In the ladies room, her mother demanded, "What do you see for yourself? He's eighteen years older than you. A boat's a complete universe. Why change your world? We're proud that you have achieved important goals in New York City, living well and safely. You've written some wonderful songs. You've got a job you love, made friends and you sing regularly at Freddy's. Stay here! We want you near."

"Mom, you have Charlotte and the grandkids."

"My darling daughter, you'll be in a box at sea! Don't waste your youth on some temporary exploration. Later on, you may not be able to get what you want. Ocean sailing is not a joke, and you'd be so far away from us if anything happened."

"Mom, there's something about him that sticks. I have a sense of well-being with him. He's smart, able, funny, and a little opinionated. A balance to my innocence."

"It is your life, honey. We want you to be happy. We don't want you to be sorry. We want you safe."

"Thank you, mom," said the ever polite Amy, screwing up her face in the mirror. She opened the door for her mother and silently followed her back to the table.

***

After dinner, the Sandlers shook hands with Dutch and retired to their hotel room. Evelyn turned to Elliott, "She'll throw her life away with this adventurer. Does he really care about her?"

"He seems like a good man. Let's hope and pray that whatever she does, she survives and blooms. It may toughen her up. You do see the way he looks at her."

***

Back aboard, Dutch said, "Your dad's pretty sharp. When I was in business, I could have used his help and advice. While the evening was nice, your mother was seriously looking me over. I don't think I passed inspection."

***

"Charlotte, I wish he wasn't going," Amy complained. "I've gotten to love this man. I don't feel there's any age difference. We're both so different."

"You're the one who decides. I know mom and dad are not pressuring you."

***

On the Stamford dock, it was an August 3-H weekend, hot, humid and hazy. Amy immersed herself in the famous compendium of sailing, *Chapman's Piloting and Seamanship* navigation text, realizing the excessive work it took to keep up *Quadriga*. How much sanding and varnishing did it take for *Quadriga*'s good looks and maintenance while she, a vital breathing young woman, only got an occasional haircut? Manicures were finished.

Amy continued to reflect on how she was busy with work, singing at Freddy's Pub, and on her deepening involvement with Dutch. His way of life or hers?

It wouldn't be what she did, but what she didn't do.

In the bathroom, her mind fluttered as she looked into the mirror. Her peeling nose, too much sun, the ever-lengthening 'Honey-Do' list. On the boat, she had fewer clothes. She again thought of Dutch's words of how her daily work at the book club was repetitive. This conflicted with her dreams of rough weather, sea monsters, tattered sails, and being swept overboard. How about the slap of a friendly whale's tail sinking the boat? Life-threatening chances aboard a forty-foot sailboat in the Caribbean. Drowning? She was doing well in the city. At Freddie's Pub, she had sold 100 more albums of Seaside Dreams and two new songs that were being recorded by emerging artists. She hardly wrote songs these days, or practiced.

"Get your ass out here!"

Hearing him stomp, she moved quickly out of the head. A mess of rotting garbage, strewn on the cabin sole, with a soaked paper bag bottom oozing banana peels and coffee grounds clung to his legs. "No paper bags for garbage! Assholes use paper bags!"

"Don't swear at me?"

"I'll swear any fucking time," he seethed. "Carry it up! It's on my varnish. Do it now!"

"I'm stunned," she wailed, and grabbed onto the center table for support. "*Quadriga*'s more important than I am!"

Defiantly, she moved into the forward cabin and grabbed her pocketbook. Dutch moved forward and put tough hands around her body, gripping her arms.

"I was stupid to get close to you," she yelled. "What makes you so obsessive about this boat?" Amy sobbed up into his sweaty face. "You're a man without class."

"You knew that! Staying alive is about control, management, being smart; the story of human history! The very survival of our ancestors and us depends on control! We need to be good at staying afloat and alive! You're a snooty, privileged Radcliffe grad with a fancy Harvard professor father. You know all about class. Going to sea means everything is in order. This is training!"

Dutch released the grip on her arm, sweat on his forehead dripping onto her face, both silent in the eruption and amazement of his behavior.

She looked up at him with a stark glaze, straining away from him; "Any dream I had of sailing to the Caribbean with you has rotted, like this stupid garbage."

He sat, listlessly, watching flies buzz around the banana peel stuck to his leg.

"Where does your rage come from? Why have I been attracted to you? My family's gentle, consistent, loving. Why are you so rude, so nasty?"

"It's about safety! Each thing must be done to our best: the ocean is indifferent."

What she did now would cast the standards for her own self-respect. She felt the unbearable sorrow of being, of failure. It tormented her to look at him. She took a deep breath.

"I must have an apology, or I cannot continue with you."

"The boat must be ready for all sailing conditions. It comes first."

"You've chosen." Declaring softly, she grabbed her bag, and hurriedly climbed up the companionway. Out on the dock, she did not look back.

Chapter Four

Logbook: *Yacht Zephyr*, **Virgin Gorda,
British Virgin Islands. June, 1980**

Name	Location	Latitude	Longitude
Zephyr	Little Dix Bay, Virgin Gorda, BVI	18° 27.576'	64° 25.929'
Quadriga	Edgartown, Martha's Vineyard	41° 23.505'	70° 29.961'

Say hello to Zoe Bainbridge, a successful travel writer based in New York, who has been continually thrilled to have the British Virgin Islands Tourist Board as her major client. Twice a year, for ten years, she's led a marvelous trip for travel writers around Tortola, Virgin Gorda, Jost Van Dyke and Anegada. Her current group sat on the veranda of Tortola's Fort Recovery Hotel, offering an expansive view of the Sir Francis Drake Channel, the narrow body of water between the islands of Tortola and St. John. The group gazed at brilliant turquoise waters as sailboats dotted the horizon.

At lunch, Zoe told them, "While the British Virgin Islands, often abbreviated to BVI, lie only 40 miles from the U.S. Virgin Islands, what romance and adventure are to be found in the languid BVI? We're on safe, sexy islands. Our vacationers can stroll along white sand beaches and snorkel in clear waters teeming with sea life."

"We got it, Zoe. That's why we're here!"

Zoe laughed, loving the BVI, her grown-up students, glad to share: "Remember, ladies and gentlemen, moonlit nights and starry skies are always on the menu in this territory."

They all knew how important affirmative writing and advertising were to their careers: never mind the robberies, hijackings, drug-running or murders that happened in the Caribbean. Savvy citizens and tourists knew to lock their cars and their homes at all times. However, the allure and accommodations in the BVI were fabulously evident.

Zoe was grateful to earn a merry, excellent living, with a closet full of designer clothes, a gym membership, great friends, and a portfolio carefully cultivated. When she had visited Virgin Gorda, more than twenty years ago, goats were shooed off the runway. Now, in 1980, it was considered a prime location with an up-to-date runway and more upscale resorts.

At forty-nine, she was healthy and sleek, with intense brown eyes that dominated her face, and her looks polished from constant exercise. She loved her work, yet was stoical, acclimatized to a certain disappointment in loneliness, dispelled by social encounters. There was nothing to hide, nothing to be ashamed of, and never a need to defend her life, she told herself. Many men. No one man. Always single. No relationship. She was aware, at times, of certain, wordless longings. Through work, she was able to travel around the world, jauntily calling herself a happily unmarried woman and enough dating stories to fill a book. Not one she would write. There were many men she never wanted. Fair to say, they had their own ideas as well.

When the busy tour was over, and her writers had departed, she took a few extra days to relax, allowing the intoxication of Virgin Gorda to move into her bones. As she sat on the porch of Little Dix Bay Resort for breakfast, breezes softly wafted through nearby bougainvillea blossoms. Yet again, in sultry Virgin Gorda, she was alone.

Strolling past Speedy's rental car yard, Zoe turned left at the gas station and slipped through the Shopping Centre, crossing to the docks. She wondered why she'd never taken a course on sailing at City Island. It was the only way to learn to sail. By taking courses and having the best instructors.

***

On Dock B, Zoe's eyes lingered on a large, exquisite sailboat. The hull was bright red, matching the color of the Canadian flag hung at the stern. The name on the transom: *Zephyr*. The hail port said Little Current. The deckhand, muscular, fit, with gray-blonde hair down to his shoulders, was on deck, coiling lines. She looked up, astonished at the rise in her eyes, and heart, at the power of the unexpected handsome ruggedness of this fellow. He smiled and gazed at her, his blue eyes crinkling.

"This is a beautiful boat," she said indisputably, looking at his tanned, naked chest.

"Yah, I think so. Bought her some months ago." He shielded his eyes against the sun. Looked at her. Lovely. "Care to come aboard and have a look? Take your sandals off and come to the stern."

***

He held her hand as she stepped aboard, and invited her to sit in the cockpit. He began talking immediately; she could tell he was lonely for company. "I can tell you *Zephyr* was the Greek god of the west wind, which was considered the gentlest wind, especially if compared to the colder north wind, Boreas? The war the west wind brought was in the spring season. Even today, the name of the god means a warm and gentle breeze. My deckhand, Simon, thinks I named the boat after the mythical Greek god of wishful thinking. False hopes and unreliable forecasts," he joked. "We'll sail for the next two years in the Caribbean. No schedule. Would you like a cold drink?"

"Please." she said, delighted.

Where are you from?"

"A fabulous, busy island. Manhattan!"

"Oh, that's a nasty city," he scowled.

"Sir," she said indignantly. "Manhattan can be the greatest, friendliest island in the world. You obviously don't know this! While my business niche in life is to study, learn and write about islands, almost every island in the world," she boasted," I love coming home to Manhattan. And I constantly study the Caribbean and if you haven't been down island, I know all the places you'd love to see."

Why was she angry with this stranger? This was ridiculous. She had spent three minutes aboard this sailboat in the Virgin Gorda Harbour. Instantly, she shut up, ashamed of herself and instead, gazed at his tanned, muscular arms. He'd gotten her message, not exactly smirking, but smiling, now charming her when he spoke. She smiled. He had her. And she had yet to identify his accent. Ashamed of her outburst, she felt grateful to sit there. Their eyes met. Thrilling and slightly disturbing. She blushed.

"I apologize. Why do I feel I have to stick up for my home? You can believe anything you want!"

He smiled. "Truce?" he asked. "Want to know about the most beautiful island in the Great Lakes?"

"Sure, if you want to tell me."

"It's Manitoulin Island, located at the top of Lake Huron, in Ontario, Canada. The largest island in a freshwater lake in the world. Ever heard of it, Miss Smarty Island Know It All?"

"Isn't Manitoulin a kind of duck?"

He laughed with delight; it had been a sweaty working day. Here was comic release with whomever this lady might be. "Manitoulin Island's a beautiful, pastoral island. You can only get there by ferry in spring, summer or fall. Or drive over the old swing bridge. But once you cross the old swing bridge to the island, your life will never be the same. Is ginger ale with ice okay?"

He went below and brought up two glasses, handing one to her. Icy, large and cold. She took a longed-for sip. "Thanks. Sorry to get so mad. That was stupid. I'm Zoe. From Manhattan."

Why did he laugh?

"Oh my, I'm Zeb. From Manitoulin."

"You're Zeb on *Zephyr*. Manhattan and Manitoulin. Zeb, we certainly belong to different islands," she said, her face luminous with discovery. He got better looking by the minute. Better ask, "Where's Mrs. Zeb?"

"I'm a widower. My wife died ten years ago. My two daughters are grown. You can learn something new, maybe. Sailing in the Great Lakes fresh water has always kept my boats clean. I'm from a family of Canadian sea dogs, a life-long sailor. Our family's worked hard. Now, I'm grateful to be in the Caribbean on my new boat," he said, holding up a glass of ginger ale, "Where the only ice you find is tinkling in your glass." He paused. "Winters are long on Manitoulin, but never dull. I'm fifty-one. Thank goodness, my two daughters inherited a love of winter. One's in Sault Ste. Marie. The other's on Manitoulin Island, in Little Current. Both are teachers and both married this year. Good men. *Zephyr*'s been waiting for me. I've been dreaming about sailing to Iles Des Saintes, south of Guadeloupe, and the Grenadines for diving."

She looked out at the calm water of the marina, pleased he was offering a genuine account of himself. Nice Canadian man.

"We're all part of enormous stories about our own lives, finding our path, searching, finding people, losing, and learning again," she said. "Each time I'm back in the Caribbean, I love it so, and I'm honored to see how people, hotels, restaurants, and tourism grow."

"You're lucky to have a life you love," Zeb said. "I am, as well, aboard *Zephyr*.

Seeming to be partners in contemplation, they sat silently, the merry sound of water slapping at the hull. No need to talk. After a time, she stood up. "I must go. I've enjoyed meeting you, Captain Zeb on *Zephyr*."

"Delightful, in fact, Miss Zoe," he said warmly. "Thanks for coming aboard. I need socialization every now and then." He offered a large hand, she took it. He held on, his warm hand encasing hers, his blue eyes directed at her brown eyes. This touch seemed not a goodbye, but an invitation. She turned to break his piercing glance and cautiously made her way to the deck. She was introduced to young Simon, Zeb's cheerful young deckhand, who arrived with fresh laundry done. He helped her off the boat. She slid a business card into Simon's hand to give to Zeb.

Slipping on her sandals, she continued walking down the dock. Don't look back, though she wanted to. Had Zoe been able to hear, she would've enjoyed the exchange between Zeb and his deckhand aboard the *Zephyr*.

"Simon, what was that tornado?"

"I think your cold's gone, boss."

***

The next day, Zoe flew back to New York. One highlight of her press trip, remembering she was Z from M and he was Z from M. She doted on these cheerful interludes, her regular encounters.

***

Three weeks later, Zeb flew from Puerto Rico, through Toronto, to fly home to Sudbury for business. He phoned Zoe in New York City from his farmhouse on Manitoulin.

"Zoe, I know we spent less than an hour on my boat. As a world-class travel writer you tell me you are, and I'm not making fun of you, it behooves you…."

"Behooves me?"

"Yes, to come visit my island of Manitoulin. I've an ancient, comfortable four-bedroom farmhouse. You'll have privacy, with your own bathroom. Why don't you fly up for at least five days, as friends, with all respect, to visit me and see the island? If you need to bring a friend, that's fine. It's lovely here in June. I've got time to show you the island. We draw a huge, happy population each summer. I have several thousand points on Air Canada you can use."

"Why?"

"Your energy and enthusiasm made me feel young. You're funny, and you need to learn more! Let me know what you'll do."

***

"You can't go, stupid girl," admonished Eunice, her friend. "You met this guy for thirty minutes."

"I'm nearly fifty. I'm a seasoned professional," Zoe said. "His Canadian manners are refreshing! There's something interesting and needy about him."

"And certainly needy about you," Eunice scoffed. "You need another island?"

"The Ontario Provincial Police are there. Sudbury's a sophisticated city. I'm a smart, peripatetic and circumloquacious writer," Zoe said.

"Stop showing off. It's me, Eunice."

"This would be a fam trip, of which I've taken many over the years. I'm an expert of islands, and maybe I have to learn this one. I'll buy my own ticket and take him to dinner a few times on the island."

"Traveling on two flights to a Canadian city and an island to spend time with a guy you met for half an hour? I've changed your name to Needy Stoooopid."

"You're jealous."

"I'm always jealous," Eunice said, "You've got guts, kiddo. Phone me every day please."

"I will not."

***

49

Zeb picked her up the following week at the Sudbury airport. Sudbury was a heavily industrial city, called the former nickel capital of the world. They drove away from the airport along Skead Road, through the city, along Highway 17 West, and two hours later, drove across the old swing bridge to the island. They had lunch at The Anchor Inn in Little Current and then drove for another forty minutes. She found the views exquisite along Highway 542, overlooking the North Shore of Lake Huron, and the pastoral fields below, green and long.

When they arrived in Kagawong, she smiled at the dusty old farmhouse. The doorknobs were built high up, many years ago, to keep the kids from opening the doors to their parents' room.

Walking carefully out back, down to the Kagawong River, she found constant fresh air and in the back forty, open, expansive green farmland. Farmers and cattlemen paid to use Zeb's farmland, which was good for everyone. Zoe looked at the cows in the distant field. Looking was enough.

Traveling further afield, they talked their way around the island, ambling along the docks at Gore Bay. Sailboats, dinghies, motorboats, all evidence of the burgeoning summer population. It was easy to appreciate this Northern Ontario Island of small towns, farmland and sailboats. Plus Zeb's quiet conversation. He drove her around to Providence Bay, to South Baymouth, to Sheguiandah and to the museums. He took her to lunch at The Garden Gate, and the early summer Farmers' Markets that had begun. He, and the island, began to enchant her.

They bought fresh vegetables and cooked together. She was pleased that he knew how to cook well; she was pleased to do the dishes.

Zeb shared his reading of Canadian authors with her, and his sailing books. A fine touring guide, he told her all about the businesses on Manitoulin, all small and independent. They kept talking, enjoying the different ways each viewed cities and countryside. She joked she was so New York and he was oh, so Canadian. Polite and truly shy.

She met Uncle Dougie, Uncle Moose, and his nonagenarian Uncle Everett Mudge, all who lived in Kagawong. Uncle Mudge knew everything; just ask him. These were charming characters, full of stories. She relaxed in the pastoral, countryside setting. And the host and his sightseeing guest were super polite, careful to stay away from each other. Learning a new island, this is business, she told herself.

***

We've done so much. Thank you, Zeb," she told him at the Sudbury airport. "I've great respect for Manitoulin and Northern Ontario."

"How about me?" he laughed.

"Absolutely! I'm going to hug you quickly. They're calling my plane."

"It was good," was all he said. "Next week, I'll be flying back to Virgin Gorda. Simon and I will head down islands."

***

Back home in New York City, she wondered if Zeb might still be interested enough to invite a city non-sailing woman to be his guest aboard. She had made him laugh most every day on Manitoulin. He was a nice Canadian man. Simon was his able-bodied, smart, deckhand and did the work aboard. What if Zeb actually invited her?

***

"For God's sake, Zoe, what do you know about sailing? You're a New York babe," chided Eunice. "You were a kick for a week. Shocked you didn't go to bed with him. His photographs are great. Get real, he's an Ontario farmer who grows Christmas trees, and sailing in the Caribbean for a year or more."

"The only way to live is to lose yourself in something new!"

"Not that floats in the ocean and you know absolutely nothing. So what if he's cute!"

"By the way, he and his brother run the Boston Whaler boat franchise on the Great Lakes."

"Have you heard from him?"

"No."

***

Logbook: of Amy. New York City, September 1980

"There's a gentleman in Reception," whispered Lara, on the phone from the front desk at the Tiny Tot Book Club. "He says to tell you he'll wait forever."

"Get rid of him."

Amy had received two sentences of praise in the New York Post, for her performance at Freddy's Folk Pub. The article was about Freddy and his iconic pub. Proceeding with her own aspirations, it was her life, not swept away by someone else's dream. Ha, swept away.

"Calm down, Amy," whispered Lara.

She'd sneak out. But the exit was in the reception area. At six o'clock, as he sat reading a magazine, Lara told him the office was closing When Amy attempted to tiptoe past, he jumped up, declaring, "Amy, I'll take out the goddamn garbage forever."

"You were an interlude," she said angrily, and looked out the window onto Fifth Avenue. The street below was empty. "You're a narcissist, a bully. Why trust you now?"

"As long as the boat's safe, not life and death, I promise, Amy, you'll come first."

"You can't promise that! We'll fight and I'll be afraid!"

"I'll give you a voucher from American Airlines for plane fare from anywhere in the Caribbean to fly home. I don't want you to be dependent on me." He begged, "Haven't you missed me? Come sailing! Me without you, is nothing! You love being aboard! When I leave, you'll be bored, packing stupid cartons. I'm prepared to take care of you. You're becoming a primo sailor. It's in your soul to do it. Life will be bigger, fabulous for you with me. Not in crummy New York City."

She sighed. Tired.

"Please let me take you to dinner."

Lara waited to lock the dock behind them. "You two, make up your damn minds!"

Dutch turned to her. "Lara, come to dinner with us?"

"Not a chance."

Chapter Five

Name	Location	Latitude	Longitude
Zephyr	Virgin Gorda Yacht Harbor, Spanish Town, BVI	18° 26.985'	64° 26.204'
	Village Cay Marina, Road Town, Tortola, BVI	18° 25.395'	64° 37.050'
	Anegada Reef Hotel, Anegada, BVI	18° 43.438'	64° 22.977'

"Eunice, you owe me fifty bucks!"

"The Canadian called, didn't he?"

"He asked me to fly down and take a week or two to sail with him and Simon? 'You'll have privacy, with the fore cabin and the head to yourself. June's a great time to sail. Since you always report on the hotels, we can

enjoy visiting the harbours and anchorages of the BVI.
You can even call it work!'" She was delighted. "Eunice,
I didn't hesitate. He was a great host on Manitoulin. And
not a New York empty suit. I told him based on his nice
Canadian manners, I'd take a chance with him."

"Giving him a break, are you?"

"Teasing, his mockery thrilled me, Eunice," Zoe said.
"And I told him I was a little nervous. And it would be
lovely to see him again."

***

Two weeks later, Zoe, with too much landlubber
luggage, set her dainty sized-seven sneakers aboard Yacht
Zephyr.

"You might like being aboard so much, I might have
trouble getting you off the boat!" He said, by way of
greeting her at the small airport on Virgin Gorda.

"Didn't I pass the Manitoulin test? So did you," she
refuted. "I brought you some gifts."

"Why, I've got everything," he said. "Let's get to the
boat."

***

She learned more about Simon, his deck hand, and
young, handsome, 27, born in Wales, a sheer plus aboard.
Simon often smiled at Zeb's addiction to writing lists and
the accomplishments to be done aboard. Since Simon had
served for a time in the British Army, he was exhausted
and retired from the service, with distinction. He had

taken a chance and had flown to the BVI to see if he could have a year living and working on a sailboat. Luckily, Zeb and Simon found each other, happily enjoying respect and constant humor between them.

***

Aboard *Zephyr*, Zeb gave her a spot at the table in the main salon, so she could work and write. She found him to be polite and quiet, while she had a gift for endless cheerful encounters. As a reporter, and a critic of hotels, restaurants and resorts, she was getting and publishing her stories, sending them by fax from local hotels. After a few days, she noticed while she could work on three tasks at the same time, Zeb's concentration was totally on her when he was with her. For a self-absorbed Boss of Her Own Life, this took guts and might be a fascinating interlude.

While after many years of writing, Zoe understood the tourism industry of twenty-six Caribbean islands, she was now with a charming Canadian friend. Aboard the 50 ft. German Freres ketch. In her own comfortable cabin and head.

What had she gotten into?

***

"Its great sport to sit and watch them all make mistakes," Simon told Zoe, his attention taken by watching inexperienced vacationing sailors coming in to dock their rented sailboats. "Every day, they come in and crash on the docks." He continued, "I served for eight years in the British Army, in the Falklands. Couldn't be happier to be here, sailing with Zeb and now you, while I figure out what to do next with my life."

Since Simon's arrival months ago, Zeb and Simon had hauled *Zephyr*, scraped her keel, painted the hull, and worked on the generator and all electrical outlets in the aft cabin. Almost all the work was done, supplies stowed.

"And you, Zoe, magically appeared on the dock," Zeb told her happily. We're so different and that's what makes you captivating to me."

"Captivating. Good word," she said, reaching to hold his hand.

"Before we leave Virgin Gorda," Zeb said. "I'll take you snorkelling at Fallen Jerusalem. The snorkeling is exquisite and I may teach you something you may not care to learn."

"I've had snorkeling lessons in the YMCA pool in New York."

***

Motoring out of the Virgin Gorda Harbour in the dinghy, Zeb and Zoe passed the dramatic, world-famous gray boulders of the Baths, with bright beige sand on the beaches and hundreds of palm trees. Sunshine and breezes. She hunkered down in the dinghy and looked at small clouds framing the sun. No matter how many times Zoe returned to Virgin Gorda, the beauty of this Island never ceased for her. A small plane droned overhead, flying toward Puerto Rico.

Zeb steered the dinghy toward the shoreline, slowed to a glide, turned the engine off, and tossed a small anchor over a patch of sandy bottom. The dinghy sat upon clear azure water, with the rocks, reefs, and purple fanlike fauna waving in the current below them. The cove was silent except for the lapping of waves on the tiny secluded beach. The ocean water was alive, with spirit and nuance, rising and falling like breath.

Donning the snorkel, mask, and fins that fit properly, Zoe slid into the water. "Almost everything I've learned," she told Zeb, laughing at herself, "has been with the best professors, teachers, instructors and analysts."

You're proud of that?"

"Sure, and I don't mind if you make fun of me!"

"Get used to it!"

They swam slowly, together, floating over red brain coral, as hundreds of blue iridescent fish glided by in the enchanted realm below them. Weightless, she floated in warm salt water, while an occasional small sea turtle slid by. She gazed at green, gold, pink, and orange shapes, the bright coral enchanting her. What bliss and freedom she felt, joined in this underwater universe, peaceful and quiet. Oh so connected with Zeb.

Gracefully, he dove deep to bring up a small conch shell and handed it to her. He threw off his bathing trunks and threw them into the dinghy. She did as well, experiencing new freedom in being naked, swimming past more bright coral, and floating over tiny sea kingdoms. Zeb dove again as she watched his wide shoulders and powerful legs move gracefully ten feet below her. His strokes were smooth and supple, seeming to stride under water. Then they swam to shore and splashed in the shallows, naked and laughing, sensuality hovering between them. Every erotic and suggestive aspect of her own fantasy life was heightened. Her skin, glossed by the water, happily showed her small white breasts with rose-colored nipples pointing upward. The water was alive, caressing her. Warm and weightless. Let this last, Zoe prayed, lingering in exquisite moments. She felt free, girlishly young, but she was almost fifty. He was fifty-one, and while it was spring, they were in the summer of their lives. Feeling so connected to him.

What would happen? The suspense, here, was terrible, she giggled.

***

On the sail to the island of Anegada, Zeb let her take the helm. He sat next to her. It was a gentle sailing day with steady winds and sails so balanced *Zephyr* practically sailed herself.

Reaching the shallows at Anegada, they threaded their way past the buoys and anchored near the Anegada Reef hotel. A pristine corridor of empty beach stretched out to the left of the island. Anegada's trees and bushes waved in the wind, beckoning to them. At anchor, *Zephyr* formed a dramatic silhouette against the setting hot orange Caribbean sun, the sky streaked with blue and pink. In the dinghy, trundling toward the dock, Zeb asked Zoe, "You know me and the boat. And my island. Would you be willing to spend the night together?"

"I've been waiting," she said shyly.

"I've reserved Room One. Total privacy for us, off the boat."

"Smart, eh?" she said. "Thanks."

"Zoe, you're beginning to sound Canadian."

***

Departing the dinghy, Zeb lifted Zoe's overnight bag, warning, "Be careful not to step on rusty nails or ragged jutting edges. Climbing rusty docks is a hazard of life in the Caribbean. With the constant handling of lines, standing in salt water, or working with chemicals to repair the boat, a cut on the hands, knees, or feet of a sailor can take weeks to heal."

Ewart, the eager young man who managed the front office at Anegada Reef, stood on the dock to greet them. "We've fresh lobsters tonight! In fact, we have them every night!"

***

A magical night of new love ensued, and later, time spent leisurely cherishing each other. Zoe could not believe the gentle, yet muscular body of Zeb and the slow lovemaking that flowed between them. This passion, his touch, her feelings; what she was aware of having missed for so long. Tears fell silently as she nestled in his arms. She began to absorb the essence of Zeb, touching him, his tanned skin, combing his hair with her fingers, laughing with him, entwining her legs around him. Surreal? Real! She couldn't even talk.

***

Waking early, Zeb took Zoe for a walk along the unspoiled Anegada shoreline, miles of pale sand seeping into the sea, scrubby foliage covering flat land. They were silent, listening to the wind, the twittering of small birds, and the surf gently welling up against the shore.

"Anegada presents me with a new sense of time," she told him. "This feels like the beginning and the end of the world. I've never stopped long enough to enjoy a simple walk. Thank you, Zeb. I've always been inspecting hotels and restaurants," she admitted, watching small fish dart at the surf line. On the horizon, heading south, their eyes rested on a schooner under full sail. She interlaced her fingers with Zeb, and enjoyed a wordless embrace.

Strolling along with him, holding hands, she felt uneasy. This was too good to be true, but alas, he lived on a sailboat and would soon be sailing down island, to many harbors. How she liked this unassuming Canadian.

Was she willing to abide in uncertainty? She knew nothing of the ocean's ever-present dangers, razor sharp reefs, sharks, tides, storms, and seasickness. She thought, don't get ahead of yourself. That's why she was here, not knowing what was coming, grateful for this new adventure. Would this suspense last?

Logbook: August, 1980

Name	Location	Latitude	Longitude
Quadriga	Chappaquiddick Island, Martha's Vineyard	41° 22.895'	70° 30.251'

Stepping back aboard *Quadriga,* Amy was tentative.

Dutch had profoundly apologized, with the promise of constant respect. In a contract, signed by him! And airline points in her pocket. It was more than that. It was him. He'd introduced her to a different world and she'd learned much. Could this adventure be a bigger life than her own in New York?

Aboard *Quadriga,* not only did she have appreciation for all that went into its upkeep, but of all the possibilities and the amazing suspense of adventure. She had the promise of respect in the man that had captured her emotions. He promised. Standing on the deck, she felt a lyrical vibration, whispering in the breeze, coming from the hull, the heart of *Quadriga*: 'Where've you been, girlie? I missed you taking care of me. Dutch's some brat of a captain. We'll train that sweet bastard. You, me and Dutch, supporting each other. Great sailing's ahead… We must be three, the power of three.' Musical Amy felt the boat was singing to her, listening to her, and she sang back.

"Hello dearest *Quadriga.*"

She stood at the bow, realizing how much sailing, the winds, the boat, were inside of her soul. 'The three Ds', she mused: Daunting Divine Dutch was a maddening, sexual, buccaneer wanting to carry her along on his adventure. The Caribbean Sea, lyrical, inviting; magical harbours of many islands beckoned, the potential of colour and splendour ahead of her. Palm-fringed coves, swimming, sailing, visiting the small islands. New songs to be sung.

After dinner, Dutch took her hand and quietly led her to the V-berth. "Amy, you've made me the happiest man." They went to bed and threw back the sheets; the front hatch opened to let in air.

After they made quiet, solemn love, they held each other quietly, as if agreeing toward the future, to be kind to each other. While she loved being held by him, she wondered if he could, indeed, be able to be captain of his moods. To keep his word. Dutch was like his sail boat: often soaring high with the wind, alternately slogging along, alone, against his own tide and the wind. Her captain.

Chapter Six

Logbook: Sailing from Anegada to St. Maarten, August, 1980

Name	Location	Latitude	Longitude
Zephyr	Anegada Reef Hotel, Anegada, BVI	18° 43.438'	64° 22.977'
	Philipsburg, St. Maarten	18° 01.215	63° 02.614'

Zeb, Zoe, and Simon were under sail, a southern passage to St. Maarten. *Zephyr*, rolling and awash with spray that kept dousing Zoe, introduced her to seasickness. Oh, the rocking and rolling. Zeb loving challenging weather, held the wheel, keeping the boat close-hauled in the midst of squall after squall. *Zephyr* pleased her captain, rising to frothy crests on top of the sea, then swooping down into troughs.

Zoe's safety line, tucked in twice around her, did not make her feel comfortable. She remained under the canvas dodger, trying to stay dry. And trying to keep smiling. Neither worked. Why did they have to sail in such a blow?

"Boss, where's your safety line," yelled Simon from below.

"Don't need it! I'll take coffee."

"No safety line, no coffee," Simon shot back.

"You win, as always," Zeb said. He made a show of affixing the clip to himself and to a stanchion. He said to Zoe, "You'll be able to steer. It's simply time and practice."

As if she wanted to, she thought, watching the sea crests, spuming white. Her eyes fixed on the lumpy horizon. Why was she aboard?

"We're in a series of zephyrs," he yelled above the wind.

"To you, everything's a zephyr," she shouted, trying to be jolly, while she smelled the aroma of beef stew. Simon handed up two bowls of Dinty Moore. Zeb put on the autopilot, accepted the bowl from him, and dug into his dinner. Zoe also accepted the bowl gratefully.

Never had canned beef tasted so delicious. Not on the return. The boat's movements through the sea sent Zoe's stomach on a figure-eight roll. Leaning over the top of the cockpit, holding on, she vomited in agony. She wasn't even embarrassed, simply exhausted. Glad for the safety line as she heaved almost over the deck. Feeling the ferocity of the indifferent ocean.

"Don't feel ashamed," Zeb consoled her. "Nothing's funny about being seasick. Don't worry, Zoe, the next wave will wash the deck clean. Even scientists don't understand how motion sickness is triggered. It's sensory conflict. Discord between visual input to the brain and signals from parts of the inner ear responsible for balance.

Do I sound like a scientist? We always want to be in control of everything we do and feel, but on the water, you must be respectful, and have to let go."

"I'm letting go of everything I know," she muttered. After her heaving ended, Zoe worked her way down the companion steps to brush her teeth. She found mouthwash, noted her exhausted face, and wondered when, if ever, they might arrive in St. Maarten. She remembered why she liked powerboats. For a moment, she lay down on the rolling bunk. Being in New York City was safer than this. There was much to competency aboard, more than any intoxication of enjoying nature. Were Zeb and Simon impervious to this roiling sea?

Simon peeked in and gently placed a small blanket over her. Asleep. Good, she's a nice lady. Earnest, patient, and seems to be, so far, accepting Zeb. While Zeb was from the Great Lakes, and Manitoulin Island was 110 miles long, this career lady from the island of Manhattan was only 10 miles long. Hmmm, could honey and salt blend?

Simon came above and hitched his safety on. Zeb unhitched his line, patted Simon's shoulder in passing as Simon took the helm. A few more hours of this. Zeb went below to sleep in the main cabin while *Zephyr* rolled through the seas.

Sure hope she makes it, Simon thought. On all counts.

***

Logbook: Early September, 1980

Name	Location	Latitude	Longitude
Quadriga	Morehead City, N.C.	34° 43.151'	76° 42.356'
	St. Thomas, USVI	18°20.109'	64° 55.607'
	Road Town, Tortola, BVI	18°25.637'	64° 36.997'

At home in Cambridge, the Sandlers sat in their book-filled den. Evelyn was crocheting a blanket with a sea-theme for a gift. Musing aloud to Elliot, "She's seduced, different, and he's filled the space in her head with sailing and adventure. We know she's a capable girl, and we have to trust her. Of course, we wish her well, and she knows she can come home at any time."

"Ev, we raised her to be just who she is, creative and smart," Elliott said. "I've had him checked out by my lawyers, and he is who he says he is."

"My brilliant husband, thank you," Evelyn said. "But it doesn't make me feel any better to know our Amy's going to sea."

"We'll fly down and visit her, I promise you, honey."

***

Amy had filled the sailboat's freezer and cupboards with food for three weeks. She was packed, ready, and Mr. Crane wished her the very best. "Your job is always here, Amy," he said kindly. And then, "Don't tell my wife, but I'm jealous of you and Dutch sailing off on your adventure."

"Mr. Crane, I have to thank you for keeping *Yellow Cat* next to *Quadriga*."

He smiled. "Remember to stay afloat, young lady."

***

From Morehead City, the first six days of life sailing the Atlantic Ocean was easy. Dutch had asked her if they ought to have extra able-bodied sailors with them on the passage. He had friends always willing to leave their work to sail with him. But, having trained her well, he thought the two of them could handle this ocean crossing together.

With steady winds, *Quadriga* averaged a daily one hundred and eight nautical miles. He kept talking to her and he seemed to have the ability to understand not only what the wind was doing, but what it was about to do. "Scan the approaching water for rough patches. When you see the height of the waves up ahead, the subtle shifts in the wind direction against the sails, and the angle of our helm, you feel better and maybe sail more safely."

No forecasts could have told how the weather would turn. One squall after another, hard rain and gusts in their path. The anemometer read forty knots, fifty, gusting to sixty. Canvas went up and down, and they were constantly wet. Careening into troughs, slamming into walls of water, they lived from one crest to another.

"I can sleep, sitting or standing, rocking and rolling," Amy crowed for the first few days on the voyage, feeling great health and buoyancy. When awake, each hour was about keeping up energy and discipline. "I'll never be stronger, tougher, skinnier, or sleepier," Amy joked.

Frequently in the height of squalls, it didn't stop her new fright, thick behind her breastbone. But each breath, she vowed, made her stronger. Amy had resolutely taken on the challenge of being tested and living sea life up and down the troughs. Yah, a new word. Resolute.

What? How'd this happen?

They lost power and refrigeration, and had to wait for weather to move past. She kept quiet and did her work, whatever he told her. When the gales passed, and blue skies and calm seas returned, Dutch was able to take sites, saying, "Amy, you're earning your sea legs every minute!"

"Woo hoooooo!" She hooted at him into the wind. Songs came to her, but she couldn't concentrate on writing them down; sailing became fascinating. She kept her mouth shut, and did everything she was told to do.

"Dutch, we know *Bravo* left Morehead City two days after us. I bet they're going through the same crap. I'd sure love to see them."

"With this weather, we've made up two hundred miles within three days," declared Dutch. "We're closing in on St. Thomas at six knots on a steady wind and flat seas. And look at the beautiful stars. I pray we meet them there."

When *Quadriga* pulled in to St. Thomas, they were given a berth at Yacht Haven. She phoned her parents in Cambridge to tell them they were fine. Nothing about the fierce voyage. Now to be on a dock, the boat still, people and the St. Thomas hills in front of them.

"Amy, you kept my sanity by coordinating, compromising, configuring and cajoling us. I declare you to be a competent sailor."

"Dutch," she slurred out of fatigue, "I deem you competent as well!"

They slept for ten hours, the boat stationary at the dock. The next day, they allowed their bodies to descend back into the world of a dock, people, and land. Taxis, restaurants, tourists, large cruise boats, shops and grocery stores, civilization, pulled them in.

"Being here squeezes my head apart," Dutch grumbled after one day. "I feel assaulted by the influx of people, mostly ugly, who scheme and rush past us. I hate the smell of Chinese food delivered on the docks. I hate listening to dopey charterers being directed to their boats. We've got to get *Quadriga* out of St. Thomas, but it's cheap to do our cleanup here."

"We haven't located *Bravo*. They ought to be in these waters."

***

A few working days became six. Only mad dogs worked out in the tropical midday sun, but sitting amidst sandpaper, paint cans and brushes, and plenty of sunscreen, a hat and sunglasses, Amy cleaned, scrubbed, re-caulked, sanded and varnished. She felt an unbelievable resonance, the accomplishment of the Atlantic Ocean crossing under her belt. She was aware how the boat had changed by the ocean passage. The boat was tired, too.

"One more day to finish up," promised Dutch. "Go to Pueblo for groceries? We'll sail to Tortola tomorrow to do the rest there."

At the Pueblo supermarket, she got what they needed, and bought fresh squid at the market to cook with pasta that night. They enjoyed a delicious dinner, enjoyed white wine, and a good night's sleep.

***

The next morning, Dutch cleared U.S. Immigration out of St. Thomas, and they cast off for the British Virgin Islands. As the morning's sail progressed, winds got higher and the seas heavier. Amy was allowed to sleep, holding onto her pillow. She awakened, thrown from her bunk. Startled by a loud ripping sound. The boat went 'thunk' into a heart-stopping halt.

Below, Amy jumped up, pulled on shorts and a top, hair dishevelled.

"How'd I do this? We hit a reef!" Dutch yelled in pain. The next second, the wind caught the sail, the boat lurched and came off the reef; Amy made it to the galley to see left-over squid in a pot flying across the cabin, spraying its contents, landing starboard and denting the newly varnished sole. From out of a drawer under the sink, Amy saw a gleaming black revolver careen across the floor directly into the mess of coagulated squid. A gun and garbage on the sole or the safety of *Quadriga*? She felt afraid picking it up, but did, carefully washing and drying it off. She quickly put it back into the cabinet. How dare he not tell her! She hadn't seen guns aboard.

"Check the bilge, Amy! Are we taking on water," Dutch yelled. Amy lifted one floorboard quickly, finding the compartment dry.

Why hadn't he told her about the gun? Guns were simply an invitation to violence. Weren't they sailing in Paradise?

"This is my own appalling evidence of sloppy seamanship," Dutch scowled. "And do me a favor, Amy, no leftovers. Squid looks lousy on my beautiful sole!"

His beautiful soul?

Logbook: Road Town, British Virgin Islands, September, 1980

Name	Location	Latitude	Longitude
Bravo	Road Town, Tortola, BVI	18°25.637'	64° 36.997'
	Belle Vue, Jost Van Dyke, BVI	18°26.555'	64° 45.115'
	Road Town, Tortola, BVI	18°25.637'	64°36.997'
	Soper's Hole, Tortola, BVI	18°23.146'	64° 42.052'
	The Dog Islands, BVI	18°28.815'	64° 27.130'
Quadriga	Soper's Hole, Tortola, BVI	18° 23.146'	64° 42.052'

	Belle Vue, Jost Van Dyke, BVI	18° 26.555'	64° 45.115'
	The Baths, Virgin Gorda, BVI	18° 26.275'	64° 26.755'
	Virgin Gorda Yacht Harbor, Spanish Town, BVI	18° 26.985'	64° 26.204'
Zephyr	Belle Vue, Jost Van Dyke, BVI	18°26.555'	64° 45.115'

Yacht *Bravo*'s Atlantic Ocean passage, under similar conditions, deeply exhausted Beth and Brad. They were grateful, in fact, jubilant, to arrive. The boat handled well and they were in the British Virgin Islands. How beautiful everything on land, fresh and green, looked to them.

After clearing Immigration in Road Town, Tortola, phone calls were made to Beth's parents on Long Island, and Brad's in Maine. They stocked up on groceries. She needed to make chicken soup for Brad, his elixir when he didn't feel well. On the passage, Brad had lost a lot of weight. He didn't have her stamina and needed to recover. Vegetate was his favored word. Interestingly, no large repairs were needed, just a quiet anchorage. They sailed to the wide harbor at Jost Van Dyke. Beth mended small items aboard, happy to work by herself, while he slept, rested and read. *Bravo* was sturdy, dependable, and wonderful to sail, but a tiny, irritating leak kept making the cabin sole damp. She was determined to locate it before their passage through the Panama Canal. Should they have waited to buy a fibreglass fifty-footer? But they were impatient to get out of the city. During the passage, they'd lost contact with *Quadriga*.

***

A week of rest in the British Virgin Islands shored up their energy. Captain Beth of *Bravo*, with her light hair, blue eyes and tons of freckles, turned beet red and then dark tan in the sun. The muscles in her arms and legs were supple as she moved about her beloved boat. Brad was feeling so much better, now tired of chicken soup. They felt well enough to go into Road Town, to socialize with other sailors at the local pub, Village Cay. One sailor at the bar invited them; "Hey mate, there's a party up the mountain road. Pile into the back of our pick-up. We'll give you a lift."

They arrived at a large house overlooking the harbor, with the party in full swing. Perspiring couples danced outside on the large deck to the raucous music of a live steel band. Stars above, a nice breeze. Older local folks sat in the garden. Beth and Brad went upstairs to look for a beer and mingle with people, aware of warm Caribbean bodies jostling them, passing by them in the low-lit house. Observing the energy pulsing around them, Brad whispered to Beth, "We've been alone at sea so long, I'm not used to so many people."

She nodded in agreement, as they went to sit on the upstairs terrace nursing their beer.

"Beth, Brad, I can't believe it! So happy to see you!" A shout from Amy arriving with Dutch.

Whoops, hollers, hugs and the story of each voyage. Blessed time to be together.

***

While Dutch's never-ending list of repairs grew, the bodies and minds of *Bravo* and *Quadriga* wound down to Caribbean time. Both sailboats lay anchored near each other at Soper's Hole on Tortola. *Quadriga's* torn jib had to be dropped in Road Town for repair. Amy looked up from playing her three-quarter guitar to see a large red ketch glide by, heading out to the Sir Francis Drake Channel.

People and boat-watching was half the fun of cruising. She looked at an attractive older man with blond white hair, steering, while a wiry, tall, young deckhand raised the sails. A pretty, older woman, wearing sunglasses, a hat, and a beautiful shirt, sat in the cockpit watching the sails unfurl. Since the boats were close, they waved cheerfully.

The name of it was *Zephyr*, the hail port, Little Current, Manitoulin Island. Where in the world was that? Bright tomato-red, *Zephyr's* hull was the same colour as *Quadriga*. And *Bravo*. Amy wondered what the inside of that lovely boat might be. The lady again waved at her. Close enough to smile at each other.

Quadriga sailed on to Jost Van Dyke for them to have dinner at Foxy's and spend the night in the harbor. The red ketch, *Zephyr*, anchored nearby. At Foxy's, guests enjoyed Calypso music, eating barbecue, and drinking various rums. Amy noticed the couple from *Zephyr* at the next table. He was big and rumpled-looking, powerful, a nice smile. Must be a tycoon on vacation, she mused. The older woman turned to Amy, not sure if she recognized her, but smiled. One could never tell who anyone was on boats. Senator Ted Kennedy had been in a slip next to Amy and Dutch for two days on the Vineyard and they never recognized him. Sailors dressed raggedly; it was the charterers who had new clothes and clean sneakers. People who lived aboard, on million dollar sailboats, wore torn shirts and shorts. Forget haircuts. Reverse status. A boat's bright work should gleam, the latest life rafts, a dinghy or two, strung like ornaments trailing astern. But owners, like Dutch and Brad, loved to camouflage themselves as bums.

The rattier the docksider shoes, the bigger the stock portfolio.

***

Logbook: On the Island of St. Maarten, September, 1980

Name	Location	Latitude	Longitude
Zephyr	Philipsburg, St. Maarten	18° 01.215'	63° 02.614'

The busy streets of Phillipsburg, St. Maarten, tinged with the smell of engine exhaust from honking cars, and noisy tourists bustling from one shop to another, welcomed Zoe and Zeb. Fresh from their voyage, with a good sleep and feeling better, they stood and watched awhile, getting land legs back.

The two sides of St. Maarten, Dutch and French, made this a wide-open port. Lax Customs provided the island with an active underworld, for those who didn't mind crime with tourism. Vacationers here sought sun, beaches, shopping, gambling, and restaurants, year after year. Zoe insisted Zeb pack an overnight bag, along with hers, and after lunch on a restaurant deck overlooking the harbor, they rented a car to drive to L'Habitation, an upscale resort on the North Coast.

"How can anyone love hotels so much?" Zeb asked, bewildered, mildly challenging her as they stood at the Reception Desk at L'Habitation.

"Pierre, the manager, invited us to stay overnight so I can inspect the hotel."

"How many times have you been to St. Maarten?"

"Fourteen."

"You exhaust me with your energy on land."

"And yours at sea," she said, glad to be back on her territory. "Are you worried about leaving the boat for a night?"

"Nah, nothing gets by Simon. By the way, you need to know we keep arms aboard. We call them 'nugs.' The Caribbean's a tough place."

"Guns aboard? How many?"

"Tell you later."

Pierre came forward, gushing; "Mlle. Zoe, we appreciate your excellent write-up. Gaston, take them to the suite on the tenth floor. Send up champagne and strawberries."

***

While Zeb took a long, leisurely bath, Zoe was happy to make the hotel inspection with Pierre, who whispered to her, "That man of yours is appealing."

They had a delicious French Creole dinner.

Falling into freshly ironed sheets in the king-sized bed, mints on the pillow, champagne and chocolates on the bureau, Zeb said, "I'm not used to this, all this elegance."

"This is what I call work," she whispered.

"What about the cuddling part?"

"You aren't work, you gorgeous man." she said. They slept in the next morning. Zeb sat on the balcony while a full breakfast was delivered.

A note was slipped under the door for her. "Dear Mlle. Zoe, if you wish to stay one more night, I am not a grand hotelier for nothing. We have the space. Write yes on this envelope and slide it out the door. Please be my guests for a massage for the two of you. At your command, Pierre."

"Zeb, please, can we be away from *Zephyr* one more day?"

"I'm awfully uncomfortable being pampered like this."

"One more night? Being here with you is dreamy."

"So is sailing, dreamy, Zoe. Sailing can be also be a way of life."

"You're making fun of me."

"I'll always make fun of you," he said. "That's easy." He paused again. "May I tell you something you're not going to like?"

She nodded. Here it was. Why now?

"Zoe, you always sound as if you're in a hurry, trying too hard, as if New York-based anxiety pushes you. Okay, I've realized you're successful and an overachiever, but you say something too New York fast. And I have not understood you. You have many gifts to give. Can you just give them slower?"

"Thank you, Zeb," she smiled ruefully, knowing this too well. "You're good for me."

***

Zoe wrote a nice feature story for her newspaper, took photographs, and faxed it all back to her office from the hotel, a no-brainer, since the hotel was charming, elegant and beyond first-class. She wanted to pay Pierre for their stay, but he declined.

"Zoe, you'd have written the same thing. We both work hard. I'm glad to see this man in your life."

"Thank you, Pierre. I'm glad I can be with him and work at the same time."

"Is this serious?"

"Don't know yet! That's the suspense."

***

Back aboard *Zephyr*, with no storms or squalls expected, they headed down-island. Sailing past St.

Martin, Zeb made a discreet adjustment at the wheel. When Zoe first came aboard, she didn't know a whatsit from a ratchet, a whoosit from a halyard.

"Isn't a Barient Winch a city in Turkey?"

It took Zeb and Simon two days to get over that one. And the pragmatist in Zeb would clearly have chosen a sailing woman. But Zoe was delightful. Funny. She listened to him and told him she was appreciative of all that he had become, a man who loved his wife through illness to her death, a patient father, a retired business man. He thought about his two daughters, managing his employees on the Christmas tree farm, his men on his three fishing boats, and his brother, George, who ran the Zodiac line of dinghies for sale. As a self-educated patriarch, Zeb had sacrificed much of himself over the years to maintain the well-being and nurturing of others. This sea journey was an overdue gift. Besides, given the adorable Zoe's other talents, the definite sexual abilities that charmed him, she might outgrow the status of novice sailor. Meanwhile, Zeb had his trusted Simon to do the heavy sailing, laundry and shopping.

"Boss, this is your time now," Simon said, cheerfully respecting his employer.

***

In the BVI, Beth and Brad boarded *Quadriga* to sail for two days to anchor at the Baths at Virgin Gorda, and to climb the gray elephantine boulders. Unruly branches of waxy sea grape leaves, cashew trees, and green vines entwined over large grey rocks, welcomed them. Under their toes on the beach, the golden sand was hot. Amy, Dutch, Beth and Brad played like children, shouting for echoes under the large rocks. They swam and dove under rock crevasses to the sea, and snorkeled. The gates at one end of the Baths marked the entrance to Toad Hall, a private home, and to Mad Dog's Pub.

Beth and Brad loved sleeping overnight on *Quadriga* at the Virgin Gorda Yacht Harbor, taking long showers at the yacht basin's bathrooms, and strolling to the Little Dix Bay Resort to have dinner. They hiked to the ruins of the old Copper Mine, aware of fragrant foliage, the exquisite air, and plants carelessly growing everywhere. Paved roads and dirt roads became friends to their feet.

When Amy slid back the panel under the stove, the gun was gone. Perhaps he cleaned it and put it in another drawer. She was furious; why hadn't he told her, or asked her?

***

The next day, they returned to the harbour at Road Town. *Quadriga* was anchored ten minutes out. The four took two dinghies and went to lunch in town together. Amy and Beth took time to shop and have a drink by themselves.

By late afternoon, nearing dusk, Amy and Dutch went to pick up the sail that needed repair. At the Moorings dock, they loaded the bulky sail into the Avon dinghy, and slowly motored through the harbor. With the weight of the sail, the dinghy labored toward their boat. A large silver flying fish flashed out of the water and across their bow in a perfect arc.

"This is why we're in the Caribbean," she said, sighing with happiness. But she turned. She screamed, "Look! Men aboard our boat!"

Unable to goad the loaded dinghy into moving faster, Dutch screamed hoarsely. "You fuckers! Get off my boat!"

Two swarthy men, both holding small bags, jumped off *Quadriga* into their waiting motorboat. A third was at the wheel. Sailors on other nearby boats stood up to see. The motorboat quickly sped away, heading towards the West End.

"God dammit, who are they? What have they done to *Quadriga*?"

Amy felt sickened as Dutch slowed to circle *Quadriga* to assess any outward damage and danger. Other sailors on nearby boats resumed their earlier attentions.

"Stay quiet, Amy," Dutch commanded.

Her heart felt razor-edged as Dutch opened the blade of his sailor's knife and silently hoisted himself aboard. The well-varnished wood planks of the hatch door were hacked open on the companionway. Shards of wood lay about. Amy grasped the rail on the big boat.

"What a mess," he yelled, stalking through the boat, cursing loudly. Dutch, dazed with the shock of his privacy invaded, his boat insulted, gnashed his teeth while he kept moving around the boat. The galley panels were open, condiment bottles overturned, evidence of rifling through the flour bin. Two of his Limoges cups were broken, but the plates, the radios, and the Loran he kept, were intact.

"Come up, Amy. Make sure the dinghy's tied solid."

She made it fast, and climbed aboard.

"I forgot how, no matter where, in our dream of escape, we're always in a world of violence," he said, furious. "Someone's been watching us. We need a new hatch door, which we'll do tomorrow. We have to be willing to live in uncertainty. How could I be so stupid?"

"We locked up," she said, staring at overturned drawers, the nav desk in a mess, the silverware drawer open and empty, the sterling silver gone. She swallowed, trying to make the scene bearable. Dutch moved to the forward cabin, finding hangers pulled out at their stress points, clothes hurled on the bed. Slipping his hand down beneath a panel, feeling for the inert steel box that held his traveler's checks and cash. Untouched.

"Makes no sense." He checked the electrical panels and bilges. "We're ordinary sailors."

Amy was unsure of what to look for, realizing the hiding places aboard *Quadriga*. Was there such a thing as an ordinary robbery? Was anyone watching them? Her mind went into fast forward, dipping into new territory of deceit and fear: "We've got a beautiful boat! Instead of taking something, do you think they planted something?"

"Why would you say a thing like that? You haven't a suspicious bone in your body?"

Dutch could not stop moving around his boat. "What an idiot I am to think we've been sailing in Paradise! We're exposed," said Dutch, berating himself into a new state of consciousness.

"Do we report this to the police?"

"We'd be balled up in red tape, forever. It's you and me. Rifle's here," he said, opening the starboard berth to reveal a drawer, "Bullets here. Another rifle's deep in the fore cabin locker. And the handgun's still here." He took a box out of the locker near the steps, opened the top, revealing a black handgun.

"Why've you kept guns hidden from me?"

"Come on. They've been here all the time. All you had to do was look! Okay," he confessed, "I did hide 'em for the ocean crossing. I didn't want to scare you. You might have had a fit. Or worse, not have come with me."

She knelt down, to hide her tears, and picked up broken pieces of the beautiful china. "You want me to know everything about the boat, but you hide guns. I was going to throw one overboard!"

"Hell, no!" He turned to her. "We need them now."

"My friend Lucy killed herself, by accident, with her father's gun, when we were sixteen."

Dutch put the gun back in the box, setting it in the locker.

"Why didn't you tell me?"

I'm sorry, Amy. I'm stupid, never thinking Caribbean waters can be a war zone, like anything else,"

"I hate guns."

He turned away. "The sail is in the dinghy." He hoisted it back up on deck.

Sleep was hard to come by.

***

The next morning, Amy silently prepared breakfast while Dutch took a mask and fins to swim under the keel, investigating the boat. While he went down and came up several times, there was nothing. How could he have missed, aft, a small signalling device placed inside the exhaust cowling, nice and high over the water?

A ferry passing by interrupted him: too much wake.

He came aboard. Taking off his mask, he said. "Nothing. We're clear. As soon as we're stowed, we've got to get out of Tortola. I'll sign us out and radio Bravo that we're leaving for St. Croix. I'll ask Beth and Brad to meet us in Christiansted harbor. And when I give you orders, or you see something, like that gun sliding out, you tell me. The boat comes first."

"Yes, Captain," she sighed, her shoulders drooping, cleaning up the mess.

She felt a new tangle; would they be struggling and grappling with something in sailing the islands that they knew nothing about. Of course, *Quadriga* was exquisite. She knew people looked at the yacht. How little did she know about this new world she was living in? Was everyone cursed with the idea of a perfect Caribbean sailing life?

During the tranquil sail, steady breezes, blowing through the front hatch into the salon, they barely spoke. Amy seethed with their inequity and what was the nature of partnership at sea. Conflict of a different nature, and could she sustain this rolling life with Dutch?

Chapter Seven

Logbook: Virgin Gorda, October, 1980

Name	Location	Latitude	Longitude
Zephyr	Virgin Gorda Yacht Harbor, Spanish Town, BVI	18° 26.985'	64° 26.204'
	Christiansted, St. Croix, USVI	17° 44.922'	64° 41.914'

Aboard *Zephyr*, Zoe wrote her reports and faxed them from different island hotels.

"Would you stay a bit longer, Zoe?"

Being her own boss, she certainly could. The beauty of *Zephyr* commanded her attention, and she was mesmerized by the lovely mood being aboard. She gulped in the sheer ubiquity of her new universe.

How long could this last, she pondered, observing Zeb and Simon and how they quickly moved around *Zephyr*, how they set the sails, anchored, and joked together. On tranquil sailing days, she loved hearing the rush of water along the hull as the ocean-going vessel sliced through the seas with authority. In her citified heart, the enchantment of *Zephyr* beguiled her, the very wood resonating with protection, a sturdy guardian. She kept away from the chocolate.

There was built-in joy in the hundreds of details comprising *Zephyr*. In the master cabin at night, their bodies mingled happily, muscles and sweat gliding together, the new bedrock of the ship. With lively Zoe during the evenings, Zeb wasn't going to sleep early any more. One evening, under a full moon, they sailed from Tortola to Christiansted Harbor on St. Croix, the red setting sun casting a ruby topping on the blue sea. A red-hulled boat on a ruby-dusted sea, and she, the loquacious New York lady, was utterly speechless. And how she respected the heavenly Simon, major domo, provisioning, cleaning, and serving meals.

"Please let me wash the dishes, I'll learn how," she said.

"Stay pretty, Zoe," the Captain said. "I'll teach you how to run the outboard in the dinghy."

Run an engine by herself? She never even started a lawn mower, how would she do this? She paid people. Simon must teach her. Slowly.

***

Boat maintenance was indistinguishable at first, Zoe seeing the boat as clean and gleaming. Yet watching Zeb and Simon daily repairing, rewiring, sanding, varnishing and polishing, she began to see distinctions, skills employed, and finished details. Completed tasks looked easy, as if results appeared invisibly. The more she observed, she understood the limitless job of upkeep. Like her body, exercise, portion control! Her suspense? Uncertainty.

***

Logbook: of *Quadriga*, *Bravo* and *Zephyr* at Christiansted, St. Croix, November, 1980

Name	Location	Latitude	Longitude
Zephyr	Christiansted, St. Croix, USVI	17° 44.922'	64° 41.914'
Quadriga	Christiansted, St. Croix, USVI	17° 44.922'	64° 41.914'
Bravo	Christiansted, St. Croix, USVI	17° 44.922'	64° 41.914'
	Buck Island, Tortola, BVI	18° 25.942'	64° 33.606'

Yacht *Bravo* slid into the slip next to *Quadriga* in Christiansted. Immediately, the Turners were invited to dinner aboard *Quadriga*. Amy prepared pasta and a salad, while Beth and Brad quickly slid into their favorite spots at the dinner table. While dining, they observed *Zephyr*, a nice ketch, designed by Germain Frers, slowly motor into the Harbor and dock next to them. Three fine-looking Nantucket red colored hulled boats.

The drama of *Quadriga*'s ransacking told and retold, the four speculated on robbery, drug running, and hijacking in the Caribbean. "We've got to safety-proof our boats and dinghies with new locks and chains," Dutch said. "We were damn lucky to get fair warning."

"As the hour grows late," slurred Bradley, on his fifth glass of wine, "a toast! To a man, a woman and a boat, the eternal triangle! To what we love the most!"

"It's always and forever the boat," Beth jested.

"How small we are on the ocean," Brad philosophized. "All the wind and water drives home how mortal we are. Humans can't live on the ocean. Only visit a short time. Beth, pour me one more."

"That's it, Brad! Bed time!"

"How this captain tells me what to do! Hand the bottle over, woman!"

Amy gave Beth credit for saying, "Aye, aye, Brad."

Beth turned to Dutch, "Dutch, you're too quiet!"

"I am furious, Beth! Life has changed. We've been ransacked, and must I to be in every conversation for you?"

"Dutch, you're brusque tonight," Beth said gently.

"Someone's after our goddamn boat."

Beth whispered to Amy, "Stay strong."

***

Dutch's withdrawn moods swung between distraction and distress. Silently, Amy observed her emotional thermometer, hinging on his moods. Their safety. Must everything she do meet with his approval? Every waking hour to be spent with the one man with whom she had chosen to go to sea? He showed her four more guns aboard.

***

On the dock, *Quadriga*, *Bravo* and *Zephyr*, similarly well-kept yet individual, looked like a Maharajah's Fleet lined up. Simon, the bright, friendly deckhand from *Zephyr* came over to *Quadriga* to say hello. He'd heard about Hinckley boats, made in Maine, but had never seen a fibreglass yawl up close. Dutch and Simon were off and running about boat gear, going below to have a beer.

As preparations for departure were being made for the two boats, continuing south, Brad and Dutch unhooked the yellow power lines and filled the freshwater tanks from the dock.

Zeb, from *Zephyr*, strolled over to chat with Brad.

***

Outside on the dock, holding two cups of coffee, Amy handed one to Beth and gently tugged her aside, hoping to steal a few moments. "Beth, I'm at the mercy of his moods. I have to learn to shoot a gun. I feel stripped of all my support systems, and I'm learning to respect fear."

That moment, passing by, the lovely looking older woman from *Zephyr* stood above them on the dock. She greeted them. "Hello, ladies, please don't mind my interruption. I'm aboard *Zephyr*! I simply wanted to say hello to you two. I hope that's not too direct."

Amy and Beth looked up, hiding their annoyance. They had to be polite.

"That's fine. Please join us," Beth said graciously.

"Would you like some coffee," Amy asked, reluctantly.

"When I saw you two, you look so nice, like you'd understand. I'm so lonely for girl talk. I'm Zoe. From New York."

"We're New Yorkers too."

"Sometimes New York City seems safer," Zoe joked.

"Coffee?"

"Please."

Amy sighed, rising to the interruption, went below, and brought up coffee in a mug shaped like a whale. She handed one to Zoe. "These silly coffee cups were on sale. I happened to buy three. Beth and I've been friends since our passage began in New York. We drink from these to remember we're having a whale of a time aboard. Since you're on a red boat, Zoe, would you accept this as a gift? It says 'BE RESOLUTE.'"

"Thank you. Not always easy," said Zoe. "What I miss most are my girlfriends. I've watched your boats when we've been on the same anchorages. Thanks for this lovely gift," Zoe said, gratefully sipping her coffee.

"Tell us about you?"

"My captain," Zoe said, "is from Northern Ontario, Canada, from an island called Manitoulin. We met in Virgin Gorda some months ago. I know nothing about sailing, but Simon, the deckhand…"

Amy and Beth gawked, in unison: "You've a deckhand aboard?"

She grinned. "Yes. Simon's from Wales. I met Zeb when I was leading a group of travel writers around the BVI. My work is writing about hotels and vacations. I've been doing it for years. My mother, bless her soul, was annoying me about how one-sided I've always been. Then along came Zeb."

"Is this a Caribbean fairy tale for you, Zoe?" teased Beth.

Zoe laughed. "You bet. We're older than you. Right now, there's no sailing pressure on me. I'm turning fifty. But with Zeb, I feel younger than springtime!"

"I love your honesty," said Beth, laughing. "That's what sitting on a dock for ten minutes with new buddies' means: reality and truthfulness."

"Zeb says he won't try to change me! I don't have to become a sailor!"

"That's the first lie," hooted Beth.

"Thanks for the coffee and the cup. Resolute!"

"That's our motto, Resolute!"

In a conspiring sense of new friendship, the three sat on the dock, their legs dangling, Glints of sun lit Beth's curly red hair, Zoe's short blonde hair, and Amy's long, brown straight hair. While Beth and Zoe chatted, Amy traced her fingers along a pattern of grainy wood on the dock. Zoe had a career. The man she was with looked gentle, kind. Amy bet Zoe didn't have to learn to shoot a gun or worry about a ransacking. And Beth was smart, in everything.

"Ladies, we're taking off!"

The three stood up, coffee cups in hand, Zoe cordially inviting Amy and Beth to visit aboard the next time they might meet. "Thanks for letting me in."

"Our pleasure," Beth said, and whispered to Amy. "You've proved yourself on the ocean passage. Dutch's scared. So, you'll learn to shoot a stupid gun, so what! Understand his point of view. He wants to protect you and the boat."

They didn't see Brad listening to them. "Amy, we've so much tied up in our boats; no one wants to be a Caribbean horror story. Dutch's bluster covers up his feelings. Remember, you're free."

"On a boat?" Amy asked, and hugged each of them. Was *Quadriga*, a cage for her, the Wannabe Songbird who didn't have enough edge? Who loved Dutch?

Anyone observing the young people, their healthy bodies, obvious styles, might envy their lives, and the three elegant sailboats docked next to each other. Out of the corner of her eye, Amy caught sight of a photographer, having breakfast in the pub on the wharf, taking a series of pictures of them.

***

Maxwell Desmond, a retired businessman from England, sat at the pub, by himself, watching the spectacular Hinckley Bermuda B40 yawl recede from the dock. A few days ago, he had been in Tortola, taking care of some business he never talked about. *Quadriga* had certainly caught his eye. His men had gotten off that boat in Tortola, before the owner and the girl came aboard. It was brilliant to put the device high in the exhaust cowling, a perfect spot. He sipped his rum, and waited. St. Croix was boring to him, an American island, where his business could not stand the least observation. He was eager to get home to St. Maarten. Or to visit his second home in Antigua. Perhaps he would see this sailboat again. He was counting on it. He put his camera away. The suspense of where *Quadriga* might sail next? He could certainly wait. The Caribbean was not so boring this week He'd look at the photographs later.

Amy glanced at the photographer, simply catching the exuberance of six sailors on a dock in St. Croix? She was tempted to tell Dutch and ask him to go and ask why the fellow was taking so many pictures, but Dutch would certainly be rude and might try to take the camera away. St. Croix was a beautiful island, a free world, and she had enough on her mind.

It was time to go.

***

Logbook: of *Quadriga*, Buck Island, November, 1980

Name	Location	Latitude	Longitude
Quadriga	Buck Island, Tortola, BVI	18° 25.942'	64° 33.606'

At the helm, Amy put her boat in reverse, turning the wheel as they moved away from the dock. She gently pushed the gear forward. Once clear of the harbor, she gave Dutch the helm and they pointed toward Buck Island where they'd spend the night.

For the next day, the plan would be to sail to St. Maarten. French cuisine and shopping for her. Both sad, that their beautiful *Quadriga*, that had seemed so safe and strong, had been attacked. They were hurting.

***

Anchored safely by Buck Island, they wound the ship's clock together as they had every Sunday since they met.

"Dutch, I'm scared."

"We're in a different game. We're safe today. And smarter."

"Your moods sour everything. I know our game has changed. But don't spoil more, especially with me."

"Don't try to change me. If you don't like it, get off. I'll get you to the next airport," he said, "If that's what you want."

His words cut through her.

"Dismissing me? You'll be on a boat going nowhere."

"There are certain decisions a Captain must make."

"I won't be controlled by your moods!"

"Amy, slough off whatever I say!" He spoke softly. "Honey, if either of us got hurt, the other has to handle the boat. Learning doesn't come overnight. Guns aboard are for safety. When you learn, you'll lose your fear and be competent! Merely a skill to be learned. No moral crap to it, except maybe to save our lives."

Swift beating rain interrupted them. Dutch closed the hatch and the portholes, moving closer to her. His mood shifted with the rain. "I'm sorry. Please, is that enough?"

"I don't know anymore."

"My golden thrush, my singer of beautiful songs, trust the process." He came to her, bending down to put his arms around her, his lips to her hair. She clung to him. "I love you Amy! Commit to learning everything you can."

"You mean submit!"

"I'm an imperfect man. This voyage is nothing without you."

He stood up, "We're here. Let's put on that old Gene Autry movie, the one you like."

***

"Good morning," whispered Dutch, kissing her, as she awakened to breezes wafting from the open hatch.

After they dressed, and had coffee, Dutch said, "Let's have a look at the Walther."

There were no other boats at Buck Island, so he took the Walther out of the box and handed it to Amy. "It's not loaded. It's simply your next skill. Get a feel for it. Make it your friend. It may save our lives. Use two hands to aim. Don't jerk the trigger, squeeze it slowly. It has recoil, and the bullet has a tendency to go to the right. Cup your left hand under your right wrist to steady it. That's right, you're doing well. Line it up with the front sight. That's the notch on the muzzle. Aim at six o'clock on any target."

"I can't do this, Dutch, I'm weak, and I'll fail — at everything!"

"Fail now, so you don't fail later, if we really need this!"

As she pointed and squeezed, he directed her; "If you need to kill, Amy, you need to aim for the center mass of the body. Always. Go for it fast, even in the dark. I want you to have an added sense of protection, though you may never have to use it."

"Only on you, if you don't behave."

"Okay, you win on this one!" He smiled, "Now I'm putting bullets in." He loaded it. She held it gingerly. She aimed at a soda can he threw aft. She supported her hands, pulled the trigger. Dreadful noise tore at her ears.

"You didn't hold it right. Try it this way." Again, she aimed in the water for the floating can. She missed it but felt steadier. Another soda can was hurled into the air. She aimed for it. After five more shots, she actually hit the can. The gun was empty.

"Good. Done for now. While you're below, make me another cup of coffee."

She laughed: even she knew the old 'While you're below' trick, as in, "While you're below, would you make a chocolate cake, do my laundry, make our dinner, clean the head!"

"Anything for the Captain," she said. While waiting for the water to boil, Amy pretended to aim at imaginary killers in the cockpit. She noted her angles, crouched around the main cabin, held the gun and played heroine against robbers boarding the boat. Dutch watched from above, relieved she had gotten into the play of it as he watched her prowl in pretend deadly frolic. She may as well get good. She heard her father's favorite saying: *chance favors the prepared mind.*

***

On the passage south toward St. Maarten, Dutch said, "Wind's died." The Westerbeke chugged smoothly over the seas that had turned to calm. The engine suddenly slowed, went out of syncopation, and failing, went dead silent.

"At it again, my dead engine," he said wanly, turning the engine switch off and going below. "I see it; a residue of dirty water's built up showing in the glass bottom of the fuel filter." He sat on the sole, cross-legged, to open the filter valve to drain it, working methodically, replacing the filter and bleeding the air out of the system, a patient task.

Back above, Dutch turned the engine on. The Westerbeke purred smoothly, running another hour before falling silent again. "We'll ruin the engine if this keeps up. We've got to have repairs done."

To their starboard side, through a gray cluster of mist on the horizon, the island of Montserrat came into view. "Let's head there, get the engine fixed, and sightsee a few days. I've always been interested in that island."

Amy got the guidebook and read aloud. "This states there's nothing to do on Montserrat. Shouldn't we continue on to St. Maarten?"

They looked out on a flat sea. Sails flapped despondently at dusk.

"We've got no time schedule. It shouldn't take long to pull in there. We'll get to St. Maarten eventually," Dutch decided, setting a new course.

"It's a small island? Maybe they don't have parts there?"

"I'm tired. It's late and we're close."

With the dinghy lashed on the aft deck, they began their westerly course heading of 280 degrees. The wind surged gently to five knots. No other boats on the horizon. Happy conditions had changed, and it was getting dark. Amy sat on the low side.

Night came on suddenly. Cold, Amy went below for warm clothes and to pull out safety harnesses. A desolate feeling came over her, as the wind picked up and rain clouds appeared. It might be a long way to Montserrat, or anywhere.

Dutch raised the main sail. Too much canvas. Together, they jumped up to reef the mainsail. New rain beat down on her foul-weather gear. She secured the safety line and took the wheel as Dutch directed a course heading. The wind rose so sharply, it howled in the rigging, followed by torrents of rain, streaming down her nose, her neck, and dribbling onto her chest. Oh shut up and zip up. There's a new song. Shut up and zip up, we're sailing in Paradise, oh yeah, wet, wild and wonderful...

Quadriga was a bronco, nosing up to the crests, down into deep troughs. The lockers below were closed, everything stowed.

"I'll take the helm while you make sandwiches and coffee," he said. She agreed instantly, and went below. As she balanced herself below, the rain beat harder on the cabin top. She looked up at him at the helm, a man in love with his boat enjoying the hell out of this passage. She brought up sandwiches, which he ate quickly. Water thrashed against his face and dripped down his Indian nose.

Flashes of lightning surrounded them. "It'll be longer than we anticipated." Then he yelled into the air, "Rocking and rolling with Neptune, and you, Poseidon!" Dutch invoked to the heavens. "While I'm no Don Quixote, fighting windmills, thank you for wind on my sturdy boat!"

"You love yelling things to the sea," she yelled.

"You betcha! We're rocking and socking!"

While Amy felt sick, she stayed under the dodger to keep him company.

"Go below and get solid shuteye, Amy. I'll need you on watch later." She nodded, went below and pulled off her damp clothes, falling into forgetful sleep.

***

The clock chimed midnight. Dutch's hand stirred her from deep slumber. It was her turn at the wheel. Unconsciously, she fought to remain asleep, but awoke, startled to her responsibility. She moved out of her bunk and dressed again. The galley light was on; the tantalizing smell of fresh perking coffee buoyed her.

"Bring up coffee," said the voice above as she retied the laces on her topsiders. She poured steaming coffee into two mugs, turned off the burner, the galley light, and balancing carefully, carried two mugs into the cockpit. Without spilling.

"Don't forget your safety harness!"

"I've got it." She handed him a mug, put her coffee in the holder, and snapped on the safety clip. The rain had passed.

"Keep her steady. Sails are trimmed. Wind shouldn't change. Wake me if there's a problem."

***

She took the wheel and watched his large frame disappear below. The binnacle light held its faint steady glow. Amy was alone. Ship's bells chimed from below, in the lonely night. Fear overwhelmed her as they made seven knots. She was responsible for this vessel in the darkness. Raging sounds of the sea clutched at her. Shivering, she put on her wool hat, gloves and zipped up her jacket. She took a look at the compass. Oops, off course with that little move. Sails were luffing. Why weren't they using the autopilot? He wanted to conserve power.

At the wheel, Amy thought about melodies now inside her head. She became deeply aware of Caribbean accents, so musical and denoting mood. Could she use that musicality of speech in her songs? The sounds of the sea and wind were inner music to her. The Caribbean use of words lilted in her tired head. In Christiansted, an old man sweeping the street had said to her, "Be remindful, Miss, you not to be walkin' in de ditch dere." She was delighted, writing later, the song:

Be reminded, Sailor, all those seas we've sailed
Miss me down the road awhile, soon I am returning,
Just give me one more smile, one more smile.

She carefully kept the wheel on course, and didn't look behind at the solid wall of darkness. If only there were stars, if only a ship would appear in the distance. She was suspended in timeless space. Alone. Taking a long, slow breath, her hands became motionless on the wheel as a sense of peace invaded her. She was alone, steering *Quadriga*. Or had she help? What an incredible universe; on course, winds steady, and Amy Sandler at the helm, finally understanding how Dutch felt.

She couldn't keep her eyes open and fought to stay awake. She heard ship's bells and Dutch appeared miraculously in the companionway. "I'll take her now." She released the wheel to him, stretched her arms, inched below to the galley and heated up a can of chow mein. It was four a.m.

The lights of Montserrat loomed brightly. The chart showed the wide harbor of Plymouth, which was more of an open roadstead, showing a depth of 300 feet, shoring up quickly to 30 feet near the beach.

"With no engine, we've got to come about and anchor quickly on a tack. We can do it."

She stayed silent, vowing to do everything he told her.

"You take the wheel. Ready about," he said, readying the port side, letting the sheet off the starboard winch.

Amy turned the wheel too fast. "Bring her back, Amy, back, back, back," he yelled. *Quadriga*'s motion slowed, becoming deathly quiet.

The sea stopped.

"Congratulations on your first 360 degree turn."

Quadriga made a complete circle.

"That actually helped us," he said, and she grinned foolishly. The sails caught the wind as they came around again, Dutch cleating the line. "This last tack will take us into the harbor. I'll get sails down fast and we'll anchor as quickly as we can."

The town lights twinkled broadly. They could see cars moving. Who drove around at 4 a.m.? The wind whistled in short gusts, swirling erratically around the mountains in front of them. Amy wrestled with the wheel to keep the sails filled, but she was unable to steer straight.

"Do the best you can," Dutch bellowed, while engaging the anchor to the rode, and winding in the genoa. The boat heeled right and then left, sails flapping. Tears of effort ran down her face, instantly dried by the wind. She was upset that she could not keep *Quadriga* straight. "Come on, come on…"

"Watch the depthometer. Chart says it'll show thirty feet in a minute or two."

She peered at the instrument scanning forty, now thirty feet. The boat hurtled through the night toward shore, and would probably run aground. Dutch heaved the anchor over, paying it out. He had reefed the main, which was still up, flapping wildly. Would the anchor catch?

"Twenty feet," she yelled, waiting for the anchor to catch. Please, Neptune, a helping hand, Amy prayed. I'm your anchorwoman and I need help.

The anchor caught. Dutch secured the line. "Give me a hand to unreef," he yelled, jumping back to the mainsail. She was behind him. The spreader lights were on, brightening the night, while they sweated, loosening the reef, and lowering the sail. She tugged at the last hanks of sail as he roughly folded and flaked it, tying it down as fast as he could. It was done. Dutch turned the spreader lights off, heaved a sigh and made one more check on the anchor. She gazed at large drum moorings nearby left for the tankers.

He dropped into the cockpit, exhausted. The mountains of Montserrat loomed atop them. "Feel the awful roll of this harbor, Amy, we wouldn't have to move if we made love!"

Dutch laughed, tearing off his sweaty clothes, his mind on a second anchor. "The rolling of this harbor would do it all for us. Multiple orgasms! I've got to get the second anchor down!"

"You bet," she slurred, hardly making it to their berth below. He followed, and both became lost in deep, grateful sleep.

***

A knock on the hull awakened them at nine the next morning. "Hullo, Captain. I am Immigration Officer Hawkins. Welcome to our island of Montserrat." He was careful to keep his boat from knocking against *Quadriga*. "May I see the yacht's papers?"

"Of course. Would you know a good engine mechanic," Dutch asked, not quite awake.

"Our Mr. Hallpike is excellent with engines. By the way, we watched you on our radar for hours last night, making your way into our port. You're in rough Christmas winds. We would have towed you in, Captain, had you radioed for our support."

They looked at each other. "We never turned the radio on!"

***

Logbook: of *Quadriga:* December and Christmas vacation, 1980

Name	Location	Latitude	Longitude
Quadriga	Plymouth, Montserrat	16° 42.220'	62° 13.311'

Amy and Dutch locked up the boat and took the dingy to the main commercial pier used for loading freighters. People bustled along the quaint streets of Montserrat. When Amy looked up, lush velvet green mountains soothed her eyes. She fairly danced along the street, glad to have her feet on land. A local man, fortyish, trim, wearing a short-sleeved shirt and long pants, likely a local businessman, approached and stopped them.

"Hello Captain, I'm Everett Hallpike. Everyone calls me Hallpike. Officer Hawkins mentioned you need an engine mechanic. I can help. I watched you come in last night from my farm on the hill. We don't have many sailors coming here. I own the Hallpike Chicken Farm and my chickens are served at the Shady Nook. Please be my guests for lunch. I need to hear conversation that is not from Montserrat. And you look very interesting. Please join me."

Dutch regarded him carefully, aware of his crisp educated, British accent. He looked at Amy and she nodded. They followed him up wide concrete steps to an old restaurant with modest tables and chairs. "Goat Water Stew is the specialty, with rice. You'll like that," Hallpike suggested. When Hallpike ordered, he changed into local patois as he talked to the waitress.

"Have you lived in London," Amy asked while they waited to be served.

"Indeed. I studied at the London School of Economics, taught there a bit, but I was eager to come back home to Montserrat. My wife and baby daughter are up at our farm in the hills. Where did you begin your journey?"

"We began from New York, but I've sailed up the East Coast to the Vineyard and Nantucket. I've wanted to sail these islands for years."

They chatted easily, enjoying lunch, with this ingratiating stranger. Hallpike was pleasant, telling them about Montserrat, and his former life in London. While the men talked engines, her attention drifted to the brown and green foliage of the hills seen out of the window. The sun streamed through, highlighting red hibiscus. Her teeth were sore from gritting while she was at the helm. The goat water stew arrived. The dark, spicy taste was hearty, as Mr. Hallpike predicted. How nice it was to have someone interested in them.

"Our mountain chicken is famous and tasty. That's what we call our high-jumping frogs in the mountain streams. We catch them and roast their legs. I'll take you to my farm and ask my wife, Cora, to cook them for us. She gets rather lonely."

Dutch protested when there was no bill. "You're guests on my island," said Hallpike as he walked them through town. They passed a bakery, where he ushered them in, picking out a loaf of bread and a large box of cashew nuts, tied with a Christmas bow. "Accept these as a welcome to Montserrat. I'll take a look at the engine with you."

"I have a pressing problem. My fifteen year old son, Nels, was going to fly to St. Maarten to join us for his Christmas vacation. I must change the arrangements to fly him here. Is there a travel agency in Plymouth?"

"I own that," said Hallpike.

"We were on our way to St. Maarten, but came here and we sail there as soon as we solve the Westerbeke problem."

"Ah, my dear friend, Maxwell Desmond lives on St. Maarten, Hallpike said. "I am sure he would be glad to show you around."

***

Dutch and Amy waited while Hallpike changed into work clothes and they took him to the boat. He admired *Quadriga*, seeming to know a great deal about Hinckley boats and Westerbeke engines. Hallpike knew just what to order.

***

At his farm in the mountains, overlooking the harbour roadstead, Hallpike picked up the phone. "Max, I've found a way to solve our problem. A perfect solution, and probably great fun for our needs. The American boat, the one you saw in Road Town, just happened to pull in to Plymouth."

***

Nels, a lanky, bright, appealing dude of fifteen, arrived, flying from Newark to St. Marten and over to Montserrat. To the delight of Dutch, Nels had an adolescent croak. Montserrat was a lovely place for an island holiday with hills to climb, waterfalls to view, a safe town to explore, and blackish sandy beaches from which to swim safely. They hiked and swam and played chess.

The road wound up a series of hills to the Hallpike Chicken Farm, overlooking the sea. His wife, Cora, was pretty, demure, and welcomed them with shy pleasure. After a delicious lunch of mountain chicken for the adults and a hamburger for Nels, the men retired to the workshop. Amy saw a young farmhand who smiled at her. He told her his name was Juan.

While Cora put her baby daughter down for a nap, Amy waited in the living room looking discreetly at old novels, Victorian romances, stacks of English fashion magazines, and scholarly journals on engineering. A sepia-toned newspaper clipping from The New York Times caught her eye. It concerned Dr. Everett Hallpike presenting a paper on NASA's advanced tracking stations in the Caribbean. She picked up a yellowed Manchester Guardian. A similar story. She heard Cora's footsteps and quickly stepped back.

"I was on a yacht once," Cora said wistfully. "You must be having a fine time. I'm from Barbados. I went to school in London where I met Everett. I've no friends here and my husband's caught up in his private world, work that I don't understand." She brought her hand to her mouth, "I have no business burdening you. Excuse me; I hear the baby."

Amy was crestfallen, hoping to have a nice girl's afternoon with her. Cora left the room and did not return until Hallpike, Dutch, and Nels came back.

During the dinghy ride back to the boat, Dutch was upset the soldering did not work on the metal piece he brought from the Westerbeke, a problem Amy would never understand. Everett ordered one from Miami.

"You should see the sophisticated short-wave set he's got in the barn, Amy, fax machines, three telephones," Nels told her. "Dad, he's too smart."

"He seems to be a man of many talents," Dutch said. "All I care about is our engine."

"I saw a newspaper clipping about Dr. Hallpike discussing NASA's tracking system in the Caribbean. It said he's a retired professor."

"I don't give a damn what he was, or is. I want to get out of here with a healthy engine."

"He was casing every inch of our boat, Dutch."

"Everyone cases this boat."

"But Dutch, you said we trust nobody; he's too friendly."

"This is Montserrat. Didn't you read that nothing happens here? And besides being bored while we wait, Nels is having a good time."

"So we're in that sailing condition called "waiting-for-parts-to-be-delivered.""

"Relax, Amy."

***

Amy had a tough time sleeping on the boat with the constant rolling swells into the shallow harbor. Each morning of Nels' visit, she took the dinghy in to go to the library in town where she could sneak in a nice nap, snuggled into a deep chair, leaving Dutch and Nels to spend time together. They met later and went hiking up to a waterfall that smelled of sulfur. "Rotten eggs," said Nels, but he loved the colors of the sand, and scooped a handful to take back to the boat.

***

Christmas passed and Montserrat's Jump-up Day hosted a joyous New Year's Carnival. Nels waited in the dinghy to get to town.

Carnival music boomed from the shore. All of the island bands with their high-powered, high-volume speakers were trying to outdo each other. "Hurry up, Daaaaaaad! Can't you hear the music?"

People linked arms to dance and sing as the co-mingling of perfume and sweat, the flashing eyes, glimpses of long legs, hips and shoulders, added to the excitement. Along with Hallpike's Chicken Legs, mango and coconut ice cream were sold on every corner, scooped up from buckets. Doors to homes were opened, welcoming neighbors and friends.

Recognizing Amy and Dutch, who had been in town a week, a wealthy Montserratian lawyer and his wife swept them upstairs, welcoming them into their home. Amy gazed at the spacious living room, kitchen, and bedrooms, wishing she could sleep soundly for a night here.

While the lawyer's wife was congenial, she was guarded. "We heard Mr. Hallpike's helping you."

"He said he grew up here," Amy said. "That he'd returned home. His accent is because he's been in London."

"Oh, did he?" She arched an eyebrow.

"Margery, be quiet," her husband said, standing next to her.

"Please, what do you mean," Amy begged.

She turned to her husband, "Selwyn, you know Hallpike's a devious fellow we do not like. He came here five years ago, conned Cora, married her and took over the farm and other businesses. We're not sure what goes on up at that farm. Raising chickens? We think his business and teaching pedigrees are made up."

"Be careful, wife," Selwyn said, moving her quickly away. "Open the door, please. We've more guests."

Nels came up the stairs to Amy, "Amy, come with me! Shake your waist and dance." He pulled Amy downstairs. "Don't tell Dad I had a few beers," he giggled.

Music filled the streets, causing the plate glass of two stores to crack. Not concerned, everyone danced. Finding their way back to the lawyer's home, they found Dutch and Selwyn saturated with rich cakes and punch, smoking Cuban cigars.

It was well after dark when Dutch and Amy returned to the dinghy, both so bleary the spray didn't annoy them. Nearing the boat, Amy thought she saw Hallpike or was it the mechanic getting off *Quadriga* into a waiting dinghy. "Look, Dutch!"

But Dutch was so mellow with good cheer, he didn't see anything.

***

Up on *Quadriga*, Amy took out her flashlight to unlock the hatch. Reaching for it… it must be her imagination. She only had three glasses of wine. She used the same procedure; nobody could get in. Was the lock opened? The wine made her tired. Everything seemed fine. Since the lights of Montserrat shone the other way, it had to be a mirage of exhaustion. The hatch door opened easily.

"How could we forget Nels?" Dutch, still in the dinghy, slapped his forehead and turned around. Here was Nels on the small Customs boat speeding their way. The officer slowed and steadied Nels to transfer him into the dinghy. With a good-natured wave, the officer sped back to town.

"Where did you go?"

"Dad, you left too early! Let's go back," Nels slurred.

"Give me fifteen minutes to rest, Nels. Lie on your bunk and sing 'Yankee Doodle.'"

"Okaaay, Daaaad."

Nels flopped on his bunk, faintly whistling strains of 'Yankee Doodle,' followed by fifteen-year-old snores. Both father and son wheezed as Amy worried about the lock. She didn't remember. The rolling of the boat in the harbor rocked her to sleep.

***

Hallpike came aboard, courtesy of the Customs Boat. The parts for the Westerbeke had finally arrived from Florida. He and his mechanic came aboard to install it. The engine rumbled anew.

"Thanks, Hallpike, you've been great," said Dutch.

"I agree, if I do compliment myself. By the way, is *Quadriga* a documented vessel?"

Instantly on alert, Dutch replied, "With Lloyds of London, and my syndicate in New York. And New Jersey. They keep close tabs on us, Hallpike. By the way, what do I owe you for your services?

"Only the cost of the parts and shipping."

Amy watched as the transaction for the payment of parts and shipping took place. She looked at him apprehensively. Why hadn't Cora ever come to town? Why did such a pretty woman have deep circles under her eyes, and so afraid to talk?

All was working and well. Satisfied, Dutch went off to clear Customs and Immigration, while Hallpike stayed on the boat. "I'll be back in a half-hour."

Hallpike went back to the Customs boat, tied up by the big boat, and brought up packages, presenting them to Amy. "If you would do a favor, Amy, my dear British friend, Max, has a home in St. Maarten. Since you're headed that way, would you mind sailing these cashew nuts over? The Customs men there love these cashews, open the boxes, and then eat them. Max never gets them. It's our standing joke."

Hallpike had been very nice to them. "Of course," she said. "With pleasure."

"I'll let him know when you'll arrive. Late this afternoon. Weather's good. Here are sweet pineapples, plus three dinners of my Fried Chicken, six boxes of cashew nuts for you, and the other six tightly wrapped in festive paper for my friend. His name and phone number are taped to the top box. I'm sure he'll drive you all around the French and Dutch sides."

Hallpike took his leave as Dutch returned and boarded the boat. "We're cleared for departure."

Dutch shook his hand. "Thank you so much, Hallpike."

"Dutch, please stay in touch. I've truly enjoyed meeting you."

Nels had asked to make the sail with them to St. Maarten. Plane reservations were made to get him home for school.

***

Quadriga rounded the coast, leaving Montserrat, with high waves hitting them from the starboard bow. The rollers started off the coast of Africa and swept directly in front of *Quadriga*. With the wind a steady twenty knots, the boat negotiated these sea troughs at six knots. Amy looked back pensively at the emerald hills, dewy-fresh from the recent rain. Time with Nels was great: she adored the kid, and would be sorry when he left. Yet the French and Dutch Island of St. Maarten awaited them.

Amy was about to go down to get her guitar to practice. "Nope, my darling, time for you to practice something new!" He put the boat on autopilot, went below, and brought up the AR-15 rifle, handing it to her.

"It's so big and heavy. I'm scared. Please don't make me learn this."

"You must. It may save our lives one day." He showed her how to load the magazine. He stood up, balancing against the large winch, showing her how to take aim out across the water. "Stand this way, hold it into your shoulder. Become one with it. When it kicks back, your body will swing back, like this. Watch the repeat as I shoot."

Exploding in sound, ratta-tat-tat.

Nels spoke up. "Dad, I know this has a 16" barrel, 6-groove, 1-in-10" RH twist, with the M16A2 pistol grip. The 50-round detachable magazine, the ribbed round hand guard, the sight radius at 19 ¾", and the flip rear sight are set for 50 and 100 meters. It has a blowback system that fires from a closed bolt, introduced in 1985. It is not a machine gun, or a shotgun. It is a Commando Arms Carbine,"

"Son, where the hell did you learn that?"

"Dad, I know things. I'm fifteen."

The task at hand was learning to hold the AR-15 with the long muzzle. She cradled it in the back of her arm to aim high where she thought he would throw the plastic bottle full of water. He threw it up. She waited to take aim, dug in for balance on the boat and slowly squeezed the trigger. Her ears exploded from the sound, but she held her stance.

Had she gone deaf? Out of five, she was able to hit one plastic water bottle. The boat suddenly lurched and she slipped over the coaming ridge, sliding into the cockpit. Holding onto the gray rifle, the long barrel unwieldy in her hands, she crooned, "Well, hello Colt AR-15 9 mm Carbine," seductively, but terrified.

"This time move with the rifle, then hold still and aim."

She did it over and over, getting familiar with the feel and heft of it, and the ear-splitting sound. "I hope I'm not deaf!"

"You've got the basics. You've already held and shot the Walther." He handed it to her. Loaded. She liked this one, cuddling the small size of it, and waited for him to pitch another plastic bottle filled with water into the air. She hit it, feeling an odd power. She might be okay with these.

"If you were boarded when you're alone, use the Walther, a winch handle, an ice pick, a kitchen knife, a wire cutter, and your rigging knife. You know how to set a course, start the engine, pull the anchor, and put on the autopilot," he said.

"Dad, can I shoot?"

"Maybe later, son."

"Amy, I smell chicken. Let's have lunch…"

Chapter Eight

**Logbook: *Bravo*, at Sea off
Guadeloupe, December, 1980**

Name	Location	Latitude	Longitude
Bravo	Deshailles, Guadeloupe	16° 18.385'	61° 47.862'

At the helm of *Bravo*, Captain Beth observed vast stretches of undulating sea that lay ahead. The misty-gray island of Guadeloupe loomed up, beckoning them to the Northwestern cove of Deshailles Bay, a well-protected harbor. The island, shaped in the form of a butterfly, had two main islands called Grande-Terre and Basse-Terre. Guidebooks promised a vivid history, lovely French wine and cheeses. *Bravo* entered the quiet harbor, and dropped anchor.

Green grass was growing on *Bravo*'s hull. They'd scrub it off in the morning. "First, we clear Immigration, take a walk on French soil and find ourselves a lovely restaurant for dinner and wine."

Immigration completed, they leisurely walked up a steep hill observing the tiny French houses, all sizes, connected tightly and encroaching onto the main street.

On top of the hill, they looked back at their red sloop in the quiet, crescent-shaped bay, agreeing that *Bravo* was a thing of beauty, theirs.

A colossal white motor yacht rumbled into the bay, dwarfing *Bravo*. The Turners could read the name, *Brindisi*. But they couldn't read the hail port. Where was it based? They watched the white-uniformed crew anchor it efficiently, its generator noise filling the harbor. "There goes our sleep," Beth sighed. "We thought we picked a quiet harbor. The money in that big fat machine would feed this town for years. At least they've given us swing room."

Beth and Brad found a small restaurant on the beach, dined, and watched as the large yacht's bright lights, strung from bow to stern, illuminated the small harbor. They saw a fast, dark boat, with deeply resonating engines, enter the bay, slowly circle *Bravo* twice, shift to neutral, and coast up next to their boat, bathing the sloop with bright searchlights.

"That looks sinister. *Bravo* looks like small prey. Who are they?" she questioned aloud. Crew from the dark boat flung a line around one of *Bravo*'s cleats. Shocked, Beth jumped up, but Brad put up a hand to stop her.

"We do nothing. Stay still."

Suddenly, from the bridge of *Brindisi,* a brilliant high-beam searchlight focused on the dark boat. It withdrew the lines and reversed its engines as its swarthy-looking crewmen moved their boat with a rude bump against the large yacht.

After dinner, the Turners walked and Beth noticed an old local fisherman sitting on shore, shaking his head worriedly, pretending not to watch the scene. They looked back and saw a uniformed deckhand hold off the offending vessel. Stomping up, four men, in some sort of dark uniform, displayed disrespect for the big boat, but they were shown aboard. They disappeared inside.

Ten long minutes later, the figures climbed back down to their small cruiser. Gunning their twin engines, they sped out of the cove, leaving a raucous wake that rocked the boats. The waves washed ashore, thrashing up on the beach, lapping at the toes of two young girls chattering at water's edge. Beth and Brad hurriedly paid the bill and rushed to the town dock to their dinghy.

The old fisherman whispered "Be careful, you young people. These Gendarmes from Pointe-a-Pitre. Rough. They poke around, guns and drugs. They not like dat big boat. I listen my radio today. They look for cocaine shipment on American red sailboat, coming from Montserrat."

"While our boat is red, we've not been in Montserrat. Thank you for telling us," Beth said, now worried.

"I have daughter in Brooklyn, nice, like you. Gendarmes always angry. I never talk to you, oui?"

"Oui, monsieur." Her mind whirled. "They could impound our boat. Keep us here. Take everything away from us."

Can we sail out tonight?"

"We can't. We have to exit with Immigration, play by their rules. And wash the algae off."

***

Hallpike and Desmond's troubles had begun recently with their relationship with the huge, deadly drug cartel. Due to their businesses on the islands, which involved importing produce with small boats, the syndicate paid them to ship the cocaine that had been refined in the Columbian jungles onto their small boats that circled the islands. Hallpike's chicken farm was a perfect dodge to store the small bags of coke for a limited period until other small boats shipped the cocaine to Mexico. This had been working for years, with authorities unable to figure out the small boat distribution of the drugs. Their problems arose from a turncoat in their organization. Wild rumours arose that authorities were now searching very small boats for drugs. Hallpike had kept the drugs on the farm, waiting for the police to give up so they could ship the cocaine. He and Desmond had been laughing over their long, quiet success. Almost boring, Desmond complained. But the cops were not giving up. They were getting desperate for a shipping method as the syndicate was annoyed as to why they were not receiving their drugs.

***

The next morning, Beth observed the big yacht, assessing that they wanted nothing to do with *Bravo*, a meager tourist sloop. Nothing of value on that small boat, just dopey young American sailors. Good.

Beth rigged a safety line from bow to stern for Brad to hold onto so he could safely scrape off the slimy hull. He put on flippers, affixed his breathing apparatus and goggles, jumped in, and swam, his long, thin legs effortlessly propelling him. She peered over the side, seeing his bubbles float up from under the hull. Freedom on a sailboat was so delusional; a funny perception dreamed by all who worked in offices in cities. She lay down in the cockpit, resting a moment. Startled awake, she felt guilty, put on her flippers and mask, and joined Brad. She and Brad crisscrossed under the boat, scraping as they went.

Taking a break, they swam to the other side of the cove to observe amber reefs and multi-colored fish teeming below them. They found a rock to sit on, feeling like strong seals in the sun. Beth played with the golden hair on Brad's arm. Resting against him, she whispered, "I love you."

He placed a gentle finger on her lower lip. "Me too."

A loud rumbling noise ruined their moment as the fast black boat they had seen earlier entered the cove making straight for *Brindisi*. Three uniformed men tied up and asserted their way aboard. Minutes later, they left with several large soiled white duffel bags.

"What do you think they're taking off?"

"In broad daylight?"

"The townspeople seem terrified to talk."

"Obviously, they're not interested in us. We better leave while we can. A red sailboat carrying cocaine? A red sailboat in the Caribbean! Not *Quadriga*, us, or *Zephyr*. How can we warn them?"

***

Logbook: of Yacht *Zephyr*, Anchored off Virgin Gorda, December, 1980

Name	Location	Latitude	Longitude
Zephyr	Virgin Gorda Yacht Harbor, Spanish Town, BVI	18° 26.985'	64° 26.204'
	Yacht Haven, Charlotte Amalie, St. Thomas, USVI	18° 20.153'	64° 55.253'
	Norman Island, BVI	18° 19.048'	64° 36.931'

Zephyr sailed back to the British Virgin Islands; Zeb loved Virgin Gorda. An eighty-foot motor sailer, *Serendipity*, purred into the harbor. A shout was heard from the deck: "Yo, Simon! Yo, man! I can't believe it! Meet me for a beer, Olde Yard Inn?"

Simon was shocked to see Malcolm, a long-lost friend from Wales. They'd served together as soldiers in The Falklands. "Okay, I'll see ya at the Olde Yard!"

The next day, Simon asked to speak to Zeb, confidentially. "*Serendipity* is looking for a First Mate, about to make the passage south, through the Panama Canal to Hong Kong and the Malacca Straits. Dutch, they want me as First Mate. You've been father and friend to me without the lectures. I'm so grateful, yet I feel in the way of you and Zoe. Would it be okay with you if I left?"

"Simon, I'd never hold you back," Zeb said sadly. "While I'll miss your snoring, you have my blessings. Do you think Zoe can hold her own?"

"She certainly can, Boss."

Before Simon left, Zoe quietly placed an envelope into his hand. "You will please me if you spend it in Hong Kong." He opened it to find five, one hundred U.S. dollar bills.

"Zoe, this is too much. I can't accept this," he stammered. "Are you staying aboard?"

"You've earned this money. I've learned from your guidance. Take this now or I'll feed the fishes. Get going, before I cry. And yes, so far I want to stay aboard. I've let my niece Debra use my apartment in New York."

***

Their dear Simon waved from *Serendipity*'s rear deck as it grandly glided out of the harbor.

How would life be without Simon? Simply the two of them aboard *Zephyr*, and now Zoe had the run of the galley. She could play house, go food shopping, and take the laundry to be done locally. Yup, read a cookbook and follow directions. Glancing at Zeb, with his windswept gray hair and muscled, tanned shoulders, she felt her blessings. She'd been able to develop skills under his benevolent eye. She could certainly meet new challenges. And she was feeling more adept, more graceful moving around the boat.

***

"Pull in that sheet," Zeb ordered, under sail.

"Which one? How much," she asked, baffled.

"Look up at the sail, Zoe. Follow that line, you'll see it! Don't wait for me to tell you. The sails teach you!"

Fortunately, she grabbed the correct one, without knowing, and hauled it in. Why did she have to wait for Zeb to tell her what to do? Vacation was definitely over. Her amazement was beginning to wear off. Maybe she couldn't learn this.

He looked at her with pity. "The trick's watching the wind and understanding how to position the sails to move the boat where you want it to go."

"Thank you," she said. To herself, "Duh." And, feeling helpless, she reasoned, "No cute little learning: I've got to listen to his every word. And also, please…talk… slower."

***

While Zoe watched the sails and trimmed the sheets, she had no ability or aptitude for feeling the wind. None. She compensated by scrubbing, sanding, cleaning, doing laundry, shopping for groceries, and washing the dishes. Zeb cooked. She was the early one off to sleep. And longed to inspect hotels at the islands where they docked, still able to do her work, but now she knew the boat came first.

Gaining her balance, but with laundry, groceries, there was no time to look fashionable. Nor was she able to finish reading *Chapman's Boat Handling*. No clues there. She asked for less writing work. How the tapestry of life changed: when might this New Yorker become competent, next to being aboard and sailing, and would she even know it? If she could sneak off one day and pay for sailing lessons from a certified teacher, one who didn't know her. What was wrong about that?

Zoe became acutely aware of other subtle tasks aboard that Simon had accomplished, one being a strong social function, of conversing with Zeb all day long about boats and maintenance. There was silence where that particular male bonding had simply been part of the rhythm of *Zephyr*. She committed to be unquestionably aboard. And while she wasn't bored, she needed the presence of other people. She studied sailing books so she could talk about sailing. Ha.

***

When *Zephyr* returned north to St. Thomas for refrigerator repairs, and docked at Yacht Haven, Zoe jumped off and into a taxi, eager for a day of shopping and calling her office in New York. At the USVI Tourist Office she set up appointments, planned her tour, and inspected two hotels. It was late in the day when she returned, flushed and happy.

"Where've you been? I've been sick with worry; St. Thomas can be a dangerous island."

Rosy with excitement, Zoe described her afternoon. "The Tourist Board gave me a car and driver. I faxed an inspection report to my newspaper. May I take you to lunch at a new restaurant tomorrow?"

"Don't make plans for me," he said, flatly. "Socialize, if you must, but don't try to live two lives at once. I'm busy with the broken fridge."

"I can't be aboard all the time."

"I get worried if you're not back on time."

"I'd love to treat you."

"We eat better aboard than those crowded, noisy restaurants."

"Because you do the cooking."

***

What refuge she found at the local Laundromat! She keenly listened "When I came aboard, the first thing my guy told me, jokingly, was 'Accept it, Gertie, you'll always be wrong aboard, that's a condition of sailing with me. I'll always be right! Take it or leave it.' And you know what, girls, I married him!" The sailing woman shook her head slowly while folding her towels. "At sea, I got nothing. My senses narrow to the two of us aboard."

"Been married forty years," piped Audrey, an elderly woman in abundant physical shape. "I miss Minnesota. My husband thinks he's a good sailor; he's terrible! He doesn't know I'm the real captain. We sail, get this, by suggestion. I suggest, he does it. We have no car, no phone, and no bridge club friends. I don't get to see my grandkids. My husband thinks we're in Paradise, and oh boy, do I need this laundry," she laughed. And folded sheets.

"My man and I charter our boat," Lorraine said. "It's always in perfect condition. He and I always look fabulous. People think we have the perfect life. You'd think we never fight? We fight all the time!" She folded pink underwear. "All his underwear got dyed pink when I put my red shirt in."

"You have no idea how you're helping me," Zoe said, folding along with them.

"We all do more laundry than we have to."

***

Striving to balance living on his boat, Zoe realized how much she had taken for granted in the convenience and accessibility of friends and business colleagues. On recollection, her New York life, the network established, woven into the fabric of everyday life, seemed easy.

The magnificent part? She loved looking at and swimming in ocean water, feeling the weight of it that could lift and set her back with force at any time. She felt in tune with the pulse of waters around the boat that alternately hugged it, and then rocked it with powerful waves. She became alive to the sound of the surf by the beaches. And her new-found deep respect for the water that rose and fell like her own breath. The dappling current, the sun sparkling on morning water, coincided with the rules she was learning about living on the ocean, surviving at sea level. The suspense and challenge of life with Zeb and at sea had become, a gift bestowed upon her.

At anchor, by Norman Island, she sat in the cockpit, gazing at still waters, hearing the bleat of invisible goats on the rocky hillsides. She swam twice a day. Zeb, indeed, had established a private world of tranquility and solitude. They both liked classical music, and read in companionable silence.

Until she cleaned the head.

"In the name of Neptune, why'd you use paper towels to clean the bowl of the Crittendon toilet?"

"I was going to pump it through to clean out the entire tube," she wailed. "I'll buy a new head!"

"That's not the point!"

The next two days, spent watching Zeb take the head apart, appalled her. Then she giggled, learning up close and personal about bilges, drains, and how the head really worked.

Collecting mail from the Virgin Gorda post office, there was a package from Zoe's college pal, Dr. Robert Solomon, a professor of ethics, who sent her a gift of his new book about love.

"The primary motive for love is not sex or companionship, or children, or the convenience of a relationship, but a sense of self-worth. To put it very crudely, when love succeeds, each lover feels better about himself or herself. When love fails, it is because one no longer likes or can tolerate the person he or she has become. Love, like most emotions, serves self-esteem, and what makes love last is not passion for the other person alone, but the maximization of self-esteem. What makes love fail is the decimation of self-esteem."

Danger was not only from the chaotic elements of the sea. Wasn't she lucky to have Zeb and these challenges in the summer of her life?

***

One evening, she said slowly, but in direct New York style, "Zeb, I have a request."

"What?"

"I'm yearning for a bit of praise, dear. Can a Manitoulin sea captain give a Manhattan lady a compliment for what she's working hard at learning and becoming?"

"What're you talking about?"

"The toilet challenge is fixed. I haven't gotten sick, tripped, or caught my fingers in the winches. When you ask for a wrench or a nail, or sandpaper, I hop to it! Gladly get it for you! I haven't wound the anchor rode over my ankles, nor broken any bones. I sand and varnish." She paused, "No more manicures. But mostly, I haven't poisoned you with my cooking."

"Aw Zoe, I show you daily I appreciate you by my actions," Zeb whined, looking up from his book. "Haven't you learned that I'm not a talker? You do take both parts of any conversation!"

She got up from the table and went above, silently.

He put his book down and climbed up after her to the cockpit. "Stupid me, I get it. You're the greatest, even if you can't tell a jib sheet from the main!"

"I would appreciate some verbal praise once in a while. Without a joke attached to it!"

"You're not a sailor," he paused, "but you will be. Ahem, I delight in you being here."

"Was that so hard?"

"Yup," he said. "By the way, weather's right for sailing to Marigot Bay, Antigua, one of my favorite anchorages. You're going to take the helm. I'll keep my eye on the compass I have in the aft cabin. Now there's something I'd like to share with you that has nothing to do with sailing, or words" he said, taking her hand, and leading the way to the aft cabin.

"You bet, my darling Captain," she said, taking his hand.

***

"Just an ordinary wet Caribbean passage," Zoe kept telling herself at the helm as rogue-sea winds whipped up, gusting to thirty knots. They double-reefed the mainsail and were using a number-two jib. Winds swept at them while foam crests at quartering seas broke behind *Zephyr*. Zeb came up to take the helm and she went below to secure clattering doors that had sprung open.

At a full gale, gray rain stung his face as *Zephyr* rode upwards at a crest. All was silent for a second as the hull was lifted halfway out of the water, then the vessel dropped hard, rolling like a hobbyhorse.

"I forgot the harness," he yelled, as *Zephyr* careened again into a trough. She leaned out of the companionway, throwing the harness to him, but she fell, portside, in the cockpit, holding on with all her might. Would this be a knockdown as the rail touched water, and the mainsail... touched...water? The roiling sea entered the low side of the cockpit, rushing aft, but with skill by Zeb, *Zephyr*, oh so slowly, righted herself. The jib and main lingered full of soggy air and rain.

"You stay back," Zoe screamed to the ocean, surprised at her strength at holding on, and that the boat was again even. She watched the excess water aboard return to the sea below them.

"Zoe," he shouted. "Release the line that's led aft in the cockpit. That one, for the main halyard!"

The mainsail came tumbling down; Zoe ably furled rough and fast, desperately holding for balance. Then as the boat careened through the breaking seas, they furled the jib to the size of a small storm jib. Finally, they had control once more and Zeb steered back on course.

Both exhausted from their efforts.

"Well, done, Zoe. I'm proud of you," he said.

"Wow, a compliment," she sighed, glad to be comfortable again.

"You're capable of handling the helm. I've got to sleep."

"Of course," she said, wishing Simon was there, scolding herself for that thought. She went quickly below. She drank a full cup of water, made a stop in the head, put candy in her pocket, tissues for her nose, and put her foul-weather jacket over her bathing suit. She came up to take the wheel. Zeb blew her a kiss and went below. The rain began again, dripping down her nose, her feet, soggy in her docksiders.

She was holding course. But nausea took over. Zoe threw up on the wheel and binnacle. Her nose dripped, eyes teared, and to add insult, she felt dark liquid running down her legs, diarrhea! The indignity of it! But she laughed; stay on course; keep the wheel steady with the small jib. Her inner waves depleted, she felt better, threw off her jacket, and wiggled out of her soiled bathing suit.

Zoe stood, naked, steering *Zephyr* through slogging seas. She wasn't cold, though rain battered her, cleaning all body fluids into the cockpit, and hopefully out to sea. The binnacle, wheel, and cockpit washed clean. This was the best joke, ever. One she'd never ever share. A strange sea-love welled up in her. She would remember this. She was a sailor, and a new thought; Zoe was *marinized*.

Suddenly, Zeb appeared below by the companionway, gazing up at Zoe at the helm, naked as a jaybird, in the rain, talking to herself!

"Look! Naked Wonder Woman sailing the Ocean Blue!"

"We're on course!"

Logbook: of *Yacht Quadriga*, Montserrat to St. Maarten, January, 1981

Name	Location	Latitude	Longitude
Quadriga	Plymouth, Montserrat	16° 42.220'	62° 13.311'
	Cruz Bay, St. John, USVI	18° 19.000'	64° 47.075'

On Quadriga's midday passage from Plymouth, Montserrat to St. Maarten, Amy pulled out fresh pineapples from two shopping bags. She brought the packages into the cockpit. Dutch, at the helm, was happy to be sailing again. But he looked at her bounty and asked "Where did you get all that?

"Hallpike brought it to us as a going-away gift. Great food."

"Why did he give us three boxes of chicken and fries and four small pineapples?" he asked irritably.

"And six boxes of those cashew nuts, all wrapped up with a note where to deliver them."

"Why the hell did you accept these from him?"

"You saw him bring them on?"

"I got on as he was getting off."

"You've had him on the boat many times."

"Always, when I've been here."

"Remember, I told you I thought I saw him getting off the boat late on New Year's Day!"

"He or that mechanic's never been on the boat without me. I'm hungry; let's see what we've got."

"Here's the paper with the address for these to be delivered." He lifted it to read aloud; "Maxwell..."

As he held it, the wind tore at the flimsy paper. It flew out of Dutch's hand, a butterfly onto the sea.... "Shit, I lost the damn address. Okay, what's in here?"

"Can we get it?"

"Nah, Hallpike'll probably call him to tell him when we're arriving."

Amy untied the ribbon, the wrapping paper, and opened the top. Luscious cashew nuts were revealed.

"Oh, that was for the man. I opened the wrong box."

"Doesn't matter. Let's have some. Give me the box."

She handed the box to Dutch, who took out a knife and opened, by mistake, the bottom of the box.

In wrapped plastic, they saw white packets. "What's this?"

Dutch took a knife and slid open the packet. He licked his finger, put it in the white powder, and then tasted it. "How stupid does he think we are?"

She looked blank.

"Dad, that's cocaine," Nels said, shocked.

"Let's sail back, rewrap the box and give it back, "Amy pleaded.

"That bastard! Conned us the whole fucking time! If we sail back, we could lose the boat. He'd say we set him up, deny this and we'd be arrested. Boat impounded. No wonder he was so agreeable. That goddamn chicken farmer's not screwing up our lives!"

"Do you think Hallpike's got the police in his pocket?"

"And this guy is waiting for us in St. Maarten?"

"What do we do, Dad?"

Dutch was livid. "What else may have been added aboard *Quadriga?*"

At the wheel, Dutch turned to his two passengers. "We're not sailing to St. Martin. Screw that. Nels, we're sending you home from Antigua, the next southern island. Take the helm while I rechart our course." He went down the companionway into the main salon. He looked around, and suddenly went forward, slipped back the Persian rug and opened the floorboard by the starboard hanging locker. Small bags of white powder.

"How could I have let that bastard on my boat?"

"Does this have to do with our being ransacked in Road Town?

"But we searched the boat in Road Town."

"We're ordinary sailors," she wailed.

"Yup, naïve and stupid," he said, counting forty small packets in one bag.

"Let's sail back to St. Croix, or San Juan, to the American authorities..."

"Why not throw it overboard, Dad?"

"Then what do we do," asked Amy, terrified. "He knows we have it."

"Some helluva game we're now playing. Take it up, Nels. Throw it over. And no, you cannot try it!

"Aw, Daaaad," he pretended to whine, but happy to help. "This is like the comics!"

***

They dropped the cashew boxes, the packets, and the chicken overboard. A path behind them, ending life as they knew it. "We've got to do a thorough search in the boat, so we have nothing to show."

"That man is waiting for us in St. Maarten."

"Let the bastard wait."

***

It was late afternoon, turning to dusk, when they entered the lee of Antigua, making their way north to the harbour of St. John's. Sails down, they slowly motored from one lit buoy to the next, following the chart.

"Marker twenty-two," Amy said, standing at the bow. "Find the red beacon on the hill."

The lights of St. John's sprang up as they entered the main channel packed with large vessels and container ships docked along the wharves. Dutch turned at the next marker into a small bight, empty of other boats. Worrying if anyone would begin looking for them here, now, she took the wheel. Putting the engine in neutral, Dutch dropped the anchor, paying out the rode. Reversing, the anchor held. Engine off, new Island. They settled into the main salon, wondering how to conduct themselves.

First was getting Nels safely off the island. In the morning, they locked up *Quadriga*, and with the ship's papers, took the dinghy in to register at St. John's Immigration and Customs. They took a taxi to the airport and put Nels on the next flight to New York. "Nels, stay cautious. You know how to do that. Talk to no one," Dutch commanded. "I'll phone you at home."

They watched him board the airplane. And wave.

Amy asked, "Can Hallpike track us down?"

"Anybody can. We're a beautiful American-made-in-Maine Hinckley sailboat."

***

Both morose, at Nels' departure and their dismay of the drugs they had thrown overboard, they spent the afternoon in St. John's, walking through town and having lunch in a local restaurant. An Antiguan torrential rain began, lasting three hours straight. Dutch and Amy sat waiting miserably for the rain to stop. Of course, the boat was locked up tight and they could see it from the restaurant. The restaurant emptied, but soon filled again with the early cocktail crowd, armed with umbrellas, and remarking that the heavy rain was unusual for the beginning of January.

"There's too much rain in the dinghy. Let's go back to the dock. We have to bail or we won't be able to navigate in the downpour."

***

"Quite a rain we're having. It is most unexpected at this time of year," said a well-dressed fellow with a British accent, ever so cheerfully, coming to sit at the table next to theirs.

"I'm having a tropical depression this minute," Dutch said.

"Perhaps I may buy you two a drink? There's nothing else to do until the rain stops."

"No thanks," said Dutch grimly.

"You seem troubled? May I be of some assistance? I live here," said the man pleasantly.

Amy sat glum with new realizations, their predicament, worried about the dinghy and if *Quadriga* would hold anchor on good ground. Already in a loop of fear, she was anxious that the winds would whip the boat in a circle.

"Are you folks from the red sailboat in the harbor?"

Startled, Dutch looked up, his mouth tight.

"Why do you ask?"

"I saw your boat arriving, from my home on the hill. I sailed around Newfoundland in a Hinckley once and I have a grand appreciation for the makers of that boat, a Hinckley fibreglass yawl. If you're worried about holding ground, the harbor has a good sand bottom. Want a ride to the dock? I'm going that way."

Amy looked at Dutch. The stranger clearly knew the value of their boat.

"No thanks," Dutch said, abruptly closing the conversation. "Let's get out of here, Amy."

***

Outside, they were drenched, but so what! Amy held on to Dutch as they rushed down the street to the wharf. The dinghy was full of water. "We've got to get the dinghy up, turn it over."

"Can we do it?" she yelled against the wind.

"What a dumb question!" he yelled back.

A large black Mercedes slid up beside them next to the wharf. The British fellow from the pub hurriedly got out. "For God's sake, it'll sink with that water! Let me help you drag it!"

The Brit got out of his car. Together, they towed the dinghy from the dock to the beach. With strain on their faces, they turned the dinghy over, dumped the overflowing water, and turned it upright.

The man was soaking wet. Smiling. "That's my adventure for the day!"

"I've got to get to the boat. Amy, I don't want you in this. You can get a hotel room for the night," Dutch said, soaked, getting into the dinghy. He was able to start the motor.

"Don't be crazy, man," yelled the stranger, "Look at the turbulence. You'll overturn. Your boat's fine. You can take a look at her from my place. Don't be proud, for God's sake, accept help!"

Amy stood under the eaves of a building, drenched, hearing them yelling at each other so they could be heard above the howling wind. "Be smart. I own this warehouse. Let's put your dinghy in there."

Dutch recognized this man was helping them. They carried the dinghy through the double opened doors, set it down, and came back to the car. Placated by the stranger's help, Dutch relented, "Thank you, sir."

"I have a huge home on the hill, and I'm always in need of the company of sailors. Good ones. Please allow me to offer you refuge and hospitality."

"No, thanks, we'll get a hotel room." Dutch was brusque. It was dark.

"It's January, height of the season. You'll pay through the nose. I have plenty of room. You'll be safe for the night. I'm lonely for smart company, and I like to talk about sailing."

Dutch nodded gruffly, the voyage of yesterday in his mind. He shook his head no. But Amy was wet, exhausted. And took over…"Thank you. We accept. Get in the car, Dutch," she ordered, shivering in her wet, cold clothes.

"I'm sick of strangers," Dutch blurted.

"I'm a stranger no more," the British fellow said, laughing. "Do get into the car. By the way, my name is Max Desmond, and I'm glad to welcome you to my home. You'll be safe and comfortable."

Dutch pulled open the back door for her, shut it, and folded himself into the front seat. While Amy felt better in the car, she realized how much she loved *Quadriga*.

"Thank you. I'm Quentin Teerstrat, Dutch for short, and this is my partner, Amy.

"Glad to have you," Desmond said, gunning the car, beginning a harrowing ride up winding roads, where gullies formed, stone fences crumbled under the wash of the torrential rain, and stones were carried down, flowing and bouncing on the road. Water on the road had risen above the ankles of a couple of townswomen as they strained, leaning into the wind, trying to get home. It was obvious Desmond could hardly see, but he knew his way by rote.

"Around this turn," Desmond said, "You'll get a glance of your boat. It can get so boring in Paradise and we're glad for the rain. And I have a chance to host you two."

***

Dutch craned his neck to see the harbor below as the car entered a driveway to a sprawling house on top of a hill that overlooked the bay where *Quadriga was* anchored. "By the way, my wife's visiting on the other side of the Island. I doubt she'll be able to get back tonight."

Desmond glanced at the rain gauge outside the garage window. It passed seven inches. Lightning forked across the sky.

***

"Where you been, Dezzie," called out a beautiful, slim, black woman, waiting in the kitchen.

"This is Femalie. She's our housekeeper. She'll make you comfortable. Bring them fresh towels. My wife Roberta's across island tonight."

The housekeeper seemed to have the run of the house, and the owner. She smiled tightly at Amy. While showing irritation at their unexpected arrival, she led them to a large living room where windows faced the harbor below. In the room stood a powerful telescope, to which Dutch instantly glued himself. In spite of rain on the window, he saw that *Quadriga* was holding anchor.

Desmond offered, "Why don't you two dry off? Take a shower. I'll have Femalie dry your clothes."

Amy and Dutch glanced at each other, grateful for their unexpected host's thoughtfulness and an awareness of Femalie.

"That's a pretty name, Femalie. Where did you get that," Amy asked, trying to be friendly.

"When I was born, the birth certificate said 'Male' and 'Female.' Since I was a girl, my mother gave that name. It was already written for me. I get you towels," she said, slinking away.

***

When the power blew, Femalie lit a large candelabra and brought out a bottle of French wine, gourmet cheeses on a board, lobster pieces, and crystal glasses. She poured the wine and sat down to chat with them. The men took turns looking through the telescope as sporadic lightning illuminated the sight of the boat, a mile below. Conversation was polite, but guarded by Dutch. Amy pled a headache and was ushered into a beautiful guest room with towels, a nightgown, and toothbrush.

***

Dutch stood at their window most of the night, willing *Quadriga* to hold her ground. Was the chafing gear around the anchor rode? Amy, dry in a comfortable bed, listened to the rain beat on the roof. She awoke at dawn, and saw Dutch standing by the window. The morning, full of sunshine and stillness, showed that *Quadriga's* anchor held, with no evidence of the storm the night before.

Discreetly, Desmond approached Amy, warning her, "Not a word about little Femalie spending the night," and then drove Dutch down to the dock, dropping Femalie at her house in the village.

Alone, Amy sat on the balcony of the silent house. Landscaping and vegetation was cultivated extensively, a rich home and grounds. She took a walk around the house and saw the water cistern overflowing. Behind the house was a sturdy concrete hut, well padlocked, with antennas and three satellite dishes of various sizes. She went closer to inspect, but there were no windows.

The luxury that morning, was using a toilet she didn't have to pump, then lying in a gleaming bathtub with hot water, new soap, and fluffy towels. She looked in the mirror, strong and lean. This Brit was so nice; they were lucky to meet nice people, if they were careful. Max seemed to have everything and enjoyed his conversations with Dutch, as Dutch loosened up. Melodies began in Amy's head. She composed a song about sailing safely, strength, stamina, smarts and enough sleep. Yup, thrive, strive and survive. Rules for survival afloat were as strict as any other discipline. With no answers, she got dressed in fresh shorts and tee shirt, laid out by Femalie the night before.

Gravel crunching; she heard a car pull up in the front. Desmond helped Dutch carry out soaked sheets, blankets and towels from the boat to put in the washer and dryer in the garage, now that the electricity was on again.

"Why are you doing laundry," she asked Dutch.

"I hate telling you," Dutch admitted sheepishly, "that I left a porthole half open. So we're getting a real wash and I showed Desmond the boat."

Roberta Desmond was last out of the car, a pretty British woman, but sullen-faced, carrying groceries into her kitchen. Amy greeted her; "May I help with anything?"

"No, thanks. Desmond thinks I don't know that she stays here when I visit on the other side of the Island. Our former maid wears my clothes."

Amy looked down. "I'm wearing your clean clothes, too."

***

They all ate lunch silently, waiting for laundry to dry. Desmond drove them back to the dock and helped stow the laundry in the dinghy. When the three of them got to the boat, all of *Quadriga*'s portholes were open and the boat was dry. While the sole looked okay to Amy, she knew Dutch would varnish it anyway. Her guitar, always covered and stowed, was safe. While Dutch and Desmond had a beer and conversation in the cockpit, Amy stowed the laundry.

"I need to get gas for the dinghy and some propane. Be right back. Amy, get Desmond another beer."

***

She came out of the fore cabin to see Desmond, alone in the salon, rummaging on top of the Nav Desk. "Looking for something? Anything I can get you," she said pleasantly. They were alone aboard *Quadriga*.

"I was told," he said slowly. "You might have some packages for me from Montserrat?"

"Montserrat?"

Eyes wide open, she stared at him. "What did you say?"

While they had changed islands, not sailing to St. Maarten, but to Antigua, so had he.

Speechless, working to keep her face calm, she moved toward the Walther held in the locker behind the companionway. She tried to be nonchalant, saying brightly, "We sailed directly from the British Virgin Islands to St. Croix to meet our friends, and then here."

"I was sure you mentioned it," he said quietly, slowly moving toward her.

"Oh, we do have something for you," she said too brightly, backing up, away from him. She moved swiftly to another hanging locker and took out two bottles of French wine, holding one in each hand. She offered them in such a manner, subtly defensive, that he needed each hand to accept them. Then she rushed up the companionway, to get away from him, to get into full air.

But Desmond did not seem to have anything in mind that she could figure, as he quietly moved up the companionway behind her in the cockpit. He had to hold the two bottles of wine, but pressed them lightly against her shoulders, whispering in her ear. "I'll say this quietly. Dutch has great taste."

"What?"

Terrified, she brushed from him, quickly moving her arms away from his pressure. And loud, saying "Thank you for your hospitality. I don't know what we would have done without you!"

She felt ready for anything, yet breathed a sigh to see the dinghy approach. Dutch cut the engine by the boat.

"Dutch!" her voice pitched high. "Come aboard this minute! I'm giving Desmond two bottles of wine for being so nice to us!"

"Why do you sound like a cackling hen," said Dutch, tying up the dinghy.

***

Dutch hopped aboard, looking at the two of them, close together. This was quizzical, something wrong. Why Amy's operatic behavior? "What's the matter? You sound awful!"

Dutch saw her face, knew something, but not yet what, and covered, "Desmond, you know how women are, I'll run you back. Come, get into the dinghy."

Turning back to her, Desmond gave her a cold, warning look, as he stepped over and into the dinghy.

***

When Dutch returned, he said, "What the hell was that all about?"

"I was frightened when you came back, he'd have a gun at us. It's him! On that paper," she said, now in a whisper. He has something to do with Hallpike! While you got propane, he asked if we had any packages from Montserrat. We never, ever mentioned Montserrat. I thought he was taking you away now, to kill you."

"That guy's in St. Maarten," said Dutch.

"He's on the dock watching us." She was adamant. "We're blessed to be anchored in full daylight. What can we do now?"

"There's something more on the boat we haven't found." Dutch shrugged.

"He said you had very good taste. And the way he talked about the Hinckley last night, it seemed like he wants *Quadriga*."

"Over my dead body!"

"Don't say that, "she cried, pulling the Walther out from the locker behind the companionway. "I'm learning to use this and the AR-15," Amy said. "Why can't we sail back to U.S. territory? St. Croix or St. Thomas?"

"Nah, we'll motor over to English Harbour. Lots going on there."

"How did he find us," she said. "What's there aboard we don't know? He'll find us again."

Chapter Nine

**Logbook: of Yachts *Bravo*, *Quadriga*
and *Zephyr* January, 1981**

Name	Location	Latitude	Longitude
Bravo	Deshailles, Guadeloupe	16° 18.385'	61° 47.862'
Bravo	Falmouth Harbor, English Harbor Town, Antigua	17° 00.831'	61° 46.497'
Quadriga	Falmouth Harbor, English Harbor Town, Antigua	17° 00.831'	61° 46.497'
Zephyr	Falmouth Harbor, English Harbor Town, Antigua	17° 00.831'	61° 46.497'

After clearing Immigration, *Bravo* slid out of the
harbor of Deshailles Bay, Guadeloupe, to sail south. Brad
set *Bravo*'s sails as Beth stood at the helm, stretching
deeply, yelling; "Yes!" She relished her own strength,
listening to the wind, the waves, and the shivering timbers
of her beloved sailboat. Listening told her everything she
needed to know, always being teased that she sailed with
her ears. She was glad to see heavy clouds and a full, fast,
rain approaching, a million cat's paws flattening the water
in front of them.

"Brad, bring up the liquid soap and scrub brushes!"

Hearing that, he came up and stripped off his shorts
and shirt to nakedness. Laughing, he poured liquid soap
over himself, as rain pelted directly on him. He turned to
see Beth out of her bathing suit. He doused her, scrubbed
her back, and they laughed, as they always did at their
welcomed freshwater rain showers.

"I love this game," he said, "Are we fast enough?"

"We can do a 360 turn to rinse off!" The rain pinged
on *Bravo*'s decks, rinsing them fully, while Beth held
their course, masterfully handling an odd, mirthful roll.
Bravo's naked owners danced in the rain.

"Look!" Through fresh, clearing morning light
surrounding them, the splendor of a full, chunky rainbow
greeted them. At the horizon line, bright bands of all the
colors of the rainbow arced ahead of *Bravo*, beginning
from the port side, up and over to starboard. The Turners
stood naked, in awe.

"That's why we're here, sailing toward rainbows, Brad," she said. "On our wonderful boat that will always bring us home."

On the radio, Beth heard the urgent call from Dutch. Her instant decision; "We must turn around."

She corrected their new course, and confirmed their estimated arrival at English Harbour.

***

Hearing the same radio call, the Captain of *Zephyr* replied, "Affirmative. Heading your way." To Zoe, he said, "We're changing plans. Sounds like a problem. We're sailing to Antigua."

"Wonderful," she said. "It's Antigua Race Week. I've covered it many times. I can write a feature and fax it to my newspaper."

"Can't you stop working, eh?"

"That's what I do," she said brightly. Zoe looked forward to seeing Amy and Beth. She could relax and catch up with her new friends; maybe go exploring and shopping. How fast could she get off the boat?

***

Logbook: of Yacht *Zephyr*, English Harbour.

The three sailboats anchored in busy English Harbour, Antigua.

While Dutch, Brad, and Zeb had taken one dinghy, going hurriedly to the Inn for breakfast, Zoe waited aboard her boat for Amy and Beth.

"Thanks for inviting us aboard," Beth said, from the dinghy, while Amy tied up. Amy and Beth brought an exchange of paperbacks, always part of their community sharing. Hoorah, just coffee and conversation.

"Coffee's ready!"

"Zoe, you look terrific," Beth said, hugging her. "Stronger than when we met you!"

"When Simon left, I started truly being aboard. See these new biceps. While I shop, do laundry, clean and do dishes, Zeb cooks. He's a good cook. If I didn't work so hard, I'd gain ten pounds." Zoe pinched her waist. "We're lucky this is Antigua Sailing Week," she explained. "I've covered this week for years, the hotels and restaurants. We get to see handsome young sailors running around. Big racers are here, with people and engine parts flying in and out all week from English Harbour."

She looked at Amy's face. "Oh God, what's happened? I'll shut up. Sit down. I'll get the coffee."

"Why'd you and Dutch call us here?" Beth was in a hurry to know.

Amy put down her cup; "I'm terrified!"

"What?"

"We meant to sail from St. Croix to St. Maarten. But the engine quit in mid passage. Near Montserrat. Easier to put in there, Dutch said, instead of trying to push on to St. Maarten."

"That old Westerbeke," Beth said. "No doubt Dutch needed to make repairs."

"Beth, stop knowing everything," Amy mocked her. Then sighed, "I'm sorry."

"I'm sorry, too. I keep learning how to shut up and listen."

"When we anchored in the roadstead harbour of Plymouth, we were told about the best mechanic, by the name of Hallpike. He turned out to be an educated guy, not a typical engine mechanic. But he had a mechanic who worked for him. He told us he was Montserratian, born there. But he attended school in England, even taught there. He had a double accent, British and island. He has three businesses, and owns his family's chicken farm."

"Get to the problem!"

"When he had to send for parts in Florida to repair the Westerbeke, he became our friend. We had to wait two weeks for parts to come in from Miami. Dutch's son was with us for vacation. That was good."

"Go on!"

"On New Year's Day, we were invited to a party at a local lawyer's home. The lawyer's wife told me she lived on Montserrat her entire life. Hallpike was not a native, but from another island. She was stiff about him. They didn't know where. But he fixed the engine, and when we were about to leave, midmorning, he brought to the boat, packages of fried chicken for us and gifts of cashews.

"That was nice."

"Wait. He asked us to deliver the gift packages of cashews, personally, to St. Maarten, where we were bound, to his friend. Apparently, because the customs men there didn't care, they themselves were eating the cashews and throwing away the boxes. When Dutch was off the boat clearing us out of Immigration, Hallpike delivered these boxes. Of course, I said yes, since he'd been so nice to us." Amy took a breath. "When we were under sail, and Dutch smelled the chicken, he was glad of that, but furious with me for accepting the packages. He opened them to find a false bottom under the cashew nuts. White powder!"

"Cocaine!" Beth gasped, remembering the radio call about a red boat possibly carrying drugs, which the old fisherman on that dock in Guadeloupe had overheard. The gendarmes were after a suspicious red American boat in their waters. Who would announce or leak a report like that? Beth's mind flashed on to *Quadriga*, already ransacked in Tortola. Might it have become entangled in a non-negotiable situation? Beth listened quietly, her extensive legal nautical expertise enabling her to know the many ways to impound a boat, to relieve it of its current owner. Her knowledge of Caribbean law, of boats stolen, sunk, or repainted and used for other purposes, was extensive. To sail well around the world, she hadn't been a seagoing brainbox for nothing.

Amy went on. "Dutch became furious, going through the boat. He found packets secretly stored under the sole in the bilge. All the time, Hallpike knew we were naïve, new to the Caribbean. I begged Dutch to sail back, return this crap to Hallpike. He insisted we drop it all overboard. And simply changed our course. Here we are. Antigua."

"Go on," said Zoe, horrified, leaning forward.

"Right now, we're all anchored well. But two days ago, Antigua had the biggest rain storm, but we got Nels safely to the airport. He's home now. The day Nels left, it rained so hard that afternoon, we couldn't get back to the boat. We sat in a pub overlooking the harbour. A handsome Brit with impeccable manners sat next to us in the pub. He introduced himself as Maxwell Desmond."

"Was he nice?"

"Charming. Handsome. First, he helped Dutch turn the dinghy over, which saved it, I think. Then he invited us to stay at his home on the hill. Dutch, still troubled, said that this was Antigua Race Week, all the hotels are full. I was so tired, I said yes for us. I felt rescued, in a way, at his beautiful home on the hill. Dutch could even overlook the harbour." She stopped to take a sip of coffee. "Well, Dutch left a porthole open and the boat got flooded, everything wet. This fucking guy was so nice he insisted we use his washer and dryer. He even folded towels with me."

"So?"

"When we were ready to leave, back aboard, Dutch was off the boat getting gas for the dinghy. I was alone with Desmond…"

She stopped.

"For God's sakes, tell us," yelled Zoe.

"He asked me, alone on the boat, if we had packages for him from Montserrat?"

"Crap, this was the same guy waiting for the boxes?" Beth demanded, "Have you searched the boat for any homing devices?" She stopped. "Oh God, I have work to do."

"What?

"You'll see. Go on."

"We never thought of this, sailing to Antigua, that a man could have a house on St. Maarten and Antigua. How stupid were we?"

"Here we are, cruising and enjoying ourselves. I'm so sorry." Zoe said.

At that moment, rocketing by *Zephyr* in a speeding dinghy, a young fellow cast his appreciative eyes on three beautiful ladies, drinking coffee, and sitting in the cockpit. How privileged these women were, enjoying ritzy Antigua Race Week. He waved at them with a big smile, and thumbs up.

To break from this urgency, each woman got up to stretch, to alleviate the fear descending upon each of them and their boats. "Come below and get more coffee! See what I have to keep clean!"

Any joke would be welcomed, as they went below.

"This boat is huge, Zoe. So many places to sleep."

But Beth kept concentrating. "With the legalities and safety of all this, we must re-inspect your boat, stem to stern. Later today. Not now. Since we're sitting here, sharing so much, how's our Senior Goddess doing aboard *Zephyr*?"

"I'll never be competent like you two."

"Are you still happy aboard," Beth asked.

Zoe allowed a small laugh. "It's the sailing I can't seem to get. It's a technical and a cultivated art. I'm learning the hard way."

"There is only the hard way," Beth laughed. "By our mistakes! What about Zeb!"

"You're tough, Beth! I'm New York City brisk and chatty, Zeb's Northern Canadian, well-mannered, whatever that means, well, most of the time we laugh. That's wearing down. Last week, we were coming into Anegada, three sails up. I was doing well on the helm, but Zeb decreed, loudly, he'd take over the helm, 'because I'd surely run it aground.' I got so mad; the depth was over sixty feet. But the Captain declared 'It'll shore up fast at the green marker, and since you might run into a reef, go below and make lunch.' I've gone from office queen to sailboat slave."

"How well we know!"

"However, the heavenly side is aboard at sunset, quietly at anchor. When we go ashore, for food shopping or laundry, I can't wait to get back aboard. I've stopped shopping because I have everything. I adore Zeb, 87% of the time. I may have to get my hearing checked: when he calls commands so Canadian politely, softly, I often don't understand."

"Will you please be kind to yourself?"

"You're used to being your own boss," Beth observed. "I see enormous differences in you since we first met. How you hold yourself and your ability to adapt. Most women start like you, as guests or onlookers. It's clear you have the will and capacity to grow into a real sailor."

"Living aboard with one soul, the Captain, and learning how to think like him is a way to tolerance, and, of course, gratitude," Zoe said. "God, I sound religious. Let's get off me, and ask you. Beth, you've got a charming man. He lets you be boss."

"Lets me! I worry constantly. Brad had a respiratory disease as a kid. Living aboard, every cough is magnified. We're so far from home, all the support systems we know are gone, our work, our neighborhoods, and our own country. On our floating homes, we carry everything aboard, pictures and memory. If we don't like the neighborhood, we raise the anchor."

Zoe added, "Every time we step off the boat on a different shore, we redefine our social identity. That's what I constantly learn."

"This feels good to talk. And listen," Beth said. We need to remember each of our men has achieved something real for himself. Each has characteristics that made them successful. Their drive to create their dream. Amy and Zoe, you're both strong. Know what I'm kicking myself for? Should we have bought a sturdier boat?"

"You're strong and smart." Zoe said.

"Well, it's moot at this point." Beth said. "Today, we have a huge, ugly problem to solve. Many facets. I'll need everybody on this one."

They sat quietly for a spell, thinking what they had, and what faced them.

"Amy, do you feel calm enough to sing one of your beautiful songs?"

"Sure." She got her guitar.

Be reminded, Captain,
all those seas we've sailed.
Miss me off the boat awhile,
soon I'll be returning.
Just give me one — more — smile.
We made an ocean passage,
all night those heavy seas.
Got into port at dawn,
landing here in St. John,
So glad to see some trees
Sun already up, fresh morning,
strolling down a country lane
From the wheel to fresh earth dawning,
gutters filled with rain.
I'm glad to get to town
and market places,
fresh fruits, flowers and faces
smiling at me, I'm a Lady Sailor
with my yellow slicker on.
So to land and laughs and people,
this sailor needs to walk down a road awhile.
Soon I'll be returning,
just give me one more smile.
Yes, soon I'll be returning,
just give me one more smile…..

Her lyrical melody brought a bright Reggae sound of the Caribbean. Within the song, the beat, was the yearning for togetherness and separation, the balancing of it all. She finished the song, and spoke. "I've already written ten songs, and mailed them to my sister, Charlotte, in Boston. She's having them copyrighted."

"We must solve *Quadriga*'s digestive problem." Beth said. "We've got plenty of trouble."

"Digestive?"

"Something's inside her we don't know about."

***

Logbook: of *Quadriga*, *Bravo* and *Zephyr*, January, 1981

Name	Location	Latitude	Longitude
Quadriga	Falmouth Harbor, English Harbor Town, Antigua	17° 00.831'	61° 46.497'
Bravo	Falmouth Harbor, English Harbor Town, Antigua	17° 00.831'	61° 46.497'
Zephyr	Falmouth Harbor, English Harbor Town, Antigua	17° 00.831'	61° 46.497'

Breakfast at the fancy Copper and Lumber Inn in English Harbour, Dutch, Brad and Zeb sat at a table decorated with a pristine white tablecloth, linen napkins, and fresh imported flowers.

"Some asshole I continue to be," Dutch said disgustedly. "Missing the obviousness of that guy? And the second guy, Desmond, right here on St. John's?" To the waitress he said, "Another double order of pancakes please, miss, plenty of extra butter and maple syrup, plus two eggs over light. Don't forget strawberry jam for the toast."

Zeb enjoyed his fifth cup of Cuban coffee, having demolished scrambled eggs with sausage, bacon, fried potatoes, and his breakfast dessert of chocolate cake. No ice cream before noon. Brad was intent on Eggs Benedict, sipping his third glass of freshly made orange juice.

"I've no idea how he found us. It's obvious that Hallpike was alone on the boat at one point. Do I have to kill people to protect my boat? Dutch was rueful. "And drop them overboard?"

"Not a bad idea. No bodies!"

"When the engine failed, why didn't you sail to St. Maarten directly? There's nothing in Montserrat?"

"We were so close to Montserrat. Seemed easy."

Zeb puffed on a cigar and stared into the distance. "This could have easily happened to any of us. Don't beat yourself up, Dutch!"

"I told you those rude gendarmes in Guadeloupe were looking for a red boat carrying cocaine," Brad said. "They mentioned the possibility of a syndicate."

'One syndicate? No kidding. Caribbean's got to be full of them."

"There aren't many red boats around. That's our syndicate."

"Do we call the local police, the authorities?"

"It depends on whether you want to live or die. No authorities. They'll fuck us up; we'd be impounded. We're learning there are no rules in the Caribbean."

"Be sure to stay away from Guadeloupe," Brad said. "Dutch, let's inspect your boat? You might have missed something."

"Not necessary. One thing I am is thorough. Thanks anyway."

"Don't be a dick, Dutch. Beth's an engineer. A scuba diver. I'll go under with her," Brad insisted. "We know how meticulous and smart she is. She'll insist on this."

"It's not necessary. I went under in Road Town. I'd know."

"I'm loaded with handguns; does anyone need an extra?" Zeb asked.

"It's 1981. How the hell do we protect ourselves? Sail together?"

"As much as I love you guys, I want sailing, solitude, and sex on my own time."

"Some hell of a New Year, eh?"

"We need to establish a network, check points, as we go our own ways. Amy's mom is in Cambridge, Beth's mom is on Long Island, one daughter is in in Sault St. Marie and the other is in Little Current. We list next-of-kin, addresses, numbers and call methodically to Amy's mom and her dad, Professor Sandler," said Zeb. "You're the Harvard Business School man, Turner. Set it up."

***

Beth demanded to search under the boat, but Dutch assured, pointedly, that he had.

"Don't fight with me, Captain Stupid!" She folded her arms in defiance.

"There's not a trace of anything on the boat. I've looked everywhere," Dutch said.

"You are an ass. Don't be stubborn," Beth insisted. "Something could be in the least likely place."

"All right, Captain Smart, I'm not going to fight you," Dutch said.

"You've been trying all morning!"

***

That afternoon, Beth put on her flippers, mask and scuba tank and went under the hull, running her hands over first the port side and then starboard. Brad went under with her. She told Dutch to crank the centerboard down. She went over that. Nothing. Near the engine, she saw a hammered-out place, a spot where something must have been. The sea may have washed it out, but there was an indentation. Nothing now. Beth had been under for 21 minutes, with her tank. It was time to come up.

"Satisfied now, Beth?" Dutch demanded.

"Maybe," she said. "There seemed to be something, attached, but it fell off. The rudder's clean.

Yet, toweling off, above on the deck, she glanced at the horseshoe life preserver, and noticed a suspicious bulge. The white cover had the name *Quadriga* painted on it, with crossed flags. She walked over, unzipped the cover and reached inside. Her fingers felt a small box of sorts. She pulled out a small battery pack. "Holy shit, here's a transmitter, battery pack and antenna. This is new: I've never seen anything like this," she declared, holding it up. Worried about being loud, she closed her hand over it and put it in the towel.

"Crap, that's how they know where you are. Don't turn it off," Brad directed.

But she failed to look in the exhaust pipe, thinking she had completed her task.

Dutch, Brad, Zeb and Beth huddled together. "How the fuck do we get rid of this? They'll find us and replace it with another pack."

Zeb laughed, suggesting, "Put it on another boat. "Look around, see what boats are heading north? "While you, Dutch, head south!"

"We could put this in someone else's dinghy."

"No, we do the right thing. For ourselves and others," Beth declared. "Before we leave, we'll slip the transmitter under the dock. They'll think we're still here."

"If they were smart, they'd have more than one transmitter aboard, so if we found one, there's still at least another."

"Whoever, they're no dummies. All this shit is expensive."

"Beth, want to look anywhere else? Want to see if there's more below?"

"I did. This life preserver's clean. Nothing hidden," Beth said, checking yet another one. "It's amazing how big a boat can get! Have you checked below, thoroughly? There are so many hiding places aboard," Beth insisted. "Let go of your ego, and don't let down your guard, Dutch. I'm warning you."

"I'll keep checking, and I can tell you, Amy will become proficient with gun handling."

"Want me to look anywhere else? This is convincing."

"Naw, Amy and I will keep looking."

"Hey, Dutch," Beth teased, "Amy may be captain one day!"

"Unlikely," he said. "She's great at cooking, singing, following my orders and other things..." He winked at Amy, who heard, and squirted him with the bottle of dishwashing liquid.

When they left, Dutch deposited the transmitter on the side of a dock, and laughing, he got back in the dinghy, and they were all bound for their next Caribbean island.

"Aw, I love you, Amy."

"Yah, Captain, I love you more!"

Chapter Ten

Name	Location	Latitude	Longitude
Quadriga	Roseau, Dominica	15° 17.510'	61° 22.892'

Each boat departed Antigua, promising to keep in touch by radio and in contact with the families at home in the U.S. and Ontario. Winds picked up and drew dramatic as *Quadriga* neared the lee of the more isolated island, Dominica, known for remote mountain ranges of over 5,000 feet.

Suddenly, *Quadriga* took an enormous blast of wind, rolling them over almost to the starboard water line.

"Knockdown," Amy screamed abruptly. She leaped up onto the coaming, the highest side in the cockpit, as her eyes met Dutch's in shock. Dutch held onto the wheel, himself falling to starboard in the cockpit. "Too much canvas," he yelled. Ever so slowly, the wind abated, allowing *Quadriga* to gently right herself. Amy jumped quickly to release the line on the main, and she packed the sail when it crumpled down.

"Good girl," he yelled.

It took her time to breathe normally again. Poles bare, engine chugging, *Quadriga* entered the Port of Roseau. They were able to smell the town before seeing it, the odor of burning coconut.

Soon, they viewed jungle trees by the beaches, while they looked for and found a smooth anchorage. They watched as fifteen Carib canoes formed a circle around a huge fishing net. The men in the boats patiently rolled the net toward the shore. Women waited on the beach to help with the catch, a silent, actually beautiful panorama of old tradition.

After anchoring, Amy kissed her captain and led him into the fore cabin to show her appreciation for the completion of the sail. To celebrate their love for each other, and that Nels was home safe, they had found the transmitter, had good friends, gotten rid of the transmitter and anchored in a new harbour that appeared to be tranquil and safe. Lunch could be amazing in the Caribbean when they had to stay out of the noonday sun.

"Can we be safe here?" she asked.

"Are we safe anywhere? We ought to paint the hull blue."

"Disguise ourselves?"

"Not here, too expensive. The deeper south we sail, the safer and better off we'll be."

***

Morne Diablotin is the rugged mountain peak capping Dominica at 4700 feet. They hiked up isolated steep hills, while beautiful cascading streams beckoned to them. With three hundred and sixty-five rivers, the guidebook told them that fierce Carib Indians fought off the British and French with cannibalistic warfare. The town offered, the book said, an old atmosphere of British Colonial influence, plus years of unrepaired hurricane damage.

When they entered the Customs building which housed the post office and jail, they were saddened to see obvious poverty in Roseau. Houses were in dire need of paint and small grocery stores exhibited bare shelves. "I only want bananas and local vegetables," she said.

"Want me to go with you?"

"No, it's a short walk," Amy said. He returned to tie up the dinghy at the town dock.

In town, Amy entered a local store and bought bananas. Back out, she walked alone, passing by four local rough-looking teenagers, leaning against an empty storefront. "Get off our island, whitey," one sneered. "Think you got everything because you got a big fucking boat?"

One boy thrust another boy in her path. She jumped away, dropping her bag of bananas.

"Follow me!" It was the high-pitched voice of a small local boy, who ran out of an alleyway. While the local teenagers menacingly advanced toward her, the child scooped up the bananas.

"You wouldn't dare hurt me!" Amy shouted, but wisely turned swiftly, and ran after the little boy, straight ahead of her. He darted into the Cable and Wireless Building, kept the door open for her, "In here!" and she ran in. Together, they peered out a window to see the gang give up their chase and move on. She looked down at the little boy. "Thank you!"

"Those boys' scary bad," he said in a small defiant voice, one of courage. "For us, too." His brown eyes were big, his body small, and clothes tattered. "They gone. We near the dock."

They ran to the dock where Dutch sat, in the dinghy.

"You've found a new friend, Amy," Dutch said.

"Sir, take me with you. My family do not miss me," the small boy implored, his eyes downcast.

"I'm sorry, son, we can't take you with us." Dutch stood up and got out of the dinghy, onto the dock. He fished in his pocket, found a twenty-dollar bill. "This is for groceries for your family."

"Sir, it isn't money I need. I ready to go now."

"Amy, get into the dinghy."

The boy stood there, watching as she got into the dinghy, sad-eyed. They left the dock. Bringing up the anchor to leave Dominica, each of the three felt sad for the inequities of life.

His young eyes followed *Quadriga*.

***

Logbook: Leaving the Island of Dominica, the Caribbean, January, 1981

Name	Location	Latitude	Longitude
Quadriga	Sailing past the southern tip of Dominica, into the Caribbean Sea Toward Martinique	15° 12.795' N	61° 22.095' W

On deck, Amy watched as the weak lights of Roseau diminished over the stern of *Quadriga*. It got dark quickly in the Caribbean and she felt happy for their night sail to Martinique. She felt relieved, and had a sense of reprieve, since they'd found the transmitter. Perhaps she could lose her fears and think about French perfume. Maybe Fort-de-France was a jolly Caribbean Paris.

With the right winds, they'd arrive in the port of Fort de France around midnight, a four to five hour sail. Relieved about the boat, and full of happy friendships with Beth and Zoe, she felt relaxed, sailing in calm conditions. How she craved the silken air, and to be here loving Dutch.

In Fort de France, he said they could swim and relax. She wanted to telephone her father in Cambridge, who could talk to a lawyer about what to do. But could she talk on a local phone?

The natural emptiness of the sea, tonight, gave Amy time to think about her growing sailing strength, whatever that was. Shifting her gaze up at the stars, then down to see the brilliant phosphorous in the water trailing the boat, she remembered that in New York City, before meeting Dutch, she'd been an aspiring performer with a day job. Dutch had thrown off her idea of normal life, so she engaged with this blue-watered world. The sea laid a pulse and a cadence on her awareness. New York City was history.

She watched Dutch steer, his broad shoulders and sturdy build, thrilling her. There was a boyishness in his face, but he was serious that everything felt right and safe on his beloved boat. While Dutch still opined on local police, business, life, fat people, food in boxes, and the government, he was masculine, with style and authority and even charm, in spite of himself. Amy wrote a song for him, titled *Stay in Your Own Lane; Leave Others Alone.* He hooted and hollered over this, kissing her.

He turned to look back at his Amy standing behind him on the stern, as she watched the land diminish behind them. He lovingly recalled first seeing her on the Stamford dock; how she had stopped walking suddenly, balancing a guitar case against her hip. Struck dumb by her beauty and grace, although she was flustered, and knocked over two sanders, he remembered watching her resign any hopes for that May afternoon last year, when she was due to sail on *Yellow Cat.* Tall, with a slimness and muscle toned by exercise, he remembered those moments. Would he ever get used to her careless beauty, now strength and surety aboard. He thrived on her vitality and humor as she listened to his commands.

He felt grateful that she did not challenge him, simply absorbing his orders and directives. He'd never admit how tough the Atlantic Crossing truly was. He'd kept kidding her along and praising her, though there were plenty of tough moments. The voucher for American Airlines for her to leave him, he was sure, was never thought of.

Amy went below to wash the supper dishes, and glanced out of the porthole directly in front of her above the galley. She took one more look at the southern lee of the island. She loved the yawl as much as she loved him. She needed to play her guitar more, but chores, sleep and this new trouble now took precedence. The Westerbeke engine chugged along, singing its own tune as it charged the batteries.

In the cockpit, Dutch let out the jib to flatten, allowing less heel, while Amy was gearing up for those large ocean rollers that originated off the coast of North Africa. Filled with a good dinner and wine, she was soulful about the vastness of their sweet Caribbean universe. How lucky was he.

"Dutch, see anything?" she yelled, habit firmly ingrained in her.

"Nothing! If you're worried, come up," he yelled over the engine noise.

"Your safety harness is on the cushion," she yelled. "PUT IT ON!" She added, "If you want sex," she shouted over the engine noise, "Put on your safety line!" She stood at the foot of the companionway, and looked up with a mean face that he laughed at. He put on the harness and clicked the metal clasp to the mizzenmast.

He raised the mizzen sail to full height, and then crouched so low in the cockpit she could not see him as he peered closely at the autopilot with his flashlight to turn it on. She knew every sound that *Quadriga* made. Even in the dark of night.

Approaching, a new sound, wide-ranging and terribly dangerous. But Dutch was crouched below and didn't seem to hear it. When he finally looked up, he saw the approach of a small, fast craft coming straight at them.

"We've got trouble! Bring me the rifle!"

Below, Amy ran to the front hanging locker and pulled out the heavy AR-15 rifle, climbed clumsily up the companionway steps and handed it to him. "Stay down. The Walther is behind the companionway. Get it."

The small, noisy boat moved so fast, it was alongside *Quadriga* in seconds. "You bastards!" He knew he could kill them all easily with the rifle. How stupid were they to attempt this? Coming on frontal to him!!! He aimed, but as the launch beat up upon the sailboat, it knocked Dutch violently over. He fell backward, letting go of the rifle as it fell onto the port cushion in the cockpit. "Damn, lost it!"

In what seemed to be less than a second, two men threw lines up and over onto the boat.

Fully vulnerable, Dutch looked up as two jumped aboard, one heading straight at him.

"You fucking bastards!"

Below, Amy was slammed against the gimballed stove. Drying dishes fell, clattering at her heels. She heard hoarse shouts. Pulling herself off the stove, she flipped off the overhead light to darkness.

Who boarded *Quadriga?* She moved to the companionway in direct sight to watch the menacing silhouette of one man jumping Dutch. She saw him quickly loop a line around Dutch's neck. Dutch moaned in utter pain. They were about to be killed as *Quadriga* hurled through the darkness.

Numb with realization, startling anger registered within her. Grabbing the Walther out of the locker under the companionway, safety off, loaded, she edged quickly up the steps. Taking a deep breath, she focused on Dutch's figure in the deadly scramble with another man. One she adored. At this moment, dark clouds shrouded the night, stars gone. The wind swirled. Acrid smells of the intruders brought scents of whiskey, sweat, and cigarettes.

Dutch was fighting for his life. And hers.

The sails stayed steady as Dutch slashed the intruder with his sail knife, even with the line tight around his neck. With all his might and strength, Dutch knocked him, directly in front of her.

Could she aim without hitting Dutch?

Gunshots rang out. The man screamed in horror. It was Amy's gun! She had shot him. She turned and aimed starboard at a second man who had jumped into the cockpit, holding on to Dutch's legs, crazed to save his partner. It was a noisy, screaming struggle among three of them. Death intention everywhere.

Amy floated further up the steps, stood tall at the open hatch, pulling the trigger again, directly focused on the back of the second man struggling with Dutch. She heard him scream in pain, as he fell back, withdrawing from the struggle. He collapsed over the coaming and fell back over on the deck. How did he gasp, "We're going to kill you!"

She looked hard at him. Oddly familiar; how did she know him? She turned back to see Dutch fighting, losing his balance. The first assailant, though hit by her bullet, fought on. The two of them struggled, entangled, staggered, and fell backwards over the stern rail, disappearing overboard.

"Nooooo," she screamed; Dutch couldn't last ten minutes in the water if he was wounded, unconscious, bleeding and entwined with that murdering guy.

She stepped above, to the deck, looking at the second assailant who lay bleeding and choking in death on her starboard side.

"We kill you stupid Americans," she heard, coming from the starboard side. A third man stepped over his wounded partner, and lunged toward her.

Turning swiftly, she aimed and shot him in the chest. Blood spattered with the full force of her shot. He staggered, falling forward on the aft starboard deck. She smelled his hot breath as he fell past her, whiskey, and blood dripping from his face and neck. Being killed in front of her. By her.

Sickened at the sight of him, she began to cry. She wasn't someone who killed people!

He fell to the deck, starboard side. Blood oozing. Stricken, she watched for a minute, realizing the young assailant was indeed dead. So furious was she now, she waited to kick him overboard. But wait, he lay, not dead!

With blood pulsing, he slumped against the safety lines, moaning and clutching his belly.

Amy was enraged, crazed; no longer a protected young woman aboard a cruising sailboat. She saw his blood seeping darkly on her clean decks. Dutch would kill her! The sounds of his collapse on the deck grew still against the sound of the wind. And the incessant knocking of their launch tied up on the port side.

Quadriga's autopilot was on, winds steady. Sails full. Moonlight and stars above. She reached over the dying man to open the lifeline at the gate. She'd push him overboard, with her left arm and right foot. But touching him with her bare feet, she felt his skin warm. Blood, sticky on her on her right foot.

His eyes flickered open. He lunged at her, gripping her right arm and hand that held the Walther, forcing her to drop it. It fell on the deck and noisily slid back. His black hair was matted around his face, his energy focused into a last effort.

"No, you don't!" She roared and fought to break his steely grasp. But he had her. He was going to break her arm, then her heart, then her body.

Amy remembered the winch handle, properly nestled in its pocket. It was so near, oh God, could she reach it? He held her with an unwavering grasp, his eyes glittering on her for that last kill.

She strained, uttering a cry, and with her left arm, reached back and back, yet further, to claw at the steel winch handle. She was able to pick it up and raise it in a high arc to keep it away from him, then cracked him over the head, again and again. Blood spurted open from his head wounds and torn, now ravaged face. He slumped over, releasing his grip. With unexpected strength, she shook off his painful death grip, or had it loosened as he moaned, gasping his final breath.

Amy took out her sailor's knife and stabbed his chest, his shoulders, and his ears. She couldn't stop, so angry. "You earned that," she whispered. Taking a deep breath for strength, she exhaled anger. When she tried to stand up, she faltered. It took a minute to find her balance. Now, she was able to move. Dragging his feet, she yelled, "You fucking bastard!"

She couldn't help laughing, her nerves jumping in the danger. Like a comic book, Nels would say. Inhaling to push away her terrible inner music, she felt her lungs stretch. The breath was there. She stood strong, kicking first, then pushing him out and overboard, watching his body fall back into the wake of the boat under full sail. Hoping sharks were nearby. She defiantly wiped his blood off her hands. How far had *Quadriga* sailed since Dutch had gone overboard?

Only the sounds of rushing water and the flapping jib answered her. She sobbed, gulping in the night air, and carefully replacing the expensive winch handle back into its cloth pocket. She was trained to put it back in its proper place. Keeping the boat immaculate. She ached with exhaustion. Her senses narrowed to the blood on the deck.

Dutch was floundering in the sea.

Quadriga sailed on.

Amy kept needing to take deep breaths for strength, exhaling unstoppable anger. It became quiet as the wind seemed to stop. She quickly turned but there was no one behind her. Again, she did a quick audit; one dead in the cockpit, one swarthy bastard pushed off starboard, and Dutch, somewhere aft, over the side. It took a few moments to sink in, these utterly mortifying moments.

Alone at sea on a 40-foot yawl under sail going nowhere, their future blown away in minutes of deadly scramble, Amy was the one alive.

The sea at night would be impossible to search for one figure. She hadn't noticed a cloud cover move in, allowing the sea to be illuminated only by white spray. The heavy ocean rollers were constant in the steady wind, the motion still smooth and predictable. They seemed to be on course, sails were staying filled, as the lovely *Quadriga* on autopilot blithely sailed on.

She prepared to make a 180-degree turn. She'd get on the course's reciprocal heading to retrace their invisible path on the sea. First, she retrieved a searchlight from the lazarette, the big holding space where they threw supplies and junk. As she swept the light, she peered aft into the horizon, seeing nothing but dark night seas.

She turned the searchlight upon the dead man's face, lying crumpled in the cockpit. Disbelief roiled inside her. He was that nice farmhand working for Everett Hallpike, dead, stuck with an awful smile. He had chatted with her as he fed the chickens. She felt so deeply sick, this destruction, failure; nothing was left. Her body was tinged with nausea. What could she do next?

'WE ARE RESOLUTE' entered her head. Those coffee cups they shared. The sailboat was intact, so was Amy. Two out of three. Resolute had three syllables.

Quadriga hobby-horsed along, not knowing her decks were bloodstained. Amy wavered as she looked around. Her head sang, 'you may pretend to be resolute, but you're no warrior. What? *"Kill for Love!"* *"Overboard with My Heart."* Please, no songs. Pieces of her life forever lodged in her musical head: they kept coming, these songs. Was there a medical term for this?

But her sailboat took a dip, as if she thought, to hug her. She yelled, *"Quadriga,* we will find Dutch!" Tears trickled down her face, drying in the wind.

Amy saw a quick silvery gleam from the stern rail. Could it be?

Chapter Eleven

Logbook: of *Bravo*, February, 1981

Name	Location	Latitude	Longitude
Bravo	El Porvenir, Panama	9° 32.834'	78° 59.120'
	Colon, Panama	9° 22.578'	79° 54.268'
	Puerto Baquerize Moreno, San Cristobal, Galapagos	0° 53.771'	89°36.850'
	Punta Pitt, San Cristobal, Galapagos	0° 42.670'	89°15.176'
	Puerto Baquerize Moreno, San Cristobal, Galapagos	0° 53.771'	89°36.850'

Landfall! The lovely coastal mountains of Panama rose out of the haze behind the Archipelago of the San Blas Islands. What a smooth passage from Falmouth, Antigua; a rolling sea, full of spray, a steady six knots, clear days and nights. Brad, relaxed at the tiller, had a deep tan burnt into the back of his neck and shoulders. His long, shaggy, blond hair was delightful to him. Beth stood at the bow, her safety line attached, as *Bravo* pointed and lowered into the sea. Peach-colored freckles dotted her face and her hair, carelessly stuck up in her cap, had turned reddish blonde. Their first stop, El Porvenir, on the peninsula, was where the Cuna people lived. They anchored, took the dinghy in, and bought fresh vegetables from the market. Then they made the eighty-mile passage to Colon, and moored near the entrance to the Canal.

They cleared Immigration and sauntered over to the Panama Yacht Club to meet other sailors and pick up their long-awaited mail. Beth loved holding fat envelopes full of news that she would linger over.

Captain Poole, their friend, the captain now living in Florida, was a chatty writer who had adopted them in spirit. Beth mused that a sailboat did not sail away from its first captain and crew; it carried their dreams. Also aboard, in letters, were the well-wishes and longings of family and friends, emotionally bound to their voyage. In the hearts of all sailors were these invisible riders, on the tide with them.

They made arrangements for their passage through the Panama Canal, the most heavily congested transit area in the world. Container ships, freighters and cruise ships loomed over them, also waiting their turn. *Bravo* would be squeezed in with a myriad of sleek yachts flying flags from all over the world. Their reservation was secure, and they were lucky, only having to wait several days to transit. They went sightseeing around Casco Veijo, the city's colonial section, cavorting along the sea wall built by the Spanish in the 1600s. "Look at the wood-trimmed buildings and iron grills, which reminds me of New Orleans," Brad said. They took a bus to Panama City to amble around El Valle's famous town square.

"We had a look at the Central America we've dreamed about," Beth wrote home. She then went to a fancy beauty parlor to get a real haircut, a manicure, and pedicure. Brad refused, loving the shaggy look.

At the Gatun Locks, *Bravo* was heavily secured as turbulent water rushed through the culverts in the bottom of the lock. They were able to motor for twenty-seven miles to the Pedro Miguel Locks for the descent toward the Pacific Ocean.

When the last gate opened, the Pacific Ocean greeted *Bravo*. Beth stood at the bow, raised her hands up and yelled to the sky, "We've made it this far. Thank you, Poseidon, for all the gifts in front of us!"

The Pacific Ocean was the ceremonial commencement of their circumnavigation. The fabled islands of Ecuador's Galapagos Archipelago beckoned to them; Fernandina, Isabella, Santiago, Balta, Santa Cruz, Floreana, Hood, Bartolome and San Cristobal; a set of island pearls Beth longed to learn, where time was still professed, by the Ecuadorians, to stand still. The Islands were a thousand miles ahead of them, twelve to fifteen days with good weather.

In a comfortable routine of life at sea, when the weather was good, Beth took daily sights with the sextant. Brad did calculations and recorded their position on the charts and in the logbook. Immersed in ship life, neither thought of other people, only tasks of survival at hand, feeling happily detached from time. Lots of good paperbacks to read were essential.

On the helm at dusk on the fourth night, Beth heard a loud series of whooshing behind her. Turning swiftly, she saw a spewing of mist rising over a large dark patch in the water, fifty feet aft. One hundred feet back, another mass surfaced. "Brad, get up here," she called urgently. His head appeared instantly in the companionway. "Are we in trouble?"

"Two mammoth whales! One's fifty feet long! Bigger than *Bravo*."

"I hope they know we're here!"

"Maybe they think we're a girly whale?" Brad giggled, out of nerves: one flip of that tail could snap their mast. Or sink them.

"Brad, our survival bags and life raft are ready; but I'm not ready. We've just begun!"

Awed by the immensity of the two whales, she took a breath and sang to them; "Go away, boys, you have the whole ocean to play in. *Bravo*'s not available. Let us be, let us be."

She slowed *Bravo*, holding their course. For thirty minutes, the whales stayed nearby, blowing air fifteen feet high. "Each is bigger than a New York subway train," Brad said in awe.

Inexplicably, one whale and the other gently sunk away, leaving a patch of smooth water to mark their spot.

"We're resolute. We've been made aware to have our survival bags ready in seconds. Those whales were sent to warn us," she said, darkly. "We're lucky this time."

"Aw, Beth, don't read drama into this. Remember your whale coffee cup from Amy."

After supper, Beth scanned their medical survival kit. Essentials were there; bandages, antiseptics, aspirin, eye lotion, skin cream, Gatorade, needles and sutures, antibiotics, and seasick pills. The food rations contained cans and packets of peanut butter, forty tins of varied canned goods, six can openers, and knives.

Another bag held hats, towels, fish hooks, line, mending equipment for the life raft, flares, two offshore life jackets, an orange distress flag, an electric distress light, necessary reference books wrapped in plastic, and a note book and pens. They had three large tightly sealed plastic jars filled with water. Her inventory done, she placed the bulging duck-cloth bundles near the ladder of the salon.

"My Brainiac, so damn compulsive at everything you do," he said.

"That's why you love me, silly." Despite his making fun of her, she put herself through a drill, by yanking each heavy duffel up into the cockpit. She practised opening the plastic canister of the life raft, holding the line away from the boat so neither she nor Brad would fly away with it. How could she get the bundles in the life raft after it's been opened? A million details of suspense. She loved it.

"Our weather's been perfect. And the forecast. You worry constantly."

"Brad," she grumbled, "Please appreciate my ability to take care of us."

"I do, Beth, every damn minute! I'm only one man," he muttered, his hand on the wheel.

"Sorry, honey," she said immediately. She moved around the boat, securing a line, reefing a sail, secure in her footing. "This is Real Ocean, not Long Island Sound. There's no one out here for us. Honey, I keep telling you that we are resolute."

Brad sighed, "Enough bullshit about being resolute."

She smiled at that. Sitting in the cockpit, she remembered she had, indeed, grown up being the smartest, most capable child on the block, in school, on a bike, and in a treehouse. With her degrees and practical sense, she had a high-paying job in a New York bank. But it was so much better here, with Brad, aboard on the Pacific Ocean. What sailing vessel isn't utterly alone, she thought. And she had learned, adoring Brad physically, to ask for what she wanted sexually. He was stronger. Several months of blue water sailing had worked sensual magic on this MIT bookworm-Harvard Business School graduate and respected egghead. And he had lovingly brought her along, ardently, to great satisfaction. Captain Beth could take care of everything else.

On watch, Brad idly gazed at the horizon, thinking how far he was from his own early life expectations, here on the Pacific. With his wife, they shared companionship and adventure on this challenge of their circumnavigation. His gray Brooks Brothers suit with the vest, Harvard tie, white shirt, dark socks, underwear, and winged-tip shoes, all folded in three casings of taped-up plastic, were ready for arrival in Australia. Both had temporary placements in banking jobs waiting for them in Sydney, whose presidents had also graduated from the Harvard Business School.

Nostalgia overtook him thinking of New York's Lincoln Center, lit up at night, with the bright Chagall paintings and the concerts he loved. He thought of Christmas crowds on Fifth Avenue, their old apartment in Greenwich Village. Then he remembered rushing with crowds of men and women, through Grand Central Station, crossroads of millions of lives, and waiting for his elevator to get to his office. While they read the New York Times every day, and attended theater on discounts, here, each minute was challenging as he viewed the austere, commanding presence of the ocean. He wondered whether they'd ever return to New York. There was so much of the world to see and sail. Did he care? A pod of porpoises cavorted at *Bravo*'s bow. How swift and silent, making graceful arcs, leaping with joy in front of his boat.

***

For two days and nights, *Bravo* hosted squalls, the wind howling at thirty knots. While Brad read an adventure novel, laughing aloud from time to time, Beth giggled over a paperback, *Thirty Ways to Love Tinned Corned Beef*. They played classical music. And chess on the magnetic board, both equal players.

Now they were five days from reaching the Galapagos. As Beth heated up oatmeal in the morning, an unexpected rogue wave and a severe roll of the vessel set her heart hammering. Would they broach? She hung on, lurching, finding herself thrown into the upper berth while loose objects fell all over the cabin. But *Bravo* rolled back. She shouted, "I love our sailing life!"

Later, when seas calmed, they were comfortable again. She watched Brad, lying comfortably as possible as *Bravo* rolled slightly now, always feeling love for him. He had rescued her from being a leftover Harvard nerd. She catalogued his beauty, tanned, and muscled, with blond hair now curling at his shoulders. Again, she thought of the delicate care he had taken in her overdue sexual awakening. His respect and slowness in making her secure, indebted her to him.

"Captain, have I told you how much I adore you?"

"Every day, honey," he said, eyes focused on his book. "And, I love you." She moved toward him, a motion turned into a lurch and she knelt by his bunk, her cool hand slipping into his shorts.

"Concentrate on your book," she teased. He lay the book down, closed his eyes, never objecting to his wife's unzipping the fly of his shorts, gently lifting his pink and blue-veined penis, nestled warm, out of his pants. The Captain brought her mouth down to fondle her First Mate, caressing him. Ocean sailing made for fascinating, unexpected sex, thrusting at wave crests, and being lowered into sea troughs. Sometimes, on the crashing seas, the ocean arched to join them, loving their reliable well-built old teak woodie *Bravo*.

***

187

The Galapagos Islands lay in front of them under the hot equatorial sun. Anchoring off San Cristobal, they received permits to enter the national park and were assigned special anchorage times at various islands. The procedure was designed to keep the islands pristine in spite of the thousands of tourists brought in by cruise ships. They were eager to see celebrated wildlife, lowlands, highlands and moonscapes made by twisted lava. Ready to explore and appreciate these prized islands.

Enjoying these special islands, they were able to dine on fresh-boiled lobster in a local restaurant. From the other side of Hood Island, they sailed to Port Pitt, where the famous red-footed boobies nested in trees, their funny feet wrapped around the branches like licorice sticks.

Beth and Brad watched sea lions cavort on beaches, barking raucously. A frisky one fancied Beth, hulking toward her, and she laughed, beating a hasty retreat.

The Blue-footed Boobies delighted Beth, while Brad was awed watching seventy turtles bask and frolic in the surf, their small backs noisily bumping against each other as the sun set. He whispered, "We're at the beginning of time. These turtles are vulnerable and the ecology delicate. We know the Ecuadorian government works hard to preserve this."

In the hot sunshine, mother sea lions nursed their babies. Beth and Brad walked along paths, while some seals, so tame, snoozed on the black rocks. They watched iguanas dart along dark crevices of rock while large birds circled overhead. Much of the black rock surfaces seemed to be painted a nice shiny white. The guide told them it was guano, animal feces, and centuries old, added to, layer by layer, and rubbed shiny by the animals themselves.

"I never saw shit look so clean and shiny," Brad whispered.

At the Darwin Station, the staff nurtured tortoise and iguanas. One ancient tortoise, they were told, his carapace was over one hundred and fifty years old. She looked at his drooping face, looking tired and somewhat human to Beth. She was sympathetic to the tortoise, learning that members of the staff cleaned and shined him daily. Brad saw two tortoises in the garden, one having climbed on the other from the back. He whispered to Beth, "I wondered how they do it? I know. Carefully."

They sailed to Floreana where they bought and sent 20 postcards home to the United States. They spent one night at Hotel Galapagos that overlooked Academy Bay. They loafed in their room, quietly resting, enjoying the bathtub, a bed that didn't rock... Sex.

What a lighthearted, relaxed night on land.

Not knowing it was their last.

Chapter Twelve

February, 1981.

Name	Location	Latitude	Longitude
Zephyr	Port-de-France, Martinique	14° 36.025'	61° 04.219'
	Marigot Bay, St. Lucia	13° 57.960'	61° 01.435'

The elegant ketch, *Zephyr*, purred slowly through the busy harbor of Fort-de-France, Martinique, threading past the outer harbor where huge cruise ships waited at anchor. Zoe saw white sandy beaches, green mountains, and banana groves amid wild tropical growth. She read that Columbus had called the Island of Martinique the most beautiful country in the world.

Zeb knew while many sailboats were anchored in the inner harbor, it was a rough port. Fully aware that *Zephyr* was an object of temptation, he assessed the local fishermen sliding by in their tiny Carib canoes with motors on the stern, observing visitors and their boats. He made his pronouncement; "This is a damn zoo. We won't stay long." But Fort-de-France was an enticing, saucy,

French up-tempo city, and Zoe knew about the newly furbished Bakoua Beach Hotel, the elegant jewel of Fort-de-France. She longed to see it, yet had written about it last season, before she met Zeb.

On Martinique, visitors could hike, snorkel, shop and dine, French-made clothes, perfumes, handbags, oh so much. She was ready. He was not. And she knew better than to try to dress him. Up or down. But oh, French wine and cheeses were entirely different. Alert from *Quadriga*'s troubles, Zeb paid a French young man he found on the dock, to sit in the cockpit, with a growling face and strict instructions to protect his locked boat. He hired another to watch their dinghy on the dock when they went to town. "These city restaurants and street vendors are delightful," she declared.

French songs from Paris wafted from speakers at sidewalk cafes, while local black girls with sparkling eyes walked with saucy, moving hips, mellifluous French running from their full lips. One beautiful dark-skinned girl startled them with blue eyes, the legacy of visiting sailors and resident planters over centuries. Zoe loved the aspect of quadroons, octoroons, alive in the many beautiful faces she saw in this fascinating port. Zeb agreed to lunch at a busy sidewalk café, tolerant being at the busy café. Yes, he did enjoy the passing parade, dining on Salad Niçoise, French bread and sipping Chardonnay. She smiled; was there ever perfection? Almost, today. Zeb was so sweet, lacking in guile. But the top of their minds, unsaid today, was what could happen to them in these tropics, like *Quadriga*. Although Zoe knew the Caribbean from a vacation side, she felt new fear. Never to be in any horrific situation, but how did you know?

He allowed her to leave him, while he went to stock up on French cheeses and wines. She sauntered forth, alone, seduced by inhaling the bliss of French civilization on glamorous Martinique, wallowing in the elegant mystique of Fort-de-France. Might she buy French perfume, or an imported French handbag? She laughed at her shopper's early-instilled mentality, knowing she needed nothing, but to look. This was research. Ha, away from the sea.

They met back on the dock and returned to the boat. To his surprise, Zoe bought nothing! "Am I taking the New York imperative to shop out of you," he teased. "But one day's enough! We're out of here."

***

They sailed leisurely south to St. Lucia, anchoring in a cove near the shore of the famous Piton Mountains, two peaks that rose sharply from the sea. From the beach, the depth sank to almost one hundred feet. No easy anchoring. She admired his seamanship and smiled when he was able to secure the boat with two long stern anchors and a line that he took, while swimming, to shore and tied it from the bow to a coconut tree. The moon shone a patina of white velvet upon the peaks. They swam, slept, read, and cooked.

Zeb loved silence, so she deliberately practiced subtle adaptation and restraint to ensure quiet aboard each day. She accumulated paperback novels, learned to clean the boat quickly, studied cookbooks, and read up on

Celestial Navigation and the Constellations. At night, bright constellations lit up across the sky. Another night, the moon was high, providing her with an extraordinary state of meditation. It felt rather well, this new state of quietness within her.

They sat in the cockpit after dinner. "This is heaven, Zoe. My daughters are doing well. So far we're lucky, no danger, and ..." he touched her face, "We've got the best things of all; each other. Shall we sail directly to Nova Scotia, after we finish in Grenada for the season?"

"Sailing north on an Atlantic Ocean passage, just us?" she quaked. "We'd need hands aboard. I'll go back to New York, while you do that."

"And miss an ocean crossing?"

She laughed. "You bet. By the way, what do you see in our future after sailing?"

"This is our future! We're healthy. Unfettered by other people. Sail where we want. You don't have to produce a thing, nor be continually myopic about working or achieving more."

She sighed. "I'm different than you. I live inside and outside, in community with family, my travel colleagues, newspaper, friends, college, neighbours, theater and music."

"All former social struts," he declared. "Which you're replacing with me. And the boat."

"You've certainly swept me away." She tried not to be sarcastic.

To soothe herself, she preserved silence and lay her head against his shoulder, their physical contact inviting their transmission of warmth. Putting her lips to his ear, she kissed him softly, her mind racing. Here in midlife, and at anchor, she had so many lessons to learn. There was so much to produce in life; but what was it? Working in Paradise for years, writing about the hotels, cruises and islands? She knew these domains. Be grateful for now.

"Zoe, if I gave you an engagement ring," he asked quietly, "Would you accept it?" He paused. "And you wouldn't try to change me, would you?"

Her eyes opened, heart racing; which was the more important question? Hadn't she struggled mightily to change, change, and change and become silent and seaworthy?

"Zeb, how wonderful that you're asking me. You admit that changing's all I've done since I came aboard! I'm reconstructing everything I know!"

"Except when you start going off on a new story," he teased.

"You're the silent, strong one," she retorted, but quickly said, "I'm glad you're that way."

"You do need to learn to take time to be still. We've so much fun together….Well?"

She shrugged, a tacit assent. Was this too soon?

"Zoe, living well requires forethought, work, health and money. I'm thinking about selling *Zephyr* and eventually buying a Little Harbor Custom 52. It's a lovely shoal draft boat. Designed by Ted Hood. Three staterooms. The interior's done in American cherry, and there's a multi-level cockpit with full headroom under the dodger, and a complete navigation center with full electronics at the forward end of the cockpit."

"That's the most you've said in three days!"

He laughed easily. "All sailing systems are electronic and are within easy reach of the helmsman. We can put one of those new computers on your desk in one stateroom, my workshop in the second. We can cruise forever, maybe gunk around Belize, sail to the San Blas Islands, and back up home to Nova Scotia and to Newfoundland."

"We'll definitely need a deckhand."

"Nope, that's the beauty of it. We do it ourselves. It lists for a million two, but I can get it cheaper with cash. It will be the next *Zephyr*, bigger, better to sail. A real home."

They were quiet. She changed the subject. "It's been some time since we've heard from *Quadriga* or *Bravo*. My mother told me on the phone she received a letter from Panama from Beth and Brad. She read it to me. There's nothing new from *Quadriga*."

"We'll try to contact *Quadriga* later."

They went below to read. Living aboard certainly made every emotion intense and she prayed that a deep acceptance of herself was taking place; nor did she continue to feel driven to accomplish and share what she'd learned; Zoe was resolute. She'd absorb, reabsorb, slow down further, and live with the currents of the sea. Yup! Live quietly. At sea level.

In the morning, Zeb turned on the single sideband and tuned in the Caribbean net, channel six-six-two-four, to hear the boats broadcast for each other. They put the call out for *Quadriga*.

No answer.

An hour later.

No answer.

Logbook: Sailing on the open Caribbean Sea towards Martinique, February, 1981

Name	Location	Latitude	Longitude
Quadriga	Boarded by Assailants beyond the southern tip of Dominica, into the Caribbean Sea…on autopilot	15° 12.795' N	61° 22.095' W

Quadriga? A boat going nowhere. Dutch had been swept away, tangled with his deadly assailant.

Was it ten, twenty seconds? Or an hour since *Quadriga* had been boarded after dusk. Within that time, Dutch was attacked in his own cockpit. Amy remembered automatically shutting off the overhead light, grabbing the Walther, rushing up the companion way and killing, two of their assailants. Pitifully, she glanced down at the swarthy young man, who lay dead on the cockpit sole. The second man, so vile, after she shot him in the chest, hot blood bursting forth at her, had lain there, and suddenly grabbed her and almost killed her. She had been able to retrieve the heavy winch handle and smashed him in the head and face. Nothing left, but blood. She had opened the lifeline, and kicked him overboard.

With momentary relief, almost pleasure, she had watched as he fell, dropping into the sea and was swept backward. She heard a tear in the jib. Oh no, another tear?

Their stupid launch was still tied to the boat. Get rid of it; what else could be in there? She couldn't turn the boat around with the launch tied. And she had to stop the boat from sailing.

She had luffed up into the wind, which basically stopped the boat. She turned the autopilot off. She released the two lines that were tied to the launch. It slid back, rolling and down, further away in the sea behind them.

When she looked again at the remaining body, it was that sweet, sour young farmhand from Hallpike's farm who lay lifeless, bloodied on the sole of the cockpit. Dutch had disappeared over the side. Reconfirming, she cut the engine, quit the autopilot and now only heard wind and water. What did she hear? Was that a moan? From where? Clouds, which had shrouded them, passed, and the moon was out again. She looked back, her eyes magnetized on a taut line, catching a glint of reflected light.

How had she missed this! She fell forward on her knees, peering over the aft transom, her eyes riveted below. Gasping, she spied Dutch's body dragging in a white rush of water, phosphorescence swirling around him. His head and torso were collapsed frontally against the transom, his legs dangling at the engine's exhaust, a broken puppet.

Dutch would have been hanged if the safety line wound around his neck. Sharks could be streaming along Dutch's legs in the water. The sails were flapping, so she ran forward to release the main sheet. She took it down fast, and folded it. Then she pulled the mizzen sail down and secured it to the boom with two gaskets. She balanced on her knees, with strength that amazed her. *Quadriga* wallowed. "Dutch, wake up!"

Impaled on his own transom, unconscious, Dutch's mouth hung open. He was heavy, drenched, and his assailant, barely hanging on, dragged and curled at Dutch's feet. Had she the strength to pull Dutch up?

Amy stared at this impossible scene. What would Beth do? Beth would tell her to find a spare sheet line, and reach down to knot it to Dutch's safety harness. Hurriedly, she stepped back over the farmhand's body to find her own safety harness, in case she fell over the back of the boat while she leaned over. She burst into insane laughter; Dutch was a big fish to be caught and brought aboard.

She looked aft at the third man dangling, hanging on to Dutch. Was he dead?

So far, beloved *Quadriga* was steady, afloat, and Amy had found Dutch. Her internal music again, *"Amy, Amy, undamaged and able, do everything to keep Dutch stable."* Or was Captain Beth talking inside her head? Inner musical voices sending lyrical courage, strength. Count the ways she hadn't gotten hurt. She hadn't shot, injured, or sank herself. She stood alone aboard. Nor had she shot any part of her precious boat that she could tell! She was it, commander of the vessel. If only Dutch could tell her what to do. It didn't matter if she did it wrong, as long as she got him.

Wrong could be right, lifesaving. Dutch had kept telling her that she only learned from mistakes.

"You won't get him," she screamed into the darkness of the roiling sea. Adrenalin firing through her, Amy looked out, checking the bouncing horizons. Nothing else coming. The big boat weltered impatiently. Leaning over him, she saw his face was ashen, dried blood was around his nostrils, eyes were closed tight. He was knocked out and lifeless. She loved him. His shirt was torn and hanging open. She must risk pulling him up. There was nothing else. The slap of water slammed nonstop against the boat, *Quadriga's* transom thumping hard. The fellow hanging on him was barely alive, but saw her and shouted, "Pull us up!"

"What?"

Infuriated, she picked up the AR-15 that had dropped on the port side of the cockpit, stood aft, balancing herself, and aimed at the bloody man. Ten shots into his belly and legs, praying to aim away from Dutch's body.

It woke Dutch, who started and kicked, which released the third intruder's body into the surf. She watched him being released. "You fucking stinker."

She carefully put the rifle down. Deftly, she unrolled the halyard and lowering herself, dangerously, struggling with every part of her body; don't fall over him! But her line was attached to a stanchion. She pushed two hands past his chest and saw the clip on the front of his safety harness. She struggled to clip it. She raised herself back up to the boat. Standing up, she wound one line around the winch and turned the handle, grunting aloud. She pulled him in, slowly, steadily, marshalling crazy strength for an endless long haul. Bless the self-tailing Barient winch, which routinely held the line as it was drawn in. How glad she was to have been raising the mainsail these past few months, acquainting herself with pulling lines and tying knots, motions familiar and competent. She pulled, her arm muscles bulging, pulled against rage, fear, anxiety and death.

Slowly, for twenty pulls as she gasped for breath, Dutch's gangling body slowly rose. The halyard shifted up to his chest. He was almost up to the lifeline rail. He was now free of the transom and his body swung in toward the mizzenmast itself. She worried about his head slamming into the mast. She slowly guided his body over the stern lifelines, and toward the cockpit. With her hand, she swung him like a pendulum over the cockpit cushions.

"You will NOT get away from me," she yelled at Dutch, suspended near the wheel. She released the line on the winch slowly, bending on her haunches, allowing her calves and thighs to take the weight and guide him, suspended, into the cockpit. As his body lowered, she momentarily lost her balance, then regained it.

Painfully, slowly releasing the halyard, she still guided him. She untied the halyard and replaced it on the head of the mizzen sail. With wet hands, she slowly undid his harness, and shifted his hanging form forward over the cockpit. Lowering him, she stretched him out as well as she could on the starboard cockpit cushion, listening for his breath. She saw a pulse beating in his neck. Gashes on his head and arms were washed clean by the sea. Blood still coming. He was breathing, now moaning. For a second, she remembered the first time they made love, on this very cushion. What if he died? Amy rushed below to get a wet cloth and get some water.

"Drink this," she murmured, putting the cup to his mouth. It dribbled down his face. She put the cup down. She stepped over the dead farmhand still laying on the sole of the cockpit. She kicked his body to a corner. Never mind the bloody sole.

Knowing she had to creep along *Quadriga's* starboard deck, she affixed her lifeline as she moved. She saw the torn jib; how had that happened? She took it down and stuffed it into the open forward hatch. Talking, singing to herself. "Be patient, be resolute. Make Beth proud!"

She knew where to find another jib and attached it to the roller-furling rod. She led the foot of the sail back to the cockpit, tied new lines, and wound them on the winch. She dropped the forward hatch, closed it and went aft to raise the sail. But where were they sailing? She checked their compass heading, which would be due south for Martinique. She put on the autopilot, forever grateful she had listened and learned how to use their Loran, satnav, sextant, RDF, depth sounder, and autopilot. Thinking now about islands, she knew that Martinique was a region of the French Republic, a modern island; she'd find a U.S. contact there. Let Dutch live.

She leaned down, kissing his face, looking at the bloody shirt covering his chest. She got alcohol and cleaned his face and chest, praying they were superficial; what could she do, anyway? His eyes fluttered.

"You went overboard."

"What's our course," he whispered, unable to move.

"Due south. Boat's steady. They're all dead," she said. Steely, not crying.

"Dead, all off the boat?"

"Yes," she lied, looking at the dead farmhand lying on the sole below him. "Are we being followed?"

"Not that I can tell. I look every two seconds."

"Any boat damage?"

"Not sure. The transom rail seems bent. The jib tore. I replaced it. Can you move?"

"My ribs ache. Maybe broken."

Dutch then passed out. She covered him with a blanket. She had him aboard, the power of three; *Quadriga*, Dutch and Amy, sailing on. She felt dark, defiant, the music of murder inside her becoming a soulmate. With him dozing and waking with a start, she constantly brought water for him. "Leave me alone," he murmured.

"Not a chance," she replied. "Drink this. She scanned the night horizon. Who else was after them? The dim grip of isolation. She slept in bits. To dawn.

Waking, she looked across the sole to see, oh crap, that dead young man, hair matted over a sweet, young face. It was Everett Hallpike's farmhand. Drifting smack into sleep, she had been too exhausted to drag him overboard. This morning, she searched his clothes and in a pocket, found a pack of cigarettes he would never smoke, and a picture of his wife and baby. She began to cry, small and larger gulps of release moving through her. She was shocked to feel the boat carrying grief, as if it had absorbed the action, every bullet shot and scream. As if Quadriga was partially wounded. Her voice became a wail.

"What's that noise," she heard Dutch whisper. "You singing?"

"No," she replied, blowing her nose.

She had to show Dutch the body of this kid. Yes, his body and dead soul. When would Dutch come-to again? He had to see for his own eyes who had attacked them. Wouldn't he believe her? Okay, crazy Amy, think this thorough. Throw him overboard. Don't be a Commander. Of an idiotic action.

But she went below, bringing up two large bath towels. Not from Porthault, the crummy ones they used for the beach. Then she opened the lazarette cover and hurriedly took out junk they had been meaning to throw out. That went over aft. Uh-oh, what if island authorities found the bodies and these pieces belonging to *Quadriga*? Only two sanders. Stop! Nothing personal. Sanders dropping off the dock had begun her life with Dutch on the Connecticut dock! She pushed everything to one side, moving the tools they still needed out of the way, making room to shove the young dead farmhand in.

She was crazy to do this, wrapping the young farmhand in two towels! How demented was she from this killing and fatigue? So fucking what! His dried blood had congealed in the wind, crusting around his body. His young wife and daughter were waiting at home for him on Montserrat. Angrier still, she put masking tape around the towels and dragged his body over to the lazarette. Up, over and down into the deep compartment, she pushed him into a fetal position. But his head was unwrapped. She had to show Dutch this kid as proof that Hallpike was behind this. She kept the cover open for air. That was stupid. But after all this, why did she have to be rational. *Quadriga* could not have discolored decks, no congealing crimson blood, yet holding steady, southward, a blessing.

Amy went below, made a peanut butter sandwich and drank three glasses of orange juice. Her crazy mind kept conjuring up phrases of melody and songs. It was an uncanny reflex, one that burdened her with no let-up. Determined to stop her brain, she got a knife, the detergent *Joy*, and sponges, to pry dried blood and to lift dark stains off *Quadriga*'s decks.

On course, she looked out periodically to scour the horizon. No boats. Might they have sailed past Martinique?

She slept intermittently in the cockpit opposite Dutch. By six the next morning, Amy turned on the radio. No traffic on channel sixteen. Then it filled with Spanish voices. Her heart skipped a beat when Dutch stirred and feebly called her.

"Dutch, we're heading due south. Boat's steady," she said. "I love you."

"My ribs ache. Maybe broken."

"We must report this to the authorities."

"We are the authorities, in charge of staying alive," he shouted hoarsely.

She felt Dutch rigid in his righteousness. "The Walther saved us. And the AR-15." She looked at it resting on port side.

He whispered, "You've kept us alive, afloat, Amy."

"What do we do now, Dutch? There have to be more, waiting for us." She heard in her mind. *We're afloat on the merry-go-round of death.*

"Are you singing, Amy? There's no morality here except survival. We won this time."

"This isn't winning." She stopped. "Dutch, I killed three men!"

"We're alive. Afloat. Sailing's about living in uncertainty..." His voice floated away.

"They'll come after us again!" She grasped at him. "You're choosing death over sailing, Dutch! We've got to do something!"

"We're more than our murders. There is no them. There's only us..." He passed out.

Amy shivered, sensing she'd break into pieces. "Please tell me what to do!" She waited, realizing, "Oh my God, I'm captain of this boat."

But Dutch heard. "I'm Captain, "he whispered, "Bring me some rum. I'll try to get up."

"I'll bring you chicken soup!"

"No chicken soup," he groaned. "Rum!"

She cradled his face in her hands. "Rum first, then chicken soup!"

"We'll head south-east and poke around Grenada 'til I recover," he said. "We'll sail over any death, Amy. I've waited too long for this dream. We'll prepare the boat. Make an Atlantic crossing to Gibraltar." He sighed, abruptly aware he felt wretched.

She slumped. It didn't matter what he was saying. They were unmistakably hunted, for the cocaine, whatever else was hidden aboard, and maybe, the Hinckley itself. The boat, in a gust of wind and wave, shuddered over her.

But now they were on course, sails trimmed, autopilot on, no other boats in sight. She felt a second of gratitude, the intensity of fatigue, yet went below, heated up chicken soup, brought him half a glass of rum, woke him, and made him eat and drink.

***

While *Quadriga* sailed south under easy conditions, Dutch lay on the port cushion in the cockpit, taking shallow breaths. With his aching shoulder, he knew he'd been strung by his lifeline across his own transom, yet it had saved him. Good thing she had yelled at him. He put his hand to his aching ribs. She couldn't keep the engine on or they'd run out of fuel. He was grateful to have her spoon chicken soup and rum into him. She dispensed an all-purpose antibiotic, and forced him to drink, with rum of course, vile Gatorade for electrolyte replacement.

When he awoke, her mood was furious. "Damn you, we should have sailed back to St. Thomas!"

"Useless thinking. We're afloat. I feel like shit."

"What are we doing," she asked, allowing her shoulders to slump, wracked with sorrow, "How are we getting out of this?"

"We don't have to be anywhere."

Her head went, *"Yea, just sail along, sail along, the lovely ocean blue...."* And, *"so what if there's a murder or two..."*

"You can't be writing a song," he said, weakly. "Minute by minute, we make up our own rules of the ocean," he said, passing into slumber.

Quadriga sailed on. Amy ate something and slept sporadically. A blessing *Quadriga* was on autopilot and winds were steady. At ten a.m., she got on the VHF, hearing voices on the Caribbean net.

Zephyr, Zephyr, Zephyr, this is *Bravo, Bravo, Bravo.*"

Nothing. Static.

Two hours later, she got on again. She lied, again. Ecstatic to hear, "*Bravo, Bravo, Bravo*, this is *Zephyr* affirmative. Are you sure this is *Bravo*, from New York?

"Yes, yes, it is, Captain Zeb. This is Amy on *Yacht Bravo* from New York!"

"That's not right. It's Amy's voice using *Bravo*'s call sign," Zoe said. "They've got more trouble! *Bravo*'s in the Pacific by now. I'll find out where they are, and tell them where we are!"

Loud on the radio, Zeb replied, "*Yacht Zephyr* is anchored in Marigot Bay, St. Lucia, awaiting your arrival."

"Bravo affirmative." Too tired for tears, Amy looked at the chart. Marigot Bay?

Scarab's Crew: Maxwell Desmond in Antigua and Everett Hallpike in Montserrat.

High on the hill at home in Antigua, Maxwell Desmond leaned back in his chair, bad-tempered and sullen. One of his two launches had been found on a local beach off Montserrat. He'd found out from his underground of suppliers. What idiots to have failed such a simple task as boarding *Quadriga* and possibly killing the two sailors aboard. He should have gone with them. His guys had not returned; he'd have to take care of their women. So what, he thought. Part of the game. Maxwell Desmond smiled, remembering when he was in Road Town, months ago, his hired men had put a transmitter in the exchange cowling. He had always known where *Quadriga* was. But this morning, he smiled with a vulpine grin, dialing a well-known phone number in Montserrat.

"Good morning, Dr. Hallpike," he said. Without waiting, he said, "I just got a bead on *Zephyr* on the short wave radio. They must know where *Quadriga* is. Not very far. What fun this is going to be, closing in. I want you to come along? *Quadriga* will soon be ours."

"You mean yours, you stinker. I'm listening too."

"Where shall I meet you?"

"Meet me on *Scarab* in Castries. That's my newest cruiser. We'll head south toward Marigot Bay."

***

Logbook: of *Quadriga*, February, 1981

Name	Location	Latitude	Longitude
Quadriga	Marigot Bay, St. Lucia	13° 57.960'	61° 01.435'
Zephyr	Marigot Bay, St. Lucia	13° 57.960'	61° 01.435'

"Dutch, we're heading for Marigot Bay."

"That's nice," he mumbled, drifting in and out of consciousness.

What was the reality of finding *Zephyr?* She swung *Quadriga* westerly on the new course. Dutch woke as she trimmed the sails, but she couldn't discuss anything with him, continually mulling incidents spinning in their nonstop horror story.

Unexpectedly, the lazarette cover popped up; Hallpike's handyman's dead face lolling at her. Bugs crawled on his face. Why had she pulled the dead body up and over into the lazarette? Stupidly, she dumped liquid kitchen cleaner over his head to keep the body clean. What did rancid mean, anyway? She would, if she could, push Dutch up to see this. Why was she so insistent on this? Should she be saving him to show him to the police, to show she had killed this man? She'd be lucky to find the police before more boats converged on them.

***

Thankfully, the silhouette, the peaks of St. Lucia loomed ahead. Sailing headlong into trade winds, Amy alternately motored and took long tacks to give the engine a rest. Long-term use of the engine had gotten them in trouble in the first place.

She thought about her songs. Hadn't the music producer in New York City, Mr. Crane's friend, counselled that young Amy Sandler needed more life experience? Did this mean death experience? Was this edge? In the middle of her revulsion, horrific dreams, new thinking, and action, musical phrases opened in her head. Unbidden verses of song knocked against her mind. In lyrical hell, this affliction, she may as well write it down. Breathe in the darkness and breathe out the coming song… After an easy tack, she put on the autopilot, brought up pen, paper and her guitar. She wrote and played, pulsing with force, fear and tears. She crooned to Dutch, lying there.

"That's nice, Amy," mumbled Dutch, lying flat in the cockpit. "You light up a note…"

Sailing into the unknown, she the inexperienced warrior in charge. The Walther was part of her, alert for the next assault. But today was calm, they were alone at sea and sailing closer to Marigot Bay…."I promised you adventure," he mumbled. "No police, Amy, no police."

She thought, "Still, I am quite prepared to kill."

***

Waves of determination kept asserting themselves in her body. Amy wasn't a murderer unless there were bodies. Get that stinking kid out of the lazarette. Did Dutch truly have to see it? But there was something to do every minute; keep herself hydrated, fed, and rested so they could get to Marigot Bay, Antigua. Glancing quickly in the mirror, she saw deep circles in her exhausted face. It was 104 nautical miles at about eight knots or so, that would be more or less thirteen hours. They were alive, and doing well on a southerly course. She picked up her guitar to help relieve her, through a song or a wail, with chords, but grief seems to pulsate through her guitar as well. It seemed the boat and the guitar had absorbed the sound of her gunshots, the wounds of her actions—yes, she was crazy to think her boat and guitar could feel with her.

Bravo was long gone to the Locks at the Panama Canal. But Zeb, anchored in Marigot Bay, would know what to do. With them, she'd get Dutch to a doctor. To the local authorities. No matter what Dutch told her.

Chapter Thirteen

**Logbook: of *Yacht Bravo* in the
South Pacific, March, 1981**

With the idyllic days visiting the Galapagos Islands
over, Beth plotted their course to the Marquesa Islands,
Tahiti, Fiji, Moorea and Tonga. They'd sail on to Sydney,
Australia, and put *Bravo* up on the hard for five months.
Australian friends from the Harvard Business School were
waiting for them, with work on land for them. Looking
forward to this, she calculated the forty-five hundred mile
sail. The weather was clear when they lifted anchor, and
they slid back into a daily shipboard routine.

"The Blue-Footed Boobies were my favorite," she
said, looking over their photographs, and asked, "Do you
ever think Bravo's alive, carrying as much as we are, the
voyage? That she has feelings?"

"Don't be silly," Brad said, "Although she's been
hurting with that constant small leak we can't seem
to fix..."

Five days out, dismal clouds hung low as showers
increased. Winds freshened to forty, gusted to fifty, and
they changed watches more often. Midmorning, the

waves became thunderous. With regularity, *Bravo* slid up, shuddered, perched in space, and then dropped. Brad loved this challenging weather, knowing his boat as well as any man who knew the nape of his woman's sweet-scented neck. But in this cauldron of a sea, their boat could broach or roll over and he kept his attention on the helm.

Below, Beth felt hot with the cabin tightly closed, the hatches secure while the swirling seas pounded their boat. Too loud to miss, she heard a cracking sound in the forepeak.

"Brad, we hit something!"

"Can't hear you," he yelled, from above, water washing over him. A rumbling sounded like the muffled engine of a car starting down the block. What was under them? A moody whale?

"Oh God, seawater's gushing in! From the bow!"

That damn spot they'd fixed so many times. Beth saw water flooding onto her sole.

"Open the hatch! This is real!"

Brad reached forward to open the hatch.

Below, she unlashed the bungee cords holding three small packed duffel bags near her. The fizzing, hissing sounds became louder, becoming a large crack from the hull, forward. She looked at the water flooding in through the crack, stunned.

The Switlik life raft, packed in its hard plastic container, was affixed above the hatch.

"We're flooding fast! Don't lose these bags," she shouted, struggling to raise the first bag up the companionway. He grabbed it from her as icy water gushed in. She hauled the second bundle up the steps, leaned back to reach a third bag. Mesmerized, she stared at water, knee-high in forty seconds. This couldn't be! The hull had cracked, but why? She moved, thigh-high in water, trying to locate the radio to put out a Mayday. But who would hear?

Bravo lurched, throwing Beth against the galley. Water rose over the radio direction finder, the sat-nav and the single sideband. No place to go, only up. Taking a last look around the cabin, she saw familiar objects floating, unthinkably. Beth hurtled up the companionway to take the full brunt of the storm in her face. Wet and stinging.

He looked below; eyes glazed, to see his boat foundering? Flooding at a chilling angle!

"Brad, open the life raft! Fling it way out from the boat. Like a Frisbee. Don't let the line get away from you," she shrieked over the turbulent rush of water, above and below her. Her words, a prayer for Brad to do exactly as she commanded.

Brad released the lashings of the canister containing the life raft. Rapidly, he hauled in the painter and triggered the release and inflation. As he did, a wave washed over *Bravo*, knocking Beth flat against the seat of the cockpit. Submerged in water, she recovered, bracing her body against the three bags still wedged, intact. As the water rose, they could hear the vessel splintering with sounds of the roaring ocean.

Paralyzed by the insult of his impending death by drowning, Brad was hypnotized, watching the rush of seawater, fully high in his cabin.

"Wake up! Hang on to the painter! We're not dying!" She shouted.

Galvanized to action, with his right hand, Brad held onto the line of the life raft with inordinate strength; how absurd it would be to let it, their life, get away? He brought the raft in close to the foundering boat. With his left hand, Brad held onto his safety line, still attached to *Bravo*. Beth took each bag, one by one, and threw them into the raft. Taking a breath, she aimed and jumped in, landing inside the opening.

"Brad, release your lifeline. Brad! Jump!" Feeling utter disbelief, he was able to yank the safety clip off, hearing the familiar release. Brad felt an unseen helping hand from the sea, as the sailboat lurched, hurling him off. He dove toward the raft now six long feet away in a deep trough. He missed, falling into frigid waters as it closed over him.

Don't be swept away, not this way. She couldn't utter a sound. Picked up by a wave, he surfaced, gasping, and propelled forward, rolling directly into the raft and landing on his back against Beth. Both of them lay there, soaked, exhausted, inert, seeing nothing, stunned.

Only a few minutes later did they realize the unbelievable success of their transfer.

***

The raft *Resolute* catapulted up and down as the storm continued. In limited visibility, they watched the death throes of *Bravo*, their mast and top of the spreader sinking until it wallowed and was swallowed without a trace. The life raft smelled of new rubber as they shook their heads, suddenly confronted by this new reality.

"No grieving, we made it," she declared. Under the eerie glow cast by its cover, its abrasion-resistant fabric grated against Beth's hands.

"This raft sure looked different at the boat show. Why didn't we test this at home, not in distress," he said bitterly as they slid up and down like a Tilt-A-Whirl in an old-time traveling carnival. Beth recalled when she was a kid, that merry carnival each summer in the vacant lot in Little Neck, Long Island. She remembered brightly colored lights, pink cotton candy melting in her mouth, and shrieks of delight with her brothers as they rode up and down.

Beth and Brad could not rest, and holding each other did not lessen the impact of careening up and down the waves. They slept in bits of time, with no possibility of being comfortable. Ever the realist, Beth determinedly shook off disbelief and apathy. She located the bailer in the survival kit near her. Anything to keep busy while she thought what to do the next minute. And the next. And the next.

"We've no food, no water, no flares," Brad groaned.

"Stop that!" She didn't want to yell at him. This was the beginning of anything they'd never done. "We've got everything we need. Open the kit marked number two," she ordered him over the din. "Get the Dramamine pills, take one, swallow it, and tie up your life jacket."

One wave after another hit them squarely as they peered out to observe the flotsam and jetsam of *Bravo*'s life. Books floated to the surface, a cereal box, and a needlepoint pillow embroidered from Brad's mother," "*Don't Forget to Stay Afloat.*"

Beth looked at her watch. Ten a.m. Eight hours of washed-out gray daylight to go. *Bravo*'s gone. Along with three intense years of their life spent building and shaping their floating home. They had provisions for twenty days, maybe longer. Captain Beth should be able to stretch them.

Soaked and cold, she wanted to sob her anguish in the life raft that slid down one angry wave after another. Instead, she sneezed five times and wiped her nose with her hand. The salt water took it. His shoulders hunched over as he sobbed. She could neither comfort nor yell at him. Of course she had packed flares. But who would see them? They had nothing that would help rescue them.

Brad, sweetheart, we'll survive this," she whispered. "We're resolute."

"Stop using that fucking word," he wailed.

Chapter Fourteen

**Logbook: of *Quadriga*, into
Marigot Bay, March, 1981**

Name	Location	Latitude	Longitude
Quadriga	Marigot Bay, St. Lucia	13° 57.960'	61° 01.435'
Zephyr	Marigot Bay, St. Lucia	13° 57.960'	61° 01.435'

Was it 4 p.m.? With sails down, Amy, at the wheel of *Quadriga*, glided into the small sheltered inlet of Marigot Bay, St. Lucia. Dutch lay in the cockpit, sleeping, with a lightweight blanket over him. Amy had cleaned up as much of the blood as she could. She put on a ridiculously bright, pink shirt, lipstick and makeup. And a sun hat and sunglasses befitting the level of a Hinckley-vacationing sailor. Condition normal. Playing the part of a visitor, Amy was just another lucky, wealthy, spoiled, vacationing sailor.

Keeping her eye on the depthometer, she made a circle in the small lagoon, not crowded at all. That was a blessing, but where, oh where, was *Zephyr*? She made three-quarters of a circle around the lovely lagoon.

There she was, *Zephyr*, anchored serenely, close by. Sitting in the cockpit, Zoe was, of all things, darning a sock. Seeing Amy, she jumped up, their eyes meeting in astonishment. Zoe could tell *Quadriga's* sails looked haphazard, though packed. Amy's back was rigid as she put her finger to her mouth to indicate silence.

Zoe bounded into her dinghy and slowly approached *Quadriga*, nimbly handing up the dinghy painter to Amy and agilely hopping aboard. Amy could not break her composure, knowing every island, and these St. Lucia Mountains, had deadly eyes and ears.

"Phew, what stinks?" Zoe asked. Immediately she saw Dutch, lying in the cockpit, white-faced and unconscious. She shut up.

"We've got to get Dutch to a doctor. Where's Zeb?"

"He went to town to pick up supplies."

That said, Zoe went to the bow to anchor *Quadriga*, at Amy's direction. Done.

Amy turned off the engine, motioning Zoe down into the cabin. Amy, strong and tall, stumbled into small and short Zoe's arms, sobbing. Zoe saw Dutch lying unconscious on the starboard cushions, a blanket over him, looking half dead.

"Amy, you're amazing. Getting yourselves here," Zoe said, hugging the tall, young woman, disbelieving the rough saga tumbling out of her mouth.

"At night, leaving Plymouth, when we got out to sea, a launch came after us and we couldn't stop them though Dutch shot at them. We were boarded..."

"What?" Zoe stuttered.

Amy fell into her arms, sobbing. "Zoe, I, er, killed three men..."

Shocked, Zoe found this impossible to believe. "What did you do with them?"

"One went over with Dutch and sank. I killed him. I killed the second. And pushed him overboard. I was able to release their launch and it fell back."

"What about the third? You're driving me crazy."

"Zoe, I can't believe how well I did, using the Walther. Dutch made me learn it. And the AR-15 as well, but it's so heavy."

"Where's the third dead guy?" Zoe was having trouble listening to this.

"I've done the most stupid thing: I placed the dead kid in the lazarette. To show Dutch."

"To show Dutch? You're kidding!" Zoe was appalled. "No wonder the boat stinks!"

"When Dutch wakes up, he must see the face of the farmhand from Montserrat. I've got to get the rotting body off the boat."

"Why didn't you?"

"I don't know..."

Zoe was dumbstruck as Amy deteriorated into confusion. "Amy, you're exhausted. I'm taking your dinghy and mine back to *Zephyr*. Zeb will know you got here. It's still afternoon. I'm coming with you, out of this harbor, and we're dumping it."

"We have to get Dutch off this boat and onto *Zephyr*," Amy pleaded. "He'll be safe."

"Not 'til dark. You know how many boats and people will see us. We need Zeb to help. Let's get Dutch below to the fore cabin, and get this idiotic thing done."

"I can't get you into this," Amy said.

"I'm in. I'll kill you if you don't let me help," Zoe declared. "This has to be done. Now!"

Amy stared at her. In disbelief, Zoe stood firm, steady with her hands on her hips looking up at her young friend. "Marigot's an easy, quick harbor. We'll get out, do it and get back in. Fast. Move!"

"Are you using your bossy, executive powers on me?"

"You bet! We're doing this," Zoe ordered. "NOW!"

***

The two women lifted, stumbled and cajoled Dutch, Zoe above him, and Amy below, as he mumbled and shouted in pain. They tried to ease his way, as they bumped him down the companionway.

"Where are we going?" He muttered, barely awake. "Oh, hello, Zoe." And back out of it. They carried him, with utter strength, onto the bed in the fore cabin. Amy straightened his long legs out toward the bow, rolling him way over to the port side.

"A real bed," Dutch uttered, then instantly fell asleep.

Zoe went forward, pulled up *Quadriga*'s anchor, stowed it, put the pin in the anchor at the bow, and walked aft to take the wheel from Amy.

"You've sure learned how to handle a boat," Amy said, a slight smile.

Ten minutes due west out of the harbor, on *Quadriga*, Zoe put on the autopilot, raised the main and unfurled the jib. Amy sat, glazed, watching her friend at the helm, the unspoken burden now shared.

"Amy, drink water, eat something," Zoe commanded. "You've kept Dutch and yourself alive."

Silently, Amy went below, drank two glasses of water, checked on Dutch, and opened a hanging locker to get him another blanket. There was the AR-15 rifle up against the wall. She was so glad of the lessons, how to hold it, aim, and well, it was armed and ready for use. She checked the Walther. Loaded.

"Amy, we're out enough. If he floats toward land, it may not be to Marigot Harbor. But I'm not sure. Beth would know the tides," said Zoe.

Amy opened the lazarette, to see an overpowering rotting reality. Zoe peered in after her.

"Oh, how horrible. I can't feel sorry, Amy. Do we have to touch this bastard? The smell is killing me. I need a clothespin for my nose."

"I'll get a line. We'll pull him up and finally dump him, "Amy said, moving toward the stern of her beautiful Hinckley sailboat on the lovely Caribbean Sea. Her exhaustion made her stumble. She was almost over the edge. Edge? Driven to the edge? Was this what the New York music producer was talking about?

Nope, it was getting through the next two hours, and back into the harbour.

***

Logbook: of the Raft Resolute, in the Pacific Ocean, March, 1981

"We're 'on' the Pacific Ocean, not 'in' it," Beth said, counting seven days and nights, drifting into what sleep she could find. Sailing had been too easy, too comfortable, too brilliant, Beth thought. Now, in how many minutes was the next challenge?

She kept engaging Brad in familiar chatter, keeping him going. He was able to make one good joke this morning, pretending to roll a movie camera; "Things happen fast here in the Pacific. Time for a Budweiser. Bring a Bud back to your life raft. Or we could go to Cambridge and get a hot fudge sundae at Brigham's?"

"Good one, Brad," she allowed, wanting to smile at the stupidity of it, while thinking that nothing was funny. Dread chased away all humor.

They peered out from their cover at vast stretches of open sea, uncluttered miles of ocean. Beth saw nothing other than the sea. The last week, they'd sent postcards from the Galapagos. It would take almost one month for mail to arrive in the U.S.

Beth clicked her brain to shipping lanes. Might a tanker see them? They'd gone down approximately thirteen-hundred miles west from the Galapagos. And she knew they were fifteen-hundred miles due north of Easter Island. Maybe a tanker would be in one of the lanes. She found the flares where she'd packed them.

"Brad, take off your life jacket, so your clothes dry. Keep away from your sores," she said, while her mind jumped erratically. Brad was holding back tears of frustration, discomfort, utter defeat. She prayed his asthma would not reappear. How could it now?

"Where's our compass, Beth?"

"Bag Three."

"How deep do you think it is here?"

"About 3,000 fathoms. Check the chart, Bag One; we should be close to the North-South routing corridor.

"Where are the flares?"

"Bag Three."

"Night and day flares?"

"Hand and parachute flares, Brad, you sudden smart ass!"

"Beth, you're the smart ass! Let's rename the dinghy. How about *Yacht Smart Ass*?

"If we were so smart, we'd have gotten a big fibreglass boat!"

"Shut up, Beth. Stop the blame; we wanted to get away." And he took the lead, "Neither of us is injured, the storm is over, and we're still afloat."

"Yes, my dear mate."

Bored, he opened Bag Two to find five spools of Gudebrod fishing wire of different weights, several sizes of hooks, and a handwritten note about which fish are edible and what weights to catch in the Pacific Ocean. "When did you do all this, Beth?"

"'Chance favors the prepared mind,'" she said, "Dr. Louis Pasteur's teaching." She looked at the Elizabeth Arden night cream she packed, to assuage their saltwater sores, almost used up. Remembering what she had read about being stranded at sea, she knew their bodies would betray them, undergoing attack and damage from the elements, no matter how high their morale and sense of survival. She kept a tight watch on Brad and prayed for strength and good conditions to do whatever they must to survive. She prayed for dry against the constant wet and the strength of the life raft that was weakening.

A photograph of her mother surfaced in Bag One. Mary, tall and aristocratic, had her arms around Beth, on a summer's day at home in Oyster Bay.

The life raft was frankly meager and shallow, the cheapest model. How irritated Brad had been at the boat show when they bought it. Nobody liked to spend money on equipment they thought they would never use. Didn't want to use. He hadn't been arrogant. Simply not touched by a thought of tragedy or even the thought of an actual challenge. Now this was the fragile shell of their total existence.

"The South Equatorial currents will bring us close to the shipping lanes," Beth said, determined to speak positively, knowing chances were slight to zero.

"We're resolute," she said, Amy-Beth-Zoe-talk.

"Will you shut up with the resolute word? I'm sick of it."

"Sorry." Rummaging in the bags, Brad found a box of condoms. "I bet you have seventeen uses for these aboard. Am I to make love to a fish?"

"Another good one, Brad."

"You're not making any jokes."

No dummies, each tried to fool the other to rise above utter despair, as long as they stayed a team.

"We need to catch a turtle, Beth. All we have to do is find one!"

Running out of fresh water, they were learning to gather in rainwater during gales.

***

Logbook: of *Quadriga*, a perilous sunset sail outside of Marigot Bay, March, 1981

"The weather's bright and calm, perfect for a burial at sea," Zoe declared, standing over the open lazarette. Why did she need to make Amy laugh? The poor girl was on empty. As Zoe leaned over the open lazarette, the stench of the decaying body, made her gag. But she said, "I'll do anything, climb in next to him and push up."

Amy had forgotten how short, spry and lively Zoe was, who quickly drew a breath and lowered herself into the lazarette. Next to the body. She stared at his dead eyes blankly open. The towels in which he was wrapped had dried and congealed, and were sucked tight onto his body. Poor, stupid thing. She pushed while Amy pulled upward. "Would it be easier if we turn him sideways?"

"Good idea."

"Hey, Amy, do you think his body is 'clean'?"

"What do you mean?"

"Any evidence left behind aboard from his dead body? Bullets from your gun? What if he floats to shore? Your fancy towels are wrapped around him."

"Those are the cheap towels," Amy said. "I hadn't gotten that far in my thinking!"

"Aw, the sharks will get him. Maybe they eat towels. Keep pushing," Zoe said.

"Holy hell, you're enjoying this," Amy exclaimed, noting the muscular changes in Zoe and her absolute willingness to be in there.

"I never pushed an evil, dead body overboard before," Zoe declared tensely. "You're on edge. We're on the edge here!"

That word hit Amy full and frontal, "This is edge, life or death!"

While pushing the body up, Amy had to talk to relieve this tense idiotic scene. She told Zoe about the dismissal of her album by the music producer in New York. About having no edge. Zoe became hysterical with nervous laughter. There was almost normal talk while they struggled with lifting the body. Back to business.

"By the way, Zoe, have you learned to shoot?"

"No, the deckhand did everything."

"This idiot's heavier dead than he may have been alive" Amy said, "We've got to keep pushing!"

"Should we have the Walther nearby?"

"He's already dead. Think he'll wake up?"

"Don't be so smart. Everything feels awful. I'm getting it for you. Just shut up and take it while you're in there." Amy reached into a side locker in the cockpit. "Zoe, put this handgun on the ledge next to you. It's a 9mm."

"Whatever you say, "Zoe said, sighing. Amy put it on the ledge near her.

"Push!"

"I am!"

Amy raised her head, her eyes checking the horizon, a sea habit well ingrained.

***

Logbook of the High-Powered Cruiser *Scarab*

Out of Castries Harbour, St. Lucia, Max Desmond, stocky and brown, stood at the wheel of his fibreglass cruiser with a beam of ten feet. He kept two heavy-duty engines rumbling at low speed to avoid undue curiosity. But every local man who lived on a dock knew almost everything in port, and wanted nothing to do with this particular vessel. Hallpike stood next to Desmond, familiar by their long association. Two Colt AR-15a2 Carbine Sporters, with a caliber of .223 Rem, and a barrel length of 20 inches, lay on the front seat with a tarp over them.

"That signal you put aboard *Quadriga* on New Year's Day's is gone. We're still working on the one from Tortola," Desmond said. "That's the one good my men did in Road Town. And you are still an idiot."

"Don't call me an idiot. Max, you're equally an idiot," Hallpike replied, in a friendly retort borne of equals. "Neither of us has the goddamn coke. Three of your men are missing, one launch is wrecked, and this whole operation, what you say is fun, has been a total waste."

"A successful smuggling mission is one you never hear about, asshole."

"Gotta keep it that way. At least we're not in human trafficking."

"I hate to think of the rude embarrassment I'd feel, my highly esteemed Dr. Hallpike, to having to tell the boys in Cartagena we lost our shipment on a no-account Hinckley sailboat from New York. Sailed by a naïve dumb guy who owned a thread factory. We need to get it back. Nobody makes me look reckless."

"Relax, the boat's outside of Marigot Bay. Twenty minutes. We still have a good signal. Not only did I do a great job of putting in that homing device, but I had another shipment placed deep under their bilge. On New Year's Day when they were out dancing in town. I'll redeem that later," Hallpike said. He looked at the radar to see their position on the small screen. "Admit it, Max, you're dying for that boat."

"I certainly am, I can taste that Hinckley. I've got a bill of sale and phony documents aboard, from my yacht broker in London. I've ordered my usual navy-blue paint from England. You and I'll sail her down tonight to Union Island. I have Frenchies waiting to refit her. They owe me."

They rode in silence for several minutes.

"Ev, you want to fuck the girl before we kill her?"

"Max, you're a bastard."

"And you're not? Those fancy degrees from Oxford never stopped you. Don't make judgments about me. You're all glory. No money. And you got fired from your professorship at Oxford and had to come back and live in Montserrat. Where'd those degrees get you before you worked for me? You terrorize your cute little wife who'd do anything to leave you. And you won't let me at her."

"You're stupid with your housekeeper in front of your wife."

"Did I tell you that Roberta caught me again," he smirked. "It was funny."

"You don't give a shit what anybody thinks, except your partners on the *Brindisi*."

Desmond paid no heed to Hallpike's insults. "I've food in cartons, lots of line, and body bags with weights for Dutch and the tall girlfriend; I'll get her first."

Desmond bent to light a cigar, then looked steely-eyed to the horizon, guiding the wheel. "I will have that Hinckley."

"You've got all kinds of money, why the hell don't you buy one?"

"Been in the Caribbean too long. No fun. No laws. Besides, there's always someone to kill."

***

Logbook: of Raft *Resolute*-15 days on the Pacific Ocean, March, 1981

Days blurred for Beth and Brad, their raft plunging into valleys, lifting sharply, small waves cresting, turning them around and around. They took turns keeping watch while the other tried to doze.

Beth knew how quickly they'd perish against the rigor of the ocean if they gave up hope, so her imagination worked overtime, searching for anything, remembering the poem from Khayyam's *Rubaiyat* about being a rider on the tide. Oh, to see a tanker in the shipping lane. She was achy, cramped, much of the time trying not to be on top of Brad. And she loved him more than ever. All the while, the raft groaned in heavy seas; the sea their jailor. But Beth worked most every minute to sustain herself, sending out cosmic messages, vibrations to nearby ships at sea and angels above. Rigour, vigour, prayers, a break. Somehow.

At night, phosphorescence swirled around them. Brad wondered how many turtles, whales, sharks, and fish lay below the delicate white meat of his not-so-smart ass. Some fish below, like tuna, could give them more life, while sharks, teeth, death. Through the opening on the raft cover, he looked up at the clear night sky, trying to study the constellations. Beth knew them all. If they had a rudder and tiller, maybe they could have steered by them.

Brad's breathing was labored; his arms and thighs had shrunk and he had no energy to do any exercise. He gazed at Beth in slumber; her long red hair cut off into a cap around her head. Scissors in Bag Two.

They must keep the inflatable strong, inspecting every seam six times a day, repairing what they could with their little kit. "If only we could fix our bodies," she said. "Our strength's deteriorated on canned food, soggy bread, crackers and tastes of peanut butter."

"Let's go to Harvard Square for a roast beef sandwich and that drippy hot fudge sundae at Brigham's," he said, again and again. Remembering student days, their only cares being passing courses with good grades. His internal camera rolled to earlier autumn days, orange and gold leaves, the tang of football and parties in the Cambridge area. He recalled being tutored by Beth, falling in love with her and putting their lives together.

Thumping began under the raft. A large dark form swam close. Beth lowered their small drogue anchor to keep them steadier. "Our luck's changing. Here's a sea turtle. I'll hold your knees. Reach under his flippers. Lasso it," she begged.

"It's too big!" Brad grabbed his sea knife and leaned over as she hung onto him. Touching its hard shell, he grabbed a flipper. But the turtle was strong, and it slid away. "It's coming back. I'll get it around the neck!"

"Go for the underbelly," she begged. It swam close, bumping the raft. Brad reached out as far as he could, but the old turtle had seen enough and again slipped away.

As if in sympathy for this loss, the skies opened up and the Turners were able to collect three gallons of rainwater in plastic bottles. They drank, bathed, and laughed with secret tears of loss mingling with rain. "This isn't a bad consolation prize for losing the turtle," Beth admitted.

"No sharks, no storms, no leaks, all calm," Beth intoned, "No ships either." Her body ached with the constant bucking movement of the raft, forcing her arms and legs to perform small exercises. "You move too, Brad."

"The fucking ocean moves me more than enough!"

They roasted by day and froze by night. Neither had a bowel movement in two weeks. "We're crusting up," he said.

"No whining, honey. Takes too much energy. Our raft and the sea will keep us afloat," Beth pontificated, sounding like a Sunday school teacher.

"You're out of your mind," he said.

"You always knew that. We should have brought cards, to play bridge."

"They wouldn't stay straight."

"Yeah, and the magnetic chess board sank."

While they looked out for a puff of smoke, a mast, the sound of engines of a tanker, they played the game called, "When rescued, I will...have a shower every hour, steak and lobster, new clothes...write a book...chocolate..."

Beth remembered a special university lecturer she had, Dr. Fernando Flores, her neuro-linguistics professor, who often chided her. He would say, in his rich Chilean accent, "You're only one human being..." He had criticized her for wanting to be everywhere at once. "You can only be in one place, Miss Braithwaite, but you can be doing many things." Here she was, doing countless things to save their lives. The only path for her to take, more difficult each hour, was that of joyful challenge. "I feel like a fool," she said, "But we're afloat.

They awoke next morning to find four flying fish inside the raft, gratefully a gift from Poseidon.

"We'll clean 'em and let the sun bake 'em." But they couldn't wait, sucking the bits from the bones.

"Damn, this tastes great."

Brad felt something on the current fishing line, a hardy pull from a glistening white fish about fifteen inches long. With hope wild in her breast, "Brad, don't lose this one!"

With total determination, he carefully reeled in the fish, muscles bulging out of his scrawny arms. Having pulled it in, Brad twisted the head, breaking its spine. Blood dripped. She held up the blue whale coffee cup to catch some of it. He cut it open and filleted the meat. "Our private sushi restaurant," he said. But glistening gray forms made rings around the boat. It had to start sometime. One surfaced and hovered nearby, passing the life raft. With a small stick, Beth leaned out and whacked its head. The shark turned swiftly.

They were down to the last of the water and foodstuffs. "We need a rainstorm, a turtle, a fish, a freighter, whatever comes first. What hurts most is that we haven't seen one ship."

But she did! A black dot moving in calm seas. Beth's throat closed, excitement and hope mounting within her. Quickly retrieving the parachute flare, she handed it to Brad to light. He unscrewed the cap on the bottom, which became the striker. "Not yet, don't waste it. Let them get closer. Aim it high."

"Tell me when." They waited thirty minutes by her working watch.

"Now!" He struck the bottom of the flare with the cap in the metal canister, holding it at arm's length, pointing upwards. It became a sharp pink flare in the early evening sky, roaring out and soaring high.

"Hold up of the white flag," she commanded. On their knees, they held the flag, waving the sail together, yelling "Over here! Over here!" Adrenalin pumped their hearts out of their bodies for fifteen minutes. The ship disappeared below the horizon.

***

Logbook: of the Ecuadorian Oil Tanker *Luciano Valez*, on the Pacific Ocean

Officer on duty, Luis Garcia, had a headache, drinking too much last night. Aboard the large oil tanker Luciano Valez, out of Guayaquil, Ecuador, he checked his speed, sixteen knots in calm, uneventful seas. Lifting his head, he saw a faint glimmer of a flash twenty degrees to port side. Looking at his radar, nothing, probably a strobe of heat lightning. The fight with his wife lingered in his mind. Big deal, he'd be seeing his girlfriend in the next port.

***

Logbook: of the Raft Resolute, on the Pacific Ocean

While the loss was a severe blow, Beth could think only one way. "We're close to the shipping lanes. Those guys run highly mechanized freighters and cargo ships, sitting high. The next one will see us."

Sore, they lay in each other's arms for solace, gritting their teeth against the constant bumping under the raft, dehydrated and praying for the next rain. Above, while the stars twinkled, their life existed minute-by-minute, hour-by-hour.

A rainsquall, another fish caught, waves breaking over the raft. Comical, almost, what they got used to. And grateful. "In this unrelenting ocean, Brad, it's truly been kind to us."

"Here's rain, Brad." She held the bucket out of the opening of the raft of their faded orange raft. With water collected, she made him drink, washed his face:" I love you so much, Brad, you're doing so well. With the raft pitching, I can tell we've another storm brewing."

"There's no fucking God," he barely whispered. He began to cough nonstop.

"Brad, we'll catch the next fish."

"I'm done. Use my body for food."

"Stop!" She said hoarsely. "Don't talk like that!"

"I hear a dog barking. That's my dog, Cappy. Mom's calling me. I'm coming, Mom!"

Beth took on his mother's voice. "Bradley, you'll play tomorrow. Time to sleep."

Her eyesight was blurry. As she adjusted the fishing line, Brad struggled to rise, placing one foot over the runner pontoon. "What are you doing?"

"Going for help, I'll be back. Road's over there," he said, attempting to slip into the sea. She dropped the line and fell in front of him to block his exit. She grabbed his legs, as he kicked, trying to evade her weight. "Bethie, look at those trees!"

She gripped his frail shoulders with her arm and reached into Bag Three, working to find a heavy object. Brad struggled against her, his new adversary. Her hand fumbled on the revolver, and she drew it out by the barrel, wanting to knock him out cold with the grip end. With all the strength she could usurp from her weak body, she cracked him over the head. While he slumped, motionless, she pulled his legs back into the raft. He could still roll over the side into the ocean, so she slip-knotted his ankles and hands, loosely, working methodically, without emotion.

Beth couldn't lose her life partner now: he was knocked out, out safe. No cut where she'd clobbered him. Tears ran down her face. She took her finger to save them, then tried to swallow the tiny droplets.

The next morning, Beth looked out. It couldn't be. A square black shape moved up and down in the horizon. "A ship, Brad," she said, the words ultra-rich on her tongue. Kneeling over Brad's motionless body, she brought out a flare from Bag Two, and holding on for balance, she took the cap off, ignited it, thrust it aloft and it soared, making a brilliant light in the morning sky.

She took a second flare, lit it, and aimed up through the canopy opening. Brad moved abruptly, destroying her aim. The flare failed to clear the canopy, fell into the life raft and exploded near her. Bright red flames began to burn one side of their raft. The explosion and smell overpowered them as waves bounced the raft. Losing her balance, she fell over Brad, trying to shield them both from burns.

One pontoon fizzled with a large burn mark, partially deflating, and taking on water. Grey smoke spiraled upwards. Three compartments were still intact, holding them up. Beth pushed Brad over to the sturdy part of the raft. Nothing food-wise was left in the three bags. Her last flare. She struggled to light it, aiming it high in seemingly slow motion. It soared up, into a bright arc.

More water entered the raft from the deflated area as waves swept them up and down. She made sure her life jacket was tight, untied Brad, and forced his arms into his jacket. It was better when he was unconscious, not ranting, nor swallowing seawater.

Both of them in the choppy sea, Beth tried to hold Brad in the Red Cross lifesaving position in the sea, and to hang on to what was left of the raft. There was no way to estimate the ship's direction. Did they see the flares?

Only death by drowning in the Pacific was left. Their bodies would never make it to the bottom.

How soon would they be given to the fishes?

Chapter Fifteen

Logbook: of *Quadriga*, March, 1981

Name	Location	Latitude	Longitude
Quadriga	Marigot Bay, St. Lucia	13° 57.960'	61° 01.435'

Aboard *Quadriga*, south of Marigot Bay, Amy stood on deck, pulling, while Zoe, deep in the lazarette, grunted and pushed up the stiff corpse. The boat's autopilot was on, and rocked slightly in the calm swells of the afternoon. The young dead farmhand was solid in position, inside Amy's beach towels. Struggling, Amy and Zoe laughed, out of nerves; "We're so stupid!"

"Where did these bugs come from? They're on me!" Zoe strained.

"He's almost out, lift harder!"

"You're lifting, I'm pushing!"

Amy glanced up and looked to the North, her ingrained habit in scanning the seas. She glimpsed a dark launch bouncing over the waves, heading straight toward them, with a rumbling sound of a furious engine, full throttle, telegraphing new terror,

Was death, again, near? Whose would it be?

Could she motor back to Marigot Bay? Too much open water before the channel. She rechecked the autopilot as *Quadriga* blithely pranced along.

"That boat's heading straight for us. Let him fall back in. I should have never taken you out here," Amy yelled, beside herself.

"Amy, I took you!" Zoe yelled back, "Can we make it back into the harbour?"

"Nah, they're coming too fast. I know who it is," Amy said coldly, not wanting Zoe to panic any more than she was. "Zoe, if they try to come aboard, you've got to hide in the lazarette. Take the gun off the ledge. Hold it. Keep still."

"I can't stay in this stinking hole," said Zoe, gagging.

"Yes, you can," Amy shouted. "It's your only place. Shut up and stay! I've got to take care of Dutch!"

Without waiting for Zoe's acceptance, Amy jumped below, grabbed three sleeping pills, a bottle of water, and hurried into the fore cabin. "Dutch dear, take these," she crooned, making him swallow and drink. He had to be knocked out. Deep out. They could kill him in his own cabin.

She turned to see the Colt AR-15 in the open hanging locker. Wow. Yes. She had reloaded it and replaced it, glad she knew how to hold and shoot. What would happen if she brought it above and needed to shoot them from her stern? No, they'd be at her, a beautiful standing target for them as well. They had to be armed, of course.

Direct war couldn't work. She needed an irresistible flash of strategic shrewdness, faced, again, with unavoidable death. On the abyss; Amy had to dare, to seduce, to live. She took the rifle down and placed it on a corner on the berth, away from Dutch. She prayed he couldn't or wouldn't sigh, wake up, or turn over.

Slowly, pretending to be an actress earning her Oscar, beautiful Amy slowly climbed the companionway, and purposely stood in full sight. Her plan was ready. Charmed offensive, she thought, undoing her long hair and letting it fly around her head as she set the jib, slowly, and turned on the autopilot. Zoe, hidden in the lazarette, and Dutch, below, not hidden, were her responsibility. Taking her now famous-to-herself deep breaths, she held onto a stanchion to steady herself. "Hands, stop shaking. Driven to the edge. Keep breathing. I'm so resolute, here's to me and my edge!"

From a small opening in the lazarette, Zoe yelled, "Can you call Zeb on the radio in Marigot? He'll come!"

"We're thirty minutes out. He can't make it fast enough."

"Any radio call may deter them. Everyone will hear the transmission!"

"Smart, Zoe, but there may be more behind them. We're on our own."

"They may be just fishermen and pass us," said Zoe, hopeful, from inside the lazarette. "I'm getting seasick!"

"Try not to throw up. Hey, Zoe, I love you!"

"I love you, too, Amy."

"Above all, stay absolutely quiet in there."

"Dearest, darling *Quadriga*, we've got to come through this," Amy whispered to her sailboat. "I love you, Dutch and we've got to stay afloat and alive…"

Standing gracefully at the stern, in a deliberate pose, she actually laughed. So they could see she was well and strong. Then she made a show of going below. Dutch would kill her if anything happened to his precious boat.

She'd know soon enough.

***

Logbook: of the *Scarab* approaching *Yacht Quadriga*

Scarab planed along the seas, getting closer to *Quadriga*. Desmond loved his fibreglass cruiser. At the wheel, he looked through his high-powered binoculars to see Amy casually leave the main deck to go below. She certainly was beautiful, every long part of her. He wanted to know more. Beneath him. Dutch must be injured or dead, or he would've surely been above, physically regarding their approach. Yes, angry and loaded, Dutch might be, calmly waiting. Something wasn't right on her boat. There had to be problem aboard. From the other day. How were they sailing now, so beautifully?

"She sauntered below," Desmond said. "Didn't seem to see us. That's odd. Would have been easy to pick her off, and board. But I want a little fun!" His eyes caressed the view of the Hinckley as sunset began to scorch the Caribbean waters red. "I don't want to ram her and have to do repairs later."

"The girl or the boat? Why're you so fucking nuts? You're rich; why'd you have me load up the boat in Montserrat?" Hallpike shook his head in disgust. "Why am I even here?"

"I've an unfulfilled passion for that boat. They don't deserve it. They'll be dead within the hour."

"What makes you so crazy, Desmond?"

"I can buy anything. These tropics are so boring," Desmond repeated, smiling. "They're the next."

"To be killed? Some sport you are!"

Desmond smiled. "Shut up, Hallpike."

Desmond was still annoyed no bodies of those who worked for him, or even bones of bodies, or parts of bodies had floated up on shore, anywhere in the region.

***

Logbook: of *Quadriga*, Ten minutes… to Death, Outside of Marigot Bay, March, 1981

Down below, inside *Quadriga*, Amy heard the vibrating power and sound of the dark launch's engines approach. She waited, working to quash the crushing anger residing inside her. She heard the launch slowing to neutral, then reverse.

"Halloooo, Amy. Max Desmond here! I come in peace. Really! I don't want to startle you. I even brought…

I hope I'm not startling you…, I brought some wine as a peace offering," he called from the launch. "May I board?"

The launch eased up against *Quadriga*'s lee side, bumping slightly. Lines were tied without hearing permission.

Below, Amy crushed the understanding that she would be treated as about to be dead. Peering through a porthole in the main salon, she saw Desmond and, oh, what? Hallpike! What? Worse than she imagined. She remembered being welcomed into each of their houses, having met their wives, eating their food, drinking their wine, and laughing with them. How could she have been so unaware, saying yes to an innocent favor that had them caught?

Twice, and what was next?

'Wait, wait," she worked in her head, standing below in the main salon. "I'm Commander of this vessel." She was ready.

Deep in the lazarette, Zoe barely breathed, between her heart pounding, praying she wouldn't faint, and suppressing a nervous giggle. She looked out, her head up against the cover, opening a tiny slit to let in some air. She held a Walther 9 mm in her hand, with the magazine, and chambered for use by Amy.

He called again. "Amy! Hope we're not startling you, I come in peace, please, and I brought you some wine. May I board?"

Clearing her throat, she yelled back, brightly. "Of course! Come aboard!"

They heard the thud of Desmond boarding. His feet stood inches from Zoe. Both women knew lines from the launch were being strung, made fast. Zoe put her hand over her mouth.

In the main salon below, Amy moved quickly to the fore cabin, closing the slim wooden door behind her. She crooned, "Dutch, stay asleep. I love you," while she rolled his huge, bulky, unconscious frame to the furthest port side of the V-berth. He must be out of any possible line of fire, her line.

She took the AR-15 out of the hanging locker, blessing Dutch for teaching her how to deal with the long muzzle. Why did Desmond play these deadly games, pretending to be upstanding? His wife, Roberta, who had loved him, was duped, dulled and deadened.

Standing silently, Amy seethed with rage, breathing quickly, but forcing herself to wait. With her new understanding of the thin veneer of Caribbean society, the subordination, the silent complicity, double standards! How dare the unctuous Max Desmond have the audacity to board! Unctuous? With Hallpike in the boat? Was that a word for a song?

Not now. The shift within her became powerful, playing a new part. It was Amy who sailed this boat upon the sea. Straightening her shoulders, she cradled the semi-automatic AR-15, sat on the bed, and rested it against her knee… Waiting… Sweat poured down her face, even though the forward hatch, cranked open, blew in fresh air.

"Hello, Amy. How are you," Desmond yelled, congenially, "I came to do some marlin fishing and recognized your boat. Hey, where's Dutch?"

She yelled up, but calmly. "He's sick with a bad cold. Who's with you, Max?"

No answer.

"What's that fucking stench, Desmond," she heard Hallpike say, oblivious to social formality.

"Everett Hallpike? Is that you? Do I hear your voice?"

"Yes, Amy," Hallpike replied in a dour tone. It was clear he didn't want to be here.

"I have those cashew boxes for you," she shouted in a friendly tone, trying not to choke on her words through the closed door, "Come below, you two and have a drink!"

With one in the lazarette hardly able to breathe, and the other stuck behind a flimsy wooden door, carbine at the ready, two female hearts beat in unison.

"I know that stink," Hallpike repeated, unable to stop himself. He had hopped on board, and stood behind Desmond.

Desmond smiled as he stood in the cockpit aboard the moving *Quadriga*. He had planned well. Dutch was either off the boat, or sick in the fore cabin. Dutch would have been right up, confronting his presence. He had to be aboard. Yup, something was terribly wrong, and in his favor. Dutch would never let Amy take this boat out by herself.

Above, Zoe barely widened the lazarette cover, narrow enough to observe the tall, dark-haired, good-looking man, with a gun in one hand, standing in the cockpit.

She recognized him! This man had shown up at several hotels she'd been inspecting. Why, he once talked to her. In a charming British accent. Shocked, she softly closed the hatch.

Hallpike stood on the aft deck, by the taffrail, backing up Desmond.

"Hallpike, we never got to deliver those boxes for you," Amy said, "Come down, Dutch's sick. I think he needs a doctor."

"So he's aboard, then? We'll take care of you," Desmond said, peering down into the main cabin at an angle, familiar with *Quadriga*'s innards. There was no one in the main salon. If Dutch was aboard, he must be in the fore cabin on his bed. Why wasn't Amy in the galley?

"Amy, come up above!"

"For God's sake, man, don't go down there," Hallpike uttered.

"Don't tell me." Max Desmond smiled disdainfully, as he did whatever Hallpike said. Putting his gun into his pocket, he climbed slowly, gingerly, facing down the companionway. He stood in the main salon. He took two steps. "Amy, where are you?"

Amy appreciated her subtle knowledge, where the floorboards creaked; she knew exactly where Desmond stood.

"Oh, Max…." She began to cry, soft and low, through the closed door to the fore cabin. She had seen him with two other women. Her life, these minutes, depended on this.

That undeniable feminine sound purred toward Maxwell, sexual and inviting from the fore cabin. That stupid beautiful girl must be in deep trouble. Well, she was, he smiled. Nearly hid. Nearly dead.

"Amy, where's Dutch," Max asked.

"In here, he's sick," she spoke softly, finding it difficult to speak softly behind the closed door with the wind blowing and water slapping at the bow.

Above, Hallpike grumbled loudly, moving around the cockpit. "I know that smell…"

"Desmond, please come in," Amy said, over the sound of the engine. "I need you… to help…me…"

Hallpike grumbled again, confused, "Oh shit! That smells like my chickens."

In the salon, past the galley, Max took two more steps on the creaking sole. He stood on the small red and gold Persian carpet. Two more steps, past the table, and his hand was on the small silver knob of the door.

Amy crouched against the hanging locker, kneeling on the bed next to Dutch's unconscious body. The carbine rifle, her new lover, lay against her shoulder, the needle nose of it almost stuck against the door. Not quite. It used to be heavy, now part of her, finger tender and ready.

Desmond stood by the closed door. He opened it slightly and it creaked. He was not in a hurry. Nor was she.

"Come in, Maxwell," she purred, sanctioning invitation.

"I thought you might be in trouble," he said soothingly at the door. "Come on out, Amy, and make me a drink. We'll take care of everything."

"Max, please open the door for me."

Maxwell slowly pushed the door open. This soon would be his boat.

She looked at his tanned, weathered face and tousled dark hair. His blue shirt and shorts, casual and easy masculinity, confident. No longer good looking.

In a millisecond, his surprise registered; she held the AR-15 straight at his chest, pumping three shots hard, into his chest, neck and face. The sound of each shot exploded through her head as she shook with the repeat of it. Rich blood spurted, reeking out of his right cheek, his neck, his chest. Oh you fucking bastard. Dying blood looks bright and good on you! Pump, pump, pump, pump!

"You cunning bitch!" He was able to shout, and fell back, crumpling near the galley.

"You're calling me cunning?"

***

Above on deck, Hallpike was so startled, he tripped over the lazarette. The thud made Zoe shriek. Shocked to hear a scream from the lazarette, he lifted the large cover. Confronted to see the wide eyes of a terrified white woman, alive, next to a corpse. He recognized the corpse, whispering "Juan, I told you not to go..."

Zoe stared up into Hallpike's stunned face, pointed the Walther and squeezed five times without stopping. Loud explosions hit Hallpike. Molten blood erupted from his face and chest.

A wave bounced the boat, throwing the lazarette cover open, wide enough for Hallpike to fall on top of

Zoe, all three in the wide-open lazarette. Zoe felt his last hot breath on her face, his blood falling on her.

From below, Amy heard the shots that rang out above!

"Zoe!" Amy shrieked.

Had Hallpike killed her?

***

In spite of being shot with three well-placed bullets, Desmond seemed to have a string that yanked him backwards, onto the Persian rug. Stricken and still, she held the long, gray machine gun, waiting to see if he moved at all. She absently looked above at the holes in the cabin overhead, and then watched him lay bleeding, all strength evaporating. Why think of the rat traps in her New York City apartment at this time? Those traps that had sticky glue, catching them. How she hated watching them struggle to death. Not this time, as she looked at Rat Max Desmond.

Her eyes squinted in a manner of triumph as she took a breath. She remembered Dutch saying he felt reverence for her ability. This was luck, not ability. Blood was all over her Persian rug, and splattered on the cushions. She glanced back at the open door to the fore cabin. Quiet. Dutch seemed still unconscious.

"Zoe, you okay," she yelled, not caring if Hallpike heard her.

"Yes, but I need you to come help me," Zoe yelled.

"Okay, okay!"

Max was dead. And she waited, watching more blood ooze onto the sole. Convinced all his breath was gone, she carefully placed the rifle on the starboard upper berth. "Coming, "she yelled, carefully stepping over the starboard couch, past his body, past the galley and up the companionway to look out.

Standing above in the cockpit, she would never forget this sight. Out of raw nerves, Amy burst forth with the deepest laughter. In the crimson rays illuminating the Caribbean sky before darkness, the sun had made a last peep of brightness. Amy stared at the formerly elegant Zoe Bainbridge, trying to stand up in the lazarette, draped in fresh blood, black bugs on her face, enveloped by two dead men. "Get me out of here."

***

"Amy, did I hear something," Dutch called out from the fore cabin.

"You're dreaming. Go back to sleep, honey!"

Amy quickly pulled the warm, dead body of Hallpike off Zoe and positioned him aft on the deck.

Quickly climbing out of the lazarette, Zoe stood up and smiled like crazy. "I followed Captain's orders," she said, still holding her gun.

"We have to drag Desmond above, before the boat's full of his blood."

"Do you believe this?"

Together, with heightened adrenalin and disbelief of them both being alive, Amy and Zoe dragged Max Desmond's body above quite easily. Amy glanced to see a spray of bullet holes by the overhang near the companionway. Oh, this precious boat. But she had missed shooting the Westerbeke engine. The engine breakdown that had begun this.

They hauled Desmond and Hallpike onto the aft deck. Amy and Zoe backed off, staring at them.

"This is unbelievable! We've killed these fucking bastards!"

"Shut up, we're alive!" Amy draped her long arms gratefully around her short friend, Zoe, who clung to her.

"We're not murderers! You won't see any bodies in five minutes," Amy said. "Three to dump. Up to this?"

"You bet," Zoe declared, straightening up. "I read plenty of mystery stories. Dead bodies float after a few hours? They fill with gas, which these bastards have plenty of."

"Our only job is to get them off this boat."

"What'll we do with their launch?"

Looking over, Amy saw foodstuffs and supplies in the *Scarab* launch. "Oh, God, I can see this now. He was going to kill us and sail *Quadriga* as his own. We're taking those." She stepped into the launch and passed bags up to Zoe. "Oh, here's blue paint. Forget that."

"Amy, let's put these bastards in and set it adrift. Westerly, to Central America!"

"When did you get to be Wonder Woman?"

"Ten minutes ago," Zoe said. "I've never been more afraid. Do we get rid of these guns?"

"We keep them. Who knows what's coming next." Amy looked up at the mast. "And all of this under full sail," Amy said, feeling in awe of *Quadriga*. "I'm turning off the autopilot. We'll head her into the wind."

While Zoe was able to take the sails down, *Quadriga* wallowed. Without speaking, they easily pulled up the petrified dead body from the lazarette.

"I want to tie up Hallpike and Desmond, separately."

"Why bother? They're dead. It's dark. We've got to get back."

"Dark's better for us."

"Zeb's worrying where I am."

"Shit, I'm worrying where we are!" Amy looked down at her friend working at something. "What the hell are you doing?"

"Making fishing lines," Zoe said, working swiftly, coiling line around each man. "Found these lines in the lazarette. These shitheads are gifts to Poseidon, a three course meal for sharks."

"Where'd you learn to tie knots?"

"Honey, I've been learning steadily. I'll get into the launch. You stay aboard."

"We need to do it together," Amy said, "Beth would be proud! We've got to drink water or I'm going to faint. Want some?"

Zoe nodded. "Anything, please. Just not hot blood.'

"Eeeewwww…"

Below, Amy lifted the floorboard covered with dried blood and that hot blood smell. What caught her eye in the bilge? Something strange; a device, a small mechanical device? Another? How could they be so stupid to miss this? Could she feel more anger? She took a breath and then took out her Leatherman. What wire to cut? Cut it all. Windex and towels to clean up now. Drink Scotch soon.

With her lifeline attached to *Quadriga*, Zoe stepped down into the launch and strung up three lines to the stern. With pleasure, Amy kicked each dead man, who had been tied up by Zoe, over *Quadriga*'s stern, paying out the lines, one on each dead man's body, careful to lead the lines away from the cruiser. They were heavy now as she handed the lines to Zoe.

She'd never forget the sound of plunk, plunk, plunk.

Aboard *Scarab*, Zoe found the starter to the engine, which rumbled loudly. She gave Amy thumbs up as Amy released the lines to the launch. Zoe set the throttle at slow speed, and was quickly helped up onto *Quadriga*. With Amy's arm around Zoe, they watched the empty running boat head due east out to sea, wondering how far the cruiser might reach toward Central America.

"They're dead is a nice way," Zoe said, putting her arms around Amy.

Both laughed hysterically, and then sobbed. "What have we done?"

"We're alive, that's what we've done! We've become the predators. Take that in, Amy."

Though it was dark, she did not turn on the spreader lights. Zoe scrubbed the aft deck with pail after pail of seawater. The boat had to look clean above. To enact the part of clean, happy sailors. Both women went below, washed up, combed their hair, put on lipstick and changed shirts.

Before Amy started the engine, Zoe dropped the main, folded the sails and put the cover on, all by herself. Amy steered *Quadriga*.

"Zoe, you've become an able-bodied sea woman."

"You bet your ass!"

"We did!"

"What we do for love," Zoe sighed. "How did you drug Dutch?"

"Three sleeping pills. Fast. He's a big guy," Amy said. Lights shone from the coastline. They headed in, smoothly west to Marigot Bay.

"We're looking somewhat clean. I'm forever indebted to you," Zoe said, astonishment creeping over her. What they had mastered.

"And I to you, although we're now killers. Me for the fifth time!"

"I don't see any bodies?"

"Karma's a bitch," Zoe said, a slight smile. Back to the moment, "What will Zeb and Dutch think?"

"Do we tell them?"

"You're kidding? Look at us!"

"Let's get in and anchored," Amy said, at the wheel. "You and I went for a quick sail, Dutch's unconscious, and who cares if *Quadriga*'s a mess below. I'll clean before Dutch wakes up. If we tell, we'll never get out of the Caribbean. Nothing's on this boat but us," Amy said, automatically scanning the horizon. There was no traffic within sight. Stars were out. "Zoe, we're now bound for life. We're strong, determined and smart. We'll figure it out. I'm not sure yet what all that means."

"We've proved we're resolute together. We're approaching the harbor."

"I hate the Caribbean."

***

"*Quadriga, Quadriga, Quadriga*....." Zeb called from his hand-held radio, sitting by the engine in his dinghy, slowly motoring out of Marigot Bay. Why would Zoe go out without him on *Quadriga?* Why weren't they anchored, having drinks, waiting for him? Zoe and Amy couldn't handle themselves out there, out of the harbor.

The dark silhouette of *Quadriga* motored serenely past Zeb, gliding by almost on top of him as they looked to anchor near *Zephyr*. The sail cover was on, laced, in its usual fashion. He looked up at them, cruising by.

"You girls always surprise me! Have a nice time out there, sailing by yourselves, eh?"

Chapter Sixteen

**Logbook: of *Quadriga* and *Zephyr*
in Marigot Bay, March, 1981**

Name	Location	Latitude	Longitude
Zephyr	Marigot Bay, St. Lucia	13° 57.960'	61° 01.435'
Quadriga	Marigot Bay, St. Lucia	13° 57.960'	61° 01.435'
	Young Island, St. Vincent	13° 7.951'	61° 12.085'
	Admiralty Bay, Port Elizabeth, Bequia, The Grenadines	13° 00.566'	61° 14.193'
	Lovel, Mustique, The Grenadines	12° 52.796'	61° 11.287'
	Tobago Cays, The Grenadines	12° 37.988'	61° 21.319'

	Palm Island, The Grenadines	12° 35.235'	61° 23.609'
	Union Island, The Grenadines	12° 35.803'	61° 24.955'
	Petit St. Vincent, The Grenadines	12° 32.101'	61° 22.983'
	The Moorings, Port Louis, Grenada	12° 02.668'	61° 44.800'
	Anegada Reef Hotel, Anegada, BVI	18° 43.438'	64° 22.977'

From the air, to be seen, were St. Lucia's resplendent mountains, spun sugar beaches and lush rain forests. Closer to be seen, wild orchids and giant ferns providing dense foliage for birds. The road to Marigot Bay made winding curves, where constant breezes moved the leafy fronds of palm trees. The calm waters of Marigot Bay glinted with sunlight, the anchorage long a favorite of sailors, offering a Caribbean island paradise.

Zeb, with his Medical Technician training in the Canadian Armed Forces, attended to Dutch's two broken ribs. There wasn't much to do. In the safety and silence of her boat, Zoe kept seeing Hallpike's shocked face. She, who thought of herself as a better sailor asleep than awake, had entered absurd mortal combat from… a lazarette.

Any tropical illusion of beaches, palm trees, glamour was finished; how could the Caribbean hold any further allure? Yet, Amy felt some huge release of her unconscious inner compliancy; she'd proven something to herself that had been invisible to her.

Zoe queried the substance of her own strength, in a state of shock that she had killed so effortlessly, never expecting to sever a life that could have been hers. Languorous days and months aboard *Zephyr* in this region could never be, now that her mind and heart flung far beyond mere concerns of the pleasure in learning to sail.

Marigot Bay was serene, with other cruising sailboats anchored in the cove, offering noises of laughter, singing, and shouts of swimming. *Quadriga* and *Zephyr* anchored close together.

Aboard *Zephyr*, Zoe took a shower, swallowed two aspirins, and sat glumly. Zeb was worried, looking at her. "I've got dinner for the four of us to take to *Quadriga*."

At dinner, a tearful hour later, Zoe sat huddled silently in Zeb's arms, listening to Amy unload the burden of their actions, behavior, and thoughts.

Zeb said in awe, "Incredible how you two…" He looked at Dutch, their eyes in disbelief and in agreement.

Dutch interjected… "You two were astonishing. How you handled yourselves."

"And the boat," Zoe added.

"We ought to leave Antigua, immediately," Dutch announced quietly.

"Dutch, you're not strong enough. We'll sail with you. And watch out for you."

"Do you think anyone may have seen us?"

"It was getting dark."

"We're not able to check out from Immigration until morning. While I'm in town, I'll try to assess any legalities of protection for us," Zeb said. "No one ever checks out what kind of political or governmental protection they might have 'til it's needed."

"No, my friend," Dutch tried to shout. "No sharing of anything. Give me a few days to rest," Dutch begged. "Then we're out of here."

"A few days, eh? And hope nothing turns up."

"We've more trouble than we imagined," Zoe said. How easy her traveling and reporting life about the islands had been. Normal life was gone.

Back on *Zephyr*, Zeb handed Zoe a gray velvet box. "This may not be the right time. It might cheer you up. I wanted to offer it to you. I bought it in St. Maarten."

She sat, miserable, in the salon, looked up, took the box and opened it. She was shocked to see a bright ruby ring set off by diamonds. "It's beautiful!"

"The diamond on each side are our two spirits," he said, taking a string from his shirt pocket and placing the ring on the string. Holding one end of the string against his shirt pocket, he slid the ring along the string, across to her finger. He placed the ring on her finger. "My heart to yours. I love you. And I can only imagine what you went through. This is for better times. You're going to learn to handle every gun aboard."

Ruefully, she smiled. This tender offer included the need to handle every gun aboard.

"This is a lot happening for one Caribbean day and night," she said.

"Zoe, it's our engagement ring?" But Zeb paused. "Maybe it's too much tonight, but after we help *Quadriga* out of here, wherever they want to sail, we're sailing north. To Lunenburg. Maybe leave her there, while we fly home to Sudbury and on to Manitoulin. If you want, we'll even drive to Alaska in my camper."

Too much. Her head spun, the beauty of the ring, the pall of Hallpike's and Desmond's death. Sending them west to the sharks. Marriage to Zeb, besides being aboard, would coordinate further her life to his. Keep breathing. The ring was beautiful. Bright ruby red like fresh blood.

***

"Dutch, for the tenth time, allow us to escort you to the Grenadines," said Zeb, over their game of chess. You know, mysteries are never fully solved, from island to island. People disappear without a trace. Why're you such a stubborn bastard? Those ribs aren't healed. You need us."

Dutch sighed. "First, I took a crack to the head, beat off a guy, fell overboard, and broke two ribs. Then I'm in the fore cabin, knocked out, and she's the one who pulled us through."

"Don't tell me your ego is at risk? For God's sake, you're a team."

Dutch grumbled, "I made the rules to protect us. None of it counted. She did it all on instinct."

"You taught her! Slough it off, for God's sake, man. This isn't a battle of domination over who's Captain.

You've a girl who adores you, and a boat that has brought you home."

"Don't be so fucking cheerful."

"Your move."

"I wish I could move."

At dinner the next night, the four made a toast to the Turners, sailing *Bravo* to Australia, invisible threads of caring, holding them together. How quiet the anchorage remained: no police boats loudly around the bay, no bodies on the beach, no news on local TV, nothing.

Being so quiet in the peaceful anchorage, Dutch realized he needed to be given a couple more days of recovery.

A week later, there was still no news, scuttlebutt on the dock, on the local TV or radio. What happens when nothing happens?

***

It was time to depart. Zoe and Amy sat together, legs hanging over on the dock at Marigot Bay, companions in contemplation, blue whale coffee cups in hand: "Remember when we met? It seems so long ago. Now we're sisters for life. I wish Dutch wasn't so determined to sail down island. And now you're leaving me, Mata Hari? "

They hugged each other.

"You know sailors always leave each other," Zoe whispered. "Amy, you were astonishing. Setting that scene for Max. I've lived life in my intellect. You've learned the art of protection. I want to scuba dive, and climb mountains. And I promise, solemnly, no remorse."

"I'm glad you're sailing north. I pray Dutch won't want to make that Atlantic Ocean passage he keeps talking about. For the rest of my life, I'll be looking around corners. Zoe, you've had a chance to be somebody."

"You're growing, Amy. You're still so young. Life's different now. Yet, we can't resent Dutch and Zeb because of their dreams," Zoe said. "When we sail *Zephyr* to Nova Scotia, will you and Dutch come?"

"Think we'll still be alive?" Amy asked sullenly. "I miss Beth and Brad. Wonder where they are?" She paused. "Zoe, while dreams seep into my sleep, I have something to tell you."

"For heaven's sake, what?"

"I've had an amazing oceanic renovation." She stood up and laughed. "*Quadriga* has transferred energy to me. She's become an extension of my soul. Bloody or clean. I've been Captain. Think a sailboat you love can give you that?"

Zoe got up to stand with her. "You were steady, during it all. But please be aware your bravado's covering pain and confusion both you and I feel."

"So how do we get forgiveness for what happened?"

"You're wrong, "Zoe said sharply. "We defended ourselves. There's no guilt. Nothing to forgive."

"Can we really feel this way? There may be more to come."

"And you'll handle it, Amy."

"How?"

"We're afloat, uninjured, and our men and boats are intact. Isn't this enough?"

***

The couple on *Zephyr* waved to the couple on *Quadriga*, as one sailed north and the other south, on the lovely Caribbean Sea

Aboard *Quadriga*, Dutch told her, "Please relax, if you can. Know you've become an irreducible force. And I love you." He paused, "But why do you think I was so knocked out, not able to hear them come aboard?"

"Do you want the truth?"

"Of course."

"You were so wounded, unable to handle anything, any knife, any gun. Zoe and I dragged you to the fore cabin. To be safe. Away. I forced sleeping pills into you before *Scarab*'s arrival."

He simply looked at her. She expected him to shout with anger, but instead he took her hand. "Thank you. After all this, I crave to swim, to sail, and to love you."

"You aren't furious?"

"Hell, no. I'm wounded, but I'll heal. For God's sake, Amy, forgive yourself. Take a fresh look at what it means to be human. How many envy us!"

"You don't get it, do you?"

"We've had two incidents. We're here and afloat." He shrugged. "Now, we stay away from people. Except for what we need to buy on shore."

"Dutch, we can't have the sailing life we dreamed about."

"We're sailing south. We'll prepare *Quadriga* for an ocean voyage."

"The lower Caribbean islands may be rougher for us and you aren't healed yet." Her eyes welled up. "With drug dealers after us, lurking behind every pier. And I took out that transmitter piece with my knife, under the sole where they'd placed the drugs. We may be clear of all that stuff now."

He hated listening to her.

"We'll sail to St. Vincent, then Union Island, Petit St. Vincent and the Tobago Cays. I've always dreamed of these islands. Give me that. We'll put the boat up in Grenada, haul her, and prepare for our next trip."

Her shoulders slumped. She turned away, realizing, oddly, she had encountered no physical bruises.

Quadriga motored out of Marigot, the destination, south to St. Vincent. On the helm, Dutch sat steering, pleased to sail past the rocky green coast under alternating hot sun and swiftly passing showers. He kept repeating himself. "Amy, I can't go back to structured life. We'll haul *Quadriga* in Grenada, have her scraped and painted, and make her right for the ocean passage."

Under sail, Amy found deep refuge in her guitar playing. Within the music, she contemplated the mystery how she and Zoe had been helped, by powerful unseen hands, to sweep them through the ordeals, at sea level, and not into the sea. When she closed her eyes, she saw Desmond, falling back, blood everywhere. She'd never get rid of that picture. No song for that. Just tears.

They pulled into the commercial docks at Kingston, St. Vincent, registered at Immigration, fueled up, talked to no one, and sailed on to Young Island.

Anchoring by the resorts, they needed two anchors, fore and aft, to hold *Quadriga* against the current. Beautiful resort cottages nestled amongst tropical shrubbery.

"Amy, let's book a night in the hotel. Stop being so glum."

"I'm cultivating caution, every minute. I'll have the Walther with me at all times."

"Aw, give it up. Have a nice lunch with me at the hotel."

"You're forcing me to be an actress. To be cheerful. What happens at the next incident?"

"We're in Paradise. So please be here. We have tropical silence, palm trees…"

"I've made lunch aboard," she said abruptly.

After lunch, they locked up and took the dinghy to visit the appealing old fort next to the resort, enjoying very slowly, the climb of three hundred steps. With a gun in her pocket, and a cane for him. The height gave them a vantage point from which to see the entire island. Rain clouds passed so they hid under branches, watching the earth turn wet and dark. It kept raining. They went down the steps, slowly, Dutch protecting his ribs. The dinghy pitched in the surf at the ancient landing below, current pulling it, eager to break it loose from its grip.

Young Island's outdoor facility allowed them the luxury of paying for fresh, hot-water showers. Dry and clean, Dutch sat happily at the bar, eating crispy plantain chips and sipping a frozen piña colada. At the bar with him, looking around, relaxing, and then out to harbour, Amy could hardly believe the two sailboats with the names, *Passing Wind* and *Wet Dream.* She even laughed with Dutch, and she saw a stunning white yacht, *Brindisi,* her hail port, Milan, Italy.

***

What happens, when nothing happens?

They sailed on to Bequia, an old whaling port, pulling into the translucent azure waters of Admiralty Bay. They docked to take on fresh water, and were startled by a skirmish in the water, a young Bequian with a mask and spear gun.

"That boy crazy," said an old man, helping them at the pump. "Moray eel live below this dock, it and my boy deadly enemies. Fight every day." The water churned again. One strong brown hand reached up to the dock, the other hand holding a spear gun with a shiny grotesque green snake, long and dangling. The snake's head was as big as Amy's. The teen-aged boy flopped it on the dock, still alive.

"Father, I did it," the boy shouted, watching the eel ebb into stillness. Amy observed another killing.

***

What happens, when nothing happens?

Silence, as they anchored at Mustique, treating themselves to lunch at the beach bar. Amy had not seen fancy, well-dressed people in a long time. The Walther was in her purse that hung over her shoulder. Easy reach.

In the Tobago Cays, Dutch was able to swim in crystal waters, while Amy, ever on alert, never mentioned her Walther within reach. A native fisherman sold them live lobsters. Standing in his small craft, he lifted the creatures onto the deck. Dutch laughed catching them, while Amy turned her head as he boiled them alive. Another death.

"Stop that long face," he ordered. "We're afloat! Enjoy life and me!"

With buttery fingers and mouths, they devoured lobster tails, feasting under a full moon. "Mysteries and murders are never, ever solved in the Caribbean. That launch has sunk. Please," he begged, "Let's get back into good dreams at night, sailing and swimming."

"Okay, okay," she said. "You're the captain."

"So let me be."

***

Dutch was well enough to make long, slow, love again, more precious and valued. They had almost lost each other, twice. She deeply welcomed cuddling with him. He slowly ran his tongue over her nipples, his tongue to her waist, below her belly. Love-making was different, teasing each other as if they had all the time in the world, always, knowing what they had been through. But she knew, that now, they didn't have all the time. He swept her away, still with joy, into her body. She wanted the old dreams, the moon bathing them in shining white-velvet luminosity.

Docking at Union Island, Dutch was disquiet with loud annoyance when the young boys demanded money to look out to guard their dinghy at the local dock. Amy and Dutch observed blacks and whites, heard spoken French, English, Dutch, German and Spanish, everyone suspicious, guarded. "Forget this place," he decreed disgustedly.

***

What happens, when nothing happens?

Another day in tropical paradise as they anchored at beautiful Petit St. Vincent, a world-famous resort, where each villa overlooked the sea. Amy bet that Zoe, the experienced travel writer, knew the owners and had stayed there. At the bar, Dutch needed man and sailor talk, allowing himself to enjoy limited conversations with other sailboat owners and captains.

In this luxurious place, Amy's mood lightened. But at times, the deaths kept clocking within her. Each day, Dutch pulled her off the boat and made her hike around Petit St. Vincent, which took some of her energy. This exercise had a short relaxing result. Was she sick? Wasn't there something she'd heard or read about soldiers, coming back from battle, recurring episodes and dreams of nausea and fear? Some post-traumatic something?

Amy's concentration was hyper-acute, focusing on every sight, sound, seeing new people, and hearing sounds at sea. Her brain worked as fast as it could to analyze all possible choices and outcomes. She was able to practice her guitar, and write songs she did not like. Full of fury, and sadness, yet with a new power. Caribbean calypso, rock, jazz, defiant, resolute, angry and sad. "Oh my God," she whispered to her guitar. "I've reached an edge. The edge. She smiled bitterly. What would the New York producer think of her music now?

The fifth day, anchored at Petit St. Vincent, he cajoled her into going ashore to have lunch at the restaurant. Amy was glad to see people in this elegant place. She talked casually with one of the young waitresses. At lunch, the young waitress pointed out a handsome gentleman at the next table. "That's the Italian captain of the *Brindisi*," she whispered to Amy. "We stay away from them."

After lunch, the *Brindisi* Captain ambled over to them. "That's a beautiful Hinckley you have. One of the first fibreglass hulls made," he said. "I thought I saw you in Marigot Bay. I meant to say hello."

"You don't want to talk to us," Dutch said. "We've come out of quarantine. You don't want to get sick."

"Oh sorry." The Captain turned away.

"He never asked what we had," Amy said.

"Look sickish, Amy," he ordered sharply.

"You know I'm sick," she gasped.

***

What happens, when nothing happens?

"I feel such pressure living in this strange exotic silent vacuum. I promise not to call the Police. I need protection and solace, and it doesn't come from being here.

"Aren't I taking care of you in Paradise? Every day that you're with me has been quiet."

"You're in Paradise; I'm not. I don't want to clean *Quadriga*. She's squeaking too."

"How many people dream of sailing where we are?"

"Why are you blind to my pain and fear?"

"We almost had our boat taken. We almost died. Life is precious, and this is what I've dreamed about, Amy."

"And I'm trapped in fear and resignation, Dutch."

"Let's take a swim. You'll get over it."

***

They sailed to the dreamy Grenadines. They did not greet any other sailors. They walked around the lesser, different islands, always alone. Even in the small villages, alone buying groceries, staying quiet.

"Dutch, it's been too quiet. Something's waiting."

"Don't talk about it."

"What about retribution, and other meaningless words," Amy said. "We're constantly hiding."

"Awhile longer, please. You're eating well, sleeping, writing your music, reading, and we swim. I'm careful where we anchor. Isn't this enough, we're living our dream, just us and the sailboat."

She sighed.

"By the way, your voice and guitar sound wonderful. I adore hearing you play and sing."

"That's all I seem to be able to do. Am I in a trance?"

"Just let me adore you and obey this Captain who loves you."

***

They motored into St. George's, the capital city of Grenada, and docked at the large dock in the Carenage harbor. People, boats, shops, restaurants, now lovely for them. "We must get off this boat and do some sightseeing," he demanded. They locked up the boat, rented a car to visit the Mona monkeys that lived near the Grand Etang National Park and saw the island's waterfalls. He took her to the St. George's market where she found ginger, cinnamon, mace, turmeric, and nutmeg, sharing space with coconuts, bananas and the star-shaped carambola. For a few hours, she forgot herself in the delights of discovery.

She called her parents, but phones were not private, all in the open room at the Cable and Wireless offices. "Yes, all is well."

"You sound awfully tired. How are you?""

"I don't know."

"Do you want to come home? What's stopping you? Dutch?" Her father demanded.

In the mornings at the dock in The Carenage, Amy felt compelled to sand and varnish, anything to keep busy. They had lunch, took short afternoon naps, and when he read, she played her guitar. The days were hypnotic for her and she often got up suddenly in the middle of the night to simply look around. She didn't tell Dutch her dreams. He knew her songs were dark and sad. Oh, to get the work done, and prepare for the Atlantic crossing.

On the way to the shower room, she bumped into a tired tourist, looking for his boat. He carried his duffel, and a copy of *The New York Times* folded under his arm. "Please, if you're finished, may I buy it?"

"Have it, young lady," he said cheerfully. "You must miss New York."

She made a sour face. "Thank you."

***

Dutch had the boat taken out of the water, and put up on the hard. He scraped the vessel and hired painters for the hull. He was about to paint the goddamn boat blue. No expense spared. She was living in mid-air, using the ladder in the boat yard. The boat did not rock. Weird.

Her eyes started to itch in the hot Grenadian sun. "I need to see an eye doctor, Dutch. I feel like I'm functioning for our survival on high alert all the time."

"It just so happened that I met a young eye doctor at the pub. He told me they're leaving the harbor on *Teddy Bear*. They're sailing up the Grenadines. Get in the dinghy right now. We might catch them."

"There he is!"

Dutch hailed the doctor who slowed his boat so they could come along side.

"Can you look at her? She needs help, Doc," yelled Dutch.

"Come aboard." The doctor reached out his hand to help her up. She perched on the cabin top while he gently held her head in his hands, examined her lids and lashes. "This happens often in the tropics. You have crabs. Get salve from the druggist. Pick them out of your lashes. Clean your bedding and the entire boat."

"Thank you, what do I owe you?"

"Nothing, take care of yourself," he said. "This condition is temporary."

"At least some conditions are temporary. Thanks, doctor."

But she knew where it came from. Lice, from Hallpike's farmhand in the lazarette, now the enemy living in the pipes and bilges. New fervor propelled action: Out with the sheets, pillowcases, pillows, towels, and dishcloths. This helped. Clothing was pulled out of the hanging locker and drawers. Amy dispatched them quickly to the local laundry where they were washed, and again.

"I'm cleaning this damn boat, fore to aft, and athwart ships," she declared. "I must use up this energy, and do laundry." And the gun was in her pocket.

There, talking with other sailors, she learned how rats and snakes in bilges were common in the Caribbean. Looking in the mirror, she said, "I'm a prisoner of nothing happening, trying to keep pleasing Dutch and myself. Acting out a sailor on vacation to please my man."

***

"Stop mulling! No grieving! Enjoy what we have!" He was tired of Amy. "Nothing has happened to us. They're all dead. We're clear."

"Why are you so reckless? Because murders are seldom solved in the Caribbean? I'm living with it, the memories, and the fear. You were unconscious most of the time. Why do you ignore our continuing danger?"

"I'm planning our ocean passage. We almost lost each other and the boat."

"Yourself, your boat and an ocean passage?"

"Spare me, Amy."

"Attack comes like lightning!"

"I don't know," he said, trying to shift her away, yet again. "You sound so good, practising your music. Your new songs are deep and rich."

"I certainly have edge now," she said humbly. "Faces of dying men, of love and loss."

"What does that mean?"

"Nothing to you, Dutch."

"Take your guitar, get out of here and go somewhere," he snapped.

***

Monsieur Pierre, the friendly French chef on the swanky French yacht, *La Reve*, found her. "Mademoiselle, I hear your zongs. You zing a French lullaby my mozza used to zing to me when I was leetle. I wait every day to hear you zing it on your boat. Come to zing at tea time, today."

"I can't."

"Please, Mademoiselle, I need you. It will be good. 3 p.m."

Amy ventured aboard the magnificent air-conditioned yacht, where the main salon on the French floating mansion was filled with oil paintings, Orrefors crystal, and brocade furnishings. "Come, zay are waiting."

He introduced her to several elderly, elegant-looking people. Lovely people. She was able to sing four songs and was invited to have tea with them. When they heard her name and that she was from Cambridge, one of the owners, an investment banker, sparked up: he had taken classes with her father at Harvard.

"It's such a small world. Please give Dr. Sandler my finest regards," said the banker. Startled, sharp thoughts of her mother and father, home in Cambridge. Safety. Stupidly, she shook her head. A conversation about Harvard, publishing, and American politics. The nice women in the party smiled at her. Tears flooded her eyes.

"Are you all right, Amy?"

Slowly coming out of a torpor, the sick inertia of the last weeks, cobwebs of anxiety, watchfulness and survival, Amy began her fifth song. As she gazed at these lovely people listening to her with pleasure, she realized they were her people. Class of people? Home?

The afternoon over, Pierre handed her an envelope; "Take zis."

"Oh no, it's for you, Pierre. I forgot I've had another life."

"Mademoiselle, zis crazy, busy boatyard, keep zinging your zongs. And be very careful."

"What do you know?" She looked sharply at him.

"Nuzzing," Pierre said, turning away.

***

276

The boat was painted blue and put back into the water. Dutch, weary and worn from his labors, fell into bed, exhausted, but said, "We start at 8 a.m."

"You're relentless, and you're always mad at me."

"You'll love the passage to Europe," he said tiredly. "We're almost out of here, and please, I'm tired of your whining."

***

La Reve sailed away the next morning, leaving a big hole beside the dock. By afternoon, everyone on the dock was aware of the new, long, white yacht that pulled into that space. The Yacht *Brindisi* berthed directly across from *Quadriga*.

Maybe there were nice, friendly women aboard, someone to be friends with, some laughter and sharing, to do laundry even for a short time. No, she had seen that boat many times. What was it? Hadn't Beth spoken about the *Brindisi* in Deshailles Bay?

Chapter Seventeen

**Logbook: of *Zephyr*, Anegada,
BVI, and March, 1981**

Name	Location	Latitude	Longitude
Zephyr	Anegada Reef Hotel, Anegada, BVI	18° 43.438'	64° 22.977'
	St. Thomas Harbor, Charlotte Amalie, USVI	18° 20.164'	64° 55.422'
	Anegada Reef Hotel, Anegada, BVI	18° 43.438'	64° 22.977'

Zeb had never been emotionally close to other men, other than his brother, Robbie, growing up in Ontario. As adults, they managed their businesses in Manitoulin and Sudbury. Yet, Zeb so genuinely liked the authentic and bold American, Dutch, he worried constantly about him. He hoped Dutch would visit him on the island and sail from his beloved North Channel on the north side of

Manitoulin, and around the island into the open waters of Lake Huron.

While *Quadriga* sailed down-island to the Grenadines, *Zephyr* sailed directly north to his favorite island, Anegada in the British Virgin Islands. They anchored *Zephyr* in the peaceful byte in front of the Anegada Reef Hotel. Springtime around Anegada, oh so quiet and pristine.

Zoe slept, and mooned around for days. There was nothing to write about. She didn't feeling like swimming. Totally mindful she had acted in support to Amy's plight, she was sad most of the time. In movies or books, or real life, the villains or the police found clues and came after you. Justice was done. But what was justice?

"Talk to me," Zeb kept asking. "You and Amy were strategically brilliant."

"I'm not," she said. "We were lucky, Zeb. While we've been able to shut the world out, and it seems safer here in the BVI, there are so many sides to these murders, and now, this daily nothingness," she said, lifting her head from a book. "I am definitely grieving, and what astounds me, for all these years, is how I've missed knowing more about the other Caribbean. I've been living in a dream world, writing about resorts and vacations. So stupidly naïve."

"Stop blaming yourself. The future is unknowable," he said. "We're on Anegada, with nothing to do. Want to take a walk?"

"No, thanks."

After making two drinks, Zeb turned, saying, "You're not in a cage. I'm not holding you captive. I only want you to feel well, rest, and be your cheerful self again."

She nodded, taking a wine glass from him. "I wonder how Amy's doing, where they are."

"They're living their life as they want to. Right now, why don't you get off this boat and have lunch with me at the hotel?"

She grimaced.

"Captain's orders. Get dressed, Zoe. We're going to lunch."

They sat outside, in the shade of a coconut tree, having lobster salad for lunch. In the Gift Shop, Zoe was thrilled to make a new friend in Sue Wheatley who ran it. The next day, Zoe was invited to have lunch with Sue at her home. When she saw the ironing board with seven purple dresses waiting to be pressed, she laughed. "Please let me iron for you," she asked. "It's something I love to do."

During this, they chatted, girl talk, resorts, business, the state of the BVI's tourists, it was a relief for Zoe. She spent relaxed time with Sue, and helped out when Sue was called to manage something in the kitchen, or reservations. Zoe pinned and sewed hems for Sue; they laughed with silliness and girl talk. "The ironing board is the best medicine. What else have you got for me to do?"

***

Zoe made a picnic lunch; cold seafood pasta and bottles of iced tea in a basket to take to the Eastern side of the island. In the dinghy, over blue waters, around coral reefs, they made their way, hauling the dinghy up on the sand. "This is peaceful," Zeb said, reminding her. Swimming with her, parallel in their synchronization, always looking out for her in the water. "You and I truly began here…"

On the beach, they sat on a towel, with an umbrella to shield them from the sun, and took out the picnic. They ate quietly, punctuated only by sounds of the wind and the surf.

"When we get to Ontario this summer, we'll have a lifetime of perfect days."

But, she looked up and sighed. "Rain clouds!"

"We'd better motor back so we can see the top of the coral heads before the sky clouds over," he said, while she gathered everything and he moved the dinghy back into the water. Maybe they'd have an afternoon nap or put on a movie.

The dinghy threaded around brown spike coral reefs poking up at the surface. Skies opened, drenching them as they slogged through the chop to the boat. Zeb didn't see her tears mingle with the rain. Tying the dinghy to *Zephyr*, they climbed aboard.

"Zoe, let's get out of here and sail directly to Nova Scotia," he said, waiting for her in the back cabin. Listening to the rain beat down on the cabin top, she nestled in to him on their bed. While Zoe knew she'd exchanged one set of rules for another, and the air she breathed was strangled by ambivalence, he was comforting. She still breathed into the seductive luxury of quiet life aboard. He said, "Maybe we've been following this dream too long."

"No kidding," she said, smiling about what it meant to be captain aboard. Neither she nor Zeb wanted to be engulfed by the other; who had the authority aboard? What was the golden rule? He who had the gold, ruled? They both had gold.

She fell asleep.

***

On the way to clearing out of the BVI, Zeb sailed to lively Cooper Island for them to have a last dinner and hear local music. The restaurant was filled with carefree vacationers, where smells of expensive perfume mixed with those from the barbecue. Zeb sat quietly, no conversation, while two ladies at their table from New York City talked avidly about the mayor, Broadway plays, and shopping. Zoe was listening, indulgent in their talk. But as she looked about the restaurant, she trembled, aware her guard had been down, plus the pang of not belonging anywhere. It was nine o'clock in the shank of a beautiful Caribbean Saturday night.

"I'm tired. Let's get back to the boat," he said.

While it seemed too early, she got up instantly. When they were aboard, down below, she erupted, saying, "You have tolerance for others only when you talk about sailing!"

"I was stuck with those gabby ladies from New York at our table; what would I say to them?" He laughed. "But it felt good to watch you with them tonight. Your old self. Before Marigot Bay, you were incredibly social."

She nodded.

"You know we lack for nothing when we're together."

She stopped herself from fighting, saying, "Yes, you're very good to me."

"When we met you said you were willing to give up all those social supports. Aren't I'm the man of your dreams?"

"Honey, you don't need reassurance," she said slowly. "We need to get away from here, and the startled existence I now have. Not safe, afraid, guilty. I'm amazed you never seem afraid."

"You didn't kill him; you saved your own life! He was out to destroy Amy and Dutch. You acted in self-defence, even if you two took such a stupid, deadly chance."

"What?"

He corrected himself quickly. "I'm sorry. You acted admirably. Forgive yourself, and please get over it!"

"When you were in the Canadian forces, did you kill anyone?"

"No."

She went up on deck, gazing at the yellow moon rising, reminding her of the first night they met, thankful for the natural beauty of the Caribbean to fall back on, to soothe fragile human moods. What was their agenda, she thought, looking up at the moon. Hers, now that she felt biologically changed, scathed. Nothing in the world had one side to it. Could she find peace? Was it still with Zeb?

When they anchored in Road Town, Zoe took laundry to be done, learning that Prince Phillip and his entourage were on an official visit. Amid the festive, local throng, she stood on the dock, waiting for a glimpse of him. She felt normal in the crowd, admiring the attire of the local ladies, wearing bright dresses or suits, large hats and white gloves. She saw him for a moment, waving to all. She wore sunglasses and a cap, and dressed down, realizing how high strung was her alert button, competing with her natural joy of people. She talked to no one, did the laundry, not even joke with other ladies. And hurried back to the boat.

***

When *Zephyr* pulled into the St. Thomas harbor and docked at Charlotte Amalie, U.S. Virgin Islands, Zoe was weary of being afraid. She dressed up, left the boat immediately, and went to the U.S. Virgin Islands' Tourist Office to be in touch with familiar topics. She learned the Grand Palazzo Hotel had opened. They invited her to stay overnight.

With the promise of a luxurious bathtub and a long soak, Zeb reluctantly was pulled along to stay with her. At breakfast the next morning, on the terrace overlooking the bay, he was irritable.

"You're withdrawn, and then you get me furious and scared when you go inspect hotels," he said. "I don't understand you. I'm happy to live aboard *Zephyr*. You are a social being in the everyday world," he said. "I'm not, and anxious to get back to the boat."

She said nothing, having enjoyed the terrace, their beautiful guest room, and sipping her perfect coffee.

***

Logbook: of *Quadriga*, on the dock in Grenada, April 1981

"Are you Miss Amy, the singer and guitar player?"

It was late afternoon. Amy was exhausted from work aboard. Alert, her hand on her pocket, she nodded to the friendly, nice middle-aged Grenadian man. "Chef Jan, on *La Reve,* docked next to you, told me about you. I have a glass-bottomed boat that takes people out daily to the reef. My entertainer's sick. I need someone to fill in. I'll pay you fifty dollars each trip, cash. You sing and talk to the guests. It is quite pleasant. We're out for less than three hours."

Was this real? She had, however, seen the crowded, happy boat go out daily. No hidden agenda. Part of her thought, what a perfect break from her mind, the boat, and Dutch. The other, exhausted with being careful, she needed lightness, and to sing. What to do?

"The Captain will give you the mic, everything you need. And we'll give you lunch and drinks."

Back on board, Amy informed "Hey, I've got a singing job tomorrow the *Caribbean Reefer.*"

"That's nice. Are you doing the lunch dishes?"

It did no good to fight in the relentless heat tied up at the dock. She looked at him, hopefully. "While I'll take the Walther with me, this may be good for me. Tomorrow, I'll get to perform my songs."

"As long as you do your work aboard. Safety! I almost died. Now I've got to live!"

"It's all about you," she whispered to herself. "Hey, I've been loyal and agreeable. I've got a chance to have some fun. I've been a cover story, and you've been Captain."

At the dock in the Careenage, boats tied up close together, one heard every argument on the dock. "Sure, go!" he shouted, and jumped off the boat to get away from her. "Remember, *Quadriga* comes first."

Dismissed, Amy took a long walk down the long pier, watching Dutch go to the machine shop. She looked across the dock to see the handsome South American crew working in their spanking white shirts and shorts on *Yacht Brindisi*. While all sailors inspect each other; these deckhands did not smile at her, at anyone. She saw the Captain on deck looking at her. But he smiled with a vulpine grin. "And how are you today?"

"Sick," she said sourly, walking hurriedly away. So weary of this distorted life, despondent, guilty, itchy, lonely; Amy felt at the bottom of her soul. Following a dream that turned rotten for too long. Deliberately returning to the boat, she threw some clothes into her duffel, went to the steel box and took out her U.S. Passport and eight hundred dollars. Her guitar and music. Up the dock, blowing a secret kiss goodbye to Quadriga, her sea sister, her refuge, who knew all the fear, longing and action that had taken place on this journey. While she was aboard Quadriga, the boat was inside her; would Amy forever feel the pang of missing Quadriga?

Her scribbled note said: "Dutch, since you cannot go, and will not go for a rest and clean-up, I must take care of myself. This way, you keep concentrating on your priorities. Mine today, is rest and singing.

At the taxi stand by the dock, she asked, "Would you know a nice guest house?"

"Mrs. Monica Black, up the road. She my good cousin. I take you."

Mrs. Black's private home, just out of town, offered a room on the second floor with a double bed, clean pink flowered sheets, new towels and an adjoining bathroom. Looking at the clean tub, she broke into tears.

"You girls work too hard on sailboats, you get overtired," Mrs. Black said, drawing water in the tub. "Miss Amy, I leave a glass of iced tea by your bed. Please take a nap. I'll look in on you."

"Thanks, Mrs. Black," she said, closing the door, dropping her clothes and getting into the tub. Before she got so relaxed she couldn't move, she forced herself out, dried off with a fluffy towel. She put on her nightgown and fell into bed. She noticed the glass of iced tea and drank it all. Weightless, she fell into deep slumber.

Dreaming, Amy was alone on a beach, eyes devouring the horizon, yearning for her lost love that was sailing away. Kneeling in the sand, she wrote, "I love you." Waves pulsed up on the beach covering the words, making her jump back. The surf receded. Here she saw "I love you too." Then she saw Desmond's corpse, the others; they loved her too. No, they couldn't love her. Max Desmond's body floated up in the surf, the written words in the sand to her; "What have you done?"

She awoke with a start! Sheer white organdie curtains fluttered in the breeze. It was ten a.m. the next morning. She looked forward to singing in the early afternoon. Quietly, she dressed and went to have coffee with Mrs. Black.

With her guitar, she walked to the *Caribbean Reefer*. Welcomed by the captain, her mini-stage was set up. She looked across at the lively open St. Georges' marketplace, filled with vendors selling vegetables, fruits and fish, grateful, ever far away, to feel the banter and joyous tropic movement of Grenadian life.

Playing cheery Caribbean music everyone knew, Amy was pleased the vacationers aboard were receptive to her. She put herself back into her cheery songs and liked herself again. A nice looking man, with his two sons, asked her if the quieter, lyrical songs she sang were original. They were. "This is Andrew and Eric, eight and six, and they would love to hear you sing "The Inky, Dinky Spider?""

She smiled, "I love that song!" They sang and laughed, and the boys hung around her, one even leaning into her, as she talked with their father.

"I'm Jimmy Bloch. Thank you for charming my children." He paused. "My wife died two years ago. I've been raising them. We have a great housekeeper who takes care of them. We have an aunt, who's retired and lives here in Grenada, so we men come down to visit her. Right kids?"

"And we like the funny ice cream here," Eric said.

"And swimming," Andrew added.

Jimmy brought her an iced tea, and they sat together. "Your voice is unique, almost haunting. What do you know? Where have you trained?"

"Taking guitar lessons since I was ten, and I've always been writing songs. I've played on the Vineyard and Nantucket during the summers." She smiled. This man was actually listening to her. She liked that about him, besides his nice looks, and evident caring for his sons, now roving around the boat. He casually told her about living in New York City, and how he loved his business.

"What is that," she asked, looking at his fine-looking face, appreciating his quiet talk. He hadn't barraged her with questions, but gave her space to harmlessly chat. He had looked at her when he spoke. And a word came to her: worthy.

"I produce records in New York. The music business keeps expanding," Jimmy said. "I wish I could talk longer, but my children are my first priority." He reached into his pocket. "I won't forget you. Take my business card, and if you ever get to New York City..."

"Thank you."

He winked at her, and put his attention back on his boys. Nice things could happen.

The pleasant afternoon over, she returned to Mrs. Black's house, went up to her room to sit dejectedly in the rocker by the window. After singing aboard, she felt good. Where had she put the airline voucher? Damn, it was still on the boat.

She stared out the window.

There was a knock at her door.

"It's open, Mrs. Black."

Dutch stood, looking gaunt. Yelling. "Gone all night? I was crazy they had you, the *Brindisi* assholes. I stormed aboard. The Captain told me they were waiting for charterers. 'Bullshit,' I said. How could you do this to me?" Without waiting for an answer, he said, "I couldn't dare call the police. *Brindisi* pulled out this morning. I was sure they had you, then I remembered your cheesy singing job. The taxi driver heard me yelling on the dock. Told me where you were. Don't you ever do this again?"

Quietly, she sat in the rocker.

"We have to protect my boat," he said, and softly, "I'm still upset you saved us."

"What?" She was dumbfounded. She implored, "Dutch, you've proved yourself many times over."

He sat down on the bed, furious and grateful to find her. He held back tears. Moments passed. He said, gently. "Please come back to the boat with me."

"Is it locked up?"

"I paid a kid to watch it."

"You need sleep. And you really need a bath," she said quietly. "I'll tell Mrs. Black that you'll stay tonight. I'll finish my singing job. Then I'm flying to New York.

***

Eyes alighting down on the Manhattan skyline, Dutch sat next to Amy on the American Airlines flight from San Juan. He'd hired Jonesy, his pal, the dock master, to look after *Quadriga*. No one messed with Jonesy.

What happens, when nothing happens? They went smoothly through U.S. Immigration and Customs in San Juan, and arrived in NY. Amy's loft had been freed up; she could have time and space there. She had no idea why she was able to relax in buzzy, busy New York City. She looked out onto Eighth Street, watching the continual hustle below. Alone one afternoon, she walked on West 44th Street, past the Harvard Club toward the theater district, happy to gulp in New York summer air, and taxi fumes!

She went with Dutch to visit Nels in New Jersey, who had grown three inches. Not a word to him, about anything, but Nels asked her why his father looked so thin and tired.

Bert Crane welcomed them to his office. The Tiny Tot Book Club was thriving with a new boss. Amy met the young woman, realized how old she herself felt, and how much she had sailed, and experienced in the last year. The office was so small.

When Dutch visited the thread factory, Angelo, his ex-foreman who owned it, was still, he laughed, happy to see him.

***

"Amy, come home to Cambridge," her father declared. "Immediately."

"I'm coming with you," Dutch insisted.

"This is for me. I'll see you in a week or so," she said.

Her sister Charlotte picked her up at Logan Airport. "You look healthy and muscled, sister. Sailing in the

Caribbean certainly agrees with you!" Her young children in the back of the car shouted Aunt Amy's name during the raucous ride to her parent's home in Cambridge.

Greeting her at their front door, her mother and father seemed much older, small and frail.

"Honey, we're happy to have you home. What's the matter?" Her mother was shocked to see sorrow cloud Amy's eyes. "We've thought of you every morning and night since you've been gone. Thank God you're safe."

Amy put her duffel bag down, and hugged, long and lingering, each of her parents. In a flurry of greetings, the three quickly kissed Charlotte and her children goodbye, and shut the front door. Amy followed her father immediately into his library. He sat in his English leather armchair, and beckoned her to the couch.

"That you're here without Dutch, there's something you need terribly to tell us. I see it in your eyes. Shall we call Mother?"

"She may not be able to listen, Dad. This is excruciating. Why haven't I come home sooner?"

His eyes narrowed. "She's a woman of enormous strength. Anything that has to do with you, I assure you, she wants to hear."

In the library of her childhood home, she quietly said, "I am a killer."

Her father heard this. "You've done what?" He said softly, "What do you mean?"

It took less than a minute to unravel, as tears and pain shuddered through her, spilling the aggregate of emotion she'd been holding in for so long. First, Amy sat on the couch. As her emotion grew, she slipped off and dropped onto the dark red Persian carpet. Another Persian rug. She crouched there, on her knees, and struck her fists repeatedly against the floor as she sobbed. Told it all. Long and chilling. Blood. Reeling them in. Pulling them up and overboard.

Her mother and father sat, silent, appalled, chilled. Stunned. He had no words at the disbelief he felt; the audacity and cleverness of his daughter in staying alive. Both, stricken with love for their beloved child, watched silently as her sobs came in waves. Oddly, Amy was aware how her strong thighs managed her weight.

"Evelyn, don't go to her. She has to get it all out," whispered Professor Sandler. Her mother pulled herself back onto the sofa, nodding, as if she understood. She, too, crying in disbelief. She put a box of tissues next to Amy. Her father's eyes focused like lasers upon Amy, watching as she beat her strong arms into the carpet, protesting the invasions on her life, and the actions she was forced to take. An amazing daughter.

"Amy, tell us everything! Keep getting it out!"

With remorse, anger, and dread, she resonated, crying for the dead men, what she'd had to do. Twice. About Dutch, injured, not understanding the complexity of her feelings. Zoe, her amazing friend, carrying her own burden.

What happens when nothing happens? Was there safety anywhere? After the crescendo of sobs, her unrelenting soliloquy, her crying abated. Her breath grew quieter. She finally lay still, quiet on the carpet. All out. They waited, silently. Was she asleep or simply exhausted?

After a while, she slowly sat up. "Daddy, what do we do now?"

Professor Sandler couldn't move. He sat soundlessly until he could talk. You've shocked us with your life aboard. And what you had to do. So powerfully," Dr. Sandler said slowly. "We're incredibly proud of you. Your mother's my life partner. We will carry this encumbrance with love and attention to you, for you. And what you, and we, will need to do in the future. There are no judgments. Let your mother put you to bed."

"Amy, are you hungry? I have chicken soup?"

For the first time, what was left of Amy was able to laugh. "Do we have any Brigham's chocolate ice cream?"

"Of course."

Dr. Sandler called his trusted friend, a well-known psychiatrist and Amy had six double sessions with him. The crazy thing was that his name was Dr. Port, who had her beating a pillow, yelling, crying and then, exhausted, as she got it out. Hours. It was his dynamic therapy, and Amy, at first startled, was able to yell. She screamed, with snot dripping from her nose, tears from her eyes, and then, then, she was grateful. Emptied.

"Thank you, Dr. Port," she said, drained. "I had no idea how light I could feel."

Dr. Sandler called his cherished buddies, powerful Cambridge and New York lawyers, who had connections with the DOA, FBI and the U.S. Information Service. They quietly investigated criminal news in Antigua, St.

Marten, Montserrat, and the southern chain, finding no information. No startling Caribbean news update in the war against drugs. No murders reported. Not even missing persons. Oh, really, Amy thought, reading a confidential report some days later. The psychiatrist told her father he was proud of Amy taking enormous courage to move through this tragic saga. Where everything happened. And nothing happened. Her father and the doctor each wanted to ask, but neither would ask why she hadn't flown home earlier.

She did say one morning, "I was pleasing Dutch, and I followed a dream too long."

"Dutch should have known better," Dr. Sandler said adamantly to his wife. But he thought he understood the compelling allure and seduction, forever, beautiful and sultry, these Caribbean Islands.

Dr. Sandler's lawyer told Amy, "Obviously, the wives of these men are terrified, not talking. That launch, *Scarab*, has not reappeared in any form, or news. We remain quite still. Our sources are plugged in to an extensive network throughout the Caribbean." He paused. "My friendship is deep and long with your father, and I've known you since you were a little girl. The minute anything that comes to the surface, I'll be informed. I've been chartering in the Caribbean for years."

"This is hard to believe, since both men were known, wealthy, and social on these islands," she said.

"While there's law, there's everything else, Amy. You and Dutch were dragged into the middle of it. You've had more than enough of the Caribbean. Did the doctor say that you've had post-traumatic syndrome.'

"No," she said. "He didn't or wouldn't tell me that."

"Of course, you're never going back." The lawyer, fond of her, still felt shocked by her catastrophic story. How thin Amy looked. Yet her body, her muscles, and long legs, seemed to be in peak condition. "Do you know what you'd like to do now that you're home?"

"Work on my music." She didn't say how she missed the wholeness of Quadriga.

***

Dr. Sandler had to talk to Dutch, alone. But that would be difficult, since Dutch was in New York City, and had not been invited to Cambridge. If he could get through, Dr. Sandler had a lot to say, and a request his daughter must never know.

"Dad, Dutch complained he wasn't invited to come with me to Cambridge," Amy said.

"I'm calling right now and inviting him," said Dr. Sandler.

Dr. Sandler met Dutch at the train station in Boston. "Quentin, we need to talk privately. At the Harvard Club, I have a private room for lunch."

"Certainly, Dr. Sandler," Dutch said. He shook his hands, but felt uneasy. Not expect a talking-down, but great praise for his great seamanship.

When they sat, Dutch told how well she managed everything, and was proud of her, ashamed of himself. Then he said, "We knew the boat comes first."

"Quentin, my daughter comes first. How did you dare to compromise my daughter's life? Do you still refuse to acknowledge that she saved your life, and insist on your narcissistic ways of sailing further and further into the Caribbean?"

"I gave her a voucher to go home," Dutch said. He'd heard about her sessions with the psychiatrist and wondered if Dr. Sandler might offer this to him. "Sir, I'm all fucked up about this. Continually shocked and sad, Not knowing what to do. I adore Amy."

"You're a smart man, a good captain, and I'm sorry this happened to you, but," Dr. Sandler said softly, "You've used her for your own purposes. You seem to have no moral response to any of it"

"Sir, I was stricken as well. And, sir, I didn't come up here for this," Dutch said, pleading. "If she needs to leave me, that's her decision, not yours." He teetered as he stood up; Dr. Sandler could see that he was exhausted as well. Did he have to be so harsh? Quickly, realizing this, Dr. Sandler said, "I apologize for my abruptness and anger. I know you love my daughter, and you've been through a horrible time."

"Thank you, Dr. Sandler, but I didn't expect this from you. We were doing the best we could. I cannot stay here. I've got to take the train back to New York. I'll talk to her in a few days."

"Thank you for bringing her home."

"Oh, Daddy, he got sick?" Amy was surprised. "I wanted him to talk to my doctor."

"He phoned and said he couldn't get on the train. Diarrhea. Maybe later this week."

She had refused to take any medication. Being alert was first and second nature to her.

Dutch had phoned her for short conversations, telling her he was edgy, driving to New Jersey every day to spend time with his son. Edgy? When would she come back? Would she come back?

She took the train back to New York, glad to be in her apartment. Here was that business card from the nice record producer whom she had met on the *Caribbean Reefer* in Grenada. The chance was one hundred to one he'd remember her, but what else was she doing in New York City. Resting, waiting. She had her music, and why the hell not format and present her new songs, written aboard in the Caribbean? She dialed Jimmy Bloch's office number, sure she would be put off, or unable to get through.

"What?" She was in disbelief.

"Ah, the pretty songbird, the hummingbird from Grenada," Joel said, remembering the mystery in her eyes and the sadness in her voice. "I never do this; we have so many artists, but I'm clearing my desk for you. Tomorrow at ten a.m. and bring all your music with you."

She sat in Jimmy Bloch's cluttered office. "How nice to see you again, Amy. Here for a while?"

"Yes, getting used to the noise and traffic, but I'm glad to be home. How are your sons?"

"They're fine. They loved that afternoon singing with you. Have you got any original songs? Do you have a cassette of songs?"

"Yes, lots of songs. I flew up from Grenada three weeks ago. It feels strange to get on an elevator in a crowded mid-Manhattan building and to be sitting in your office," she said.

Jimmy Bloch gazed at the young lady, suntanned, her dark brown hair hanging over her shoulders, which she brushed off her pretty face. While he felt a connection to her, there was something held back in her way of being; hidden, lovely. What was her allure?

"Let's hear how you sound in a studio," Jimmy said, buzzing his secretary to block Studio A. "Put Stan in charge. Amy, are you able to sing right now?"

She nodded. "Why're you being so nice to me?" she asked. "Don't you get thousands of cassettes?"

"You were good to my sons," he said quickly. "Here's Stan. Go with him."

"Studio's free, boss. Two hours. Pipes warmed up? We'll make a start, a rough cut. Follow me."

"Do you have an acoustic guitar there?"

"Lady, we're an instrument store," Stan said, escorting her toward the studio. "We have Sadowsky electric guitars and basses. You name it, we got it!"

Stan fixed microphones around her and did voice checks. "Run through each song. Do each twice if you want, but then go on to the next. We'll work around you. Remember to enjoy yourself!"

"You're very kind, Stan."

"You've got something, young lady," he said, smiling at her.

Amy sat in the New York City recording studio, doing scales, warming up. Losing her self-consciousness, she became smitten again with nuances to polish her music. Could she give a silky performance? Heaven here, this week, after all her outpouring in therapy, feeling empty. And now replacing this, able to give her energy to her voice. She was surprised to find she moved effortlessly through her chord playing.

She ran through *Sailor Woman, Come with me to the Caribbees, The Barnacle Blues, Yellow Slicker, Those Seasick Blues, On Blue Waters, Nights with You*, and *Sail to the Rising Sun*. She sang *Anchors and Angels, Morning Mists on Seas of Gold, Blow Ye Gales of Summer and Fall, Sails and Sinners,* and her funny ones, *Sloop of the Day*, and *Davy Jones is No Friend of Mine.*

Stan and his colleagues listened, wondering, who, indeed, was this? They heard a resonant, husky, vulnerable voice. Singing haunting stories. When he played the tape back, Amy heard a full vocal sound, a beguiling sensuousness that had depth, even in the first cuts.

Incredulously, she asked, "Stan, do you hear *edge* in my voice?"

"Dunno about that. I heard something real fine, Miss. A bond between what you sang and what I heard. You have barnacles in the bottom of your voice," he said, busy with the levers on his electronic board.

She sat, musing, barnacles and bullets. Not even a 35-pound Danforth anchor could hold her down.

"You'll hear from Mr. Bloch," Stan said. "Wish you luck, Miss Amy. Thanks."

"You're thanking me?"

***

Where was *Bravo?* Had the sea swallowed them up? An unthinkable mystery.

In Oyster Bay, Long Island, NY, no news. Nothing for the Braithwaite family from *Bravo*, other than one postcard from Panama and three from the Galapagos Islands many weeks ago. Beth's eldest brother, Stewart, had flown to Ecuador, and took a boat to the Galapagos, returning with copies of *Bravo*'s exit documents.

Dutch and Amy took the Long Island Railroad to Oyster Bay to visit Mary and Chauncey Braithwaite, Beth's sickened parents. The taxi drove them to an elegant turn-of-the-century home on a bluff facing Long Island Sound. Their feet felt the crunch of gravel, and they saw the riotous colors of summer flowers tended carefully by the gardeners. She grabbed Dutch's hand, silent, wanting to be solid with the Braithwaite family.

Two English spaniels played in front of the veranda where the family gathered. Amy talked with Chauncey, a banker, who was part of the Long Island Power Squadron. With his senior connections with banks around the world, he had tried to get help on cargo ships and cruise ships ongoing in the Pacific Rim. So lonely for his daughter, he couldn't stay away from Amy and what she had to say about Beth, and the glow in Amy's eyes as she spoke of Beth. Where was his daughter, the light of his life?

Dutch sat at the side of the large porch, surrounded by several young women, friends of the family, who listened to his stories. Amy observed her Captain, his dashing masculinity; how splendidly salty he could be. But after catching a look on Mary's tortured face, Dutch promptly shut up. He took Amy aside. "I talk too damn loud, and I offended Mary. Amy, I can't stay here much longer."

"We'll take the train back to the city. I'm ready."

"I don't mean that."

Chauncey intervened, "I appreciate you two coming. Beth often spoke of you. Please stay for lunch."

During the quiet lunch, no one dared utter those three words.

Lost at sea.

***

Logbook: on Land at the Much More Sound Studio, Midtown, and NYC. May, 1981

"Nice talent, Amy Sandler. Original, powerful. She doesn't know it. Potential, but don't push, Jimmy."

"Saul, I sent *Sailor Woman* to three metro radio stations. They've given her good rotation. Libby's pushing it in five discos."

"Get her permission first. You don't want problems."

"She's actually an outstanding talent," Jimmy said. "Needy."

"Everybody's needy. Don't get to like needy, Jimmy."

"One thing, Jimmy, is that I need a stage name." Amy sat across from him at the desk. "For reasons too long, I'd like to use the name MAYA. I think it is exotic, and combines Calypso, and country, and you said you thought I'd invented a new genre?"

"Just MAYA?" He looked at her, realizing there was always more to Amy. In their dealings, she was reliable, constant and authentic. This, actually, was a small request. Easy. He was used to this. "I see that MAYA has your name Amy in this. It's interesting. And mysterious. Yah, okay, and we better put some steel drums into your next songs."

"You agreed so easily. Thank you, Jimmy. And it will be a long while before I publicly perform. You've agreed to that. I have to get used to all this."

He laughed. "You're doing fine, MAYA of the Caribbean. Each step at a time. We'll make you look exotic on the album cover. It will be called '*Sail to the Morning Sun.*'"

Outside the realm in becoming a money making talent, Jimmy found he was interested in her. Amy was smart, reclusive, and there was a depth he wanted to know. Perhaps in comforting her. It seemed as if she had been through much she'd never talk about. It was two years after his wife's death of cancer, and bright ladies were bringing stuffed cabbage to his door. Was he ready to date? Not yet. His sons came first.

Amy went back and recorded ten songs with two back-up musicians, bass, and another guitar, skillfully handled by Stan.

"There are three metro stations playing your songs," Jimmy told her. While there was no request for a preliminary contract, Jimmy knew her songs were copyrighted.

"We want a make-up artist to do your face and hair," he said, and arranged photographs of her in shorts and a tee shirt, then a black leather dress, a shirt and low-cut jeans. There was a sales display board and trial songs to be tested at selected music stores. He said nothing about a contract, but she felt lucky to hear her music sound so professional.

"They're treating me like Cinderella with a voice," she said to Dutch. "I'm grateful."

Dutch didn't like it. "The guy wants to get you in bed!"

"Can't you be glad for me that a bit of my dream is coming true?"

"I'm glad for you."

"You're lying," she said, surprised at herself.

"I'm sorry, I apologize," he recanted. "I'm jealous, and I'm also glad you went home to Cambridge and saw the doctor. You've come back changed."

"You never came to Cambridge? You could have seen the doctor as well?"

"Amy. I can only look forward," he said, lying to her. Still fuming about Dr. Sandler's accusations.

"When I was in Cambridge," she said slowly. "I began to understand the unspeakable horrors of my grief. How complicated it was. The more I let it out, chunks of sadness started to break up inside of me. It melted. I was able to become absorbed into my songs. Now the energy's within the new activity of producing songs."

"I'm glad this is happening for you," he surrendered. "I was so caught up in what I wanted and there it was, being taken away from us. I'm sorry, Amy."

"You're apologizing?"

"Yes."

In Studio One again, Amy wondered what unseen hand created this wonderful mystery in having her record her songs. Crazy luck? Nothing happened this fast, but didn't it happen on her boat? It was time to forget about the word *edge*.

While impatiently waiting for Amy in New York, Dutch spent time with Nels, his investment advisors, had a mailing service ready, and arranged bank drafts in Europe. When he heard *"Sailor Woman"* on the car radio twice in one day, he listened with ambivalence.

Late in the evening, at her loft, he said, "Amy, you're on the way to having your talents confirmed. I want every success to unfold for you."

"That's awfully formal. Not like you," she demanded.

He took a deep breath. Said it. "I've decided to fly Nels down to Grenada when school ends. He wants to make the ocean crossing with me. I know you can't go with me. I've booked my ticket to leave tomorrow morning for Grenada. I'm caged here. I hate New York City. Oddly, you've earned a chance. You must take it."

"You're breaking up with me?"

"Yes. I owe you my life and *Quadriga*. I'm doing this for you, giving you space."

They tumbled into bed, angry love, clawing each other. He thrust into her, and she ached for more, or was it to let him the hell go. Each moved apart and fell into deep sleep.

At dawn, Dutch held her, whispering, "I have such gratitude we've survived together. Whatever you do, I'm for you. I hate feeling this pain of leaving you."

She lay there, listening. Abruptly, she sat up, facing him. "Look at me. I don't know where this is coming from, but I forgive you and myself. We've lived and had others die on our boat." She touched his face, "I know you tried, with every breath, every moment, to do your best."

Unexpectedly he choked. "Thank you." Clearing his throat, he commanded "Coffee, woman. Strong."

She got up and made the goddamn strong morning coffee.

"I'll call you from St. George's before we sail." He stood by the door, his strong arms enveloping her. A fleeting kiss. He picked up his two duffel bags. Demanding one more kiss, she couldn't let him go until she felt his impatient arms stiffening. He would, indeed, sail from Grenada on the Atlantic, with his son.

She closed the door gently and from her fifth floor window, Amy watched Dutch hail a taxi on Eighth Street.

He did not look up.

Chapter Eighteen

Yacht *Zephyr*, June 1981

Name	Location	Latitude	Longitude
Zephyr	Road Town, Tortola, BVI	18° 25.471'	64° 36.760'
	Virgin Gorda Yacht Harbor, Spanish Town, BVI	18° 26.951	64° 26.191

In Road Town, Zeb returned to the boat, troubled. "It's bad; my brother Robbie's been diagnosed with lung cancer. He can't stop smoking those shit cigarettes. He's getting radiation. With certain investments frozen in Canada and international agreements weakening…"

"You're going home."

"We've worked so hard for our independence."

A long silence. Nothing else.

Carefully, Zoe said, "While you take care of him and handle things, I'll go back to New York." She tried not to feel fear, to keep breathing; this new event, being wrenched away from Zeb. She turned away, the uneasy anticipation in getting back into New York in her stomach. With her burden of grief, maybe at home, she might be able to cure her sad, murderous heart.

"What will you do with the boat?"

They sailed *Zephyr* back to Virgin Gorda where he put the boat up on the hard. It looked strange up on stilts. She had gotten her suitcases out of the storage bin at the Yacht Harbour. They cleaned and locked the boat up. She made his plane reservations and hers for the day after, wanting to spend the night alone at Little Dix Bay. Funny, eh?

The morning was overcast, drizzly. Standing at the small airfield, part of her yearned to hold on to Virgin Gorda, and Zeb. She reached deep inside to remember how to leave.

Her small commuter plane rose from the runway, swinging in a graceful arc over the Copper Mine, Toad Hall, and The Baths. She peered through the window for a last look at the bight, her world below on *Zephyr*. She felt cast off and borne on uncomfortable higher breezes.

The plane droned on to Puerto Rico. The docking lines, those gossamer threads of her emotion that had held her taut, snapped. Their sailboat in the British Virgin Islands, far below, was now a brooding memory.

At JFK Airport, Zoe easily went through Immigration and Customs, holding her back straight, pretending she was her former self. All normal. She waited for her luggage. An editor from one of the newspapers she worked for, saw her. "Hey Zoe, is that you? I've got a car waiting; want a lift into New York?"

Zoe settled into the limo with Steve, talking about newspapers, and Caribbean hotels. Back on her street, she opened the front door to her building, remembering her sovereignty in her own apartment. Her niece was glad to see her, and immediately moved a blow-up bed for herself into the living room.

In her own bed, Zoe thought about the courage and confidence, now, not to be loved. All the ways of the boat, and the sea, had been an aphrodisiac, learning to love, and accepting the big, burly, sandy-haired, sweet smelling, crabby, cranky Canadian. And to sail, taking care of herself, and the horror of being pulled in to help Amy. And staying alive. Keeping the secret. Or should she?

***

The Burgeoning Songbook: in New York City, July 1981

Amy was happily crafting her songs in the studio, becoming fast friends with her accompanists on drums, bass, and piano. And steel drums. These musicians were friends of Jimmy's, and supported her so beautifully, she realized her music was being elevated to places, sounds, nuances and meanings that she herself was learning.

"I want to give her comfort as she produces her first album," Jimmy told his business colleagues. "I'm interested in who she is, as well as taking care of her professionally. She seems to have a trunk of music that's been sunk. Sorry for the pun," he said," But there's more to her and her creativity."

"You're a sucker, Jimmy," said his business partner. "What is this comfort crap?"

"She needs a certain level of softness. Of being listened to, being heard in her music. I have the ability and patience to do this," Jimmy said. "I'd like to sign her and represent her as she grows. And perhaps become someone she can lean on."

"She doesn't talk very much when she's not in the studio."

"That's okay. I seem to be on some sort of path with her."

"You're taking needy to a new level."

"Sam, stay in your own lane, and manage your own talent. Shut up, my friend, and let's get lunch."

***

The Surprising Logbook: in New York City, July, 1981

"How amazing each of us is here in New York! I happened to call your mom, and she said you were here," Zoe said to Amy, arriving at the loft on Eighth Street. "I'm coming over. I've got Thai food. Can't wait to see you!"

Opening the door, Amy hugged Zoe tightly. "Hey, let me put the food down!"

"How's your music coming along?"

"Astonishing! Jimmy Bloch is managing my songs. The album will be ready in a month. How fast this is happening. Boy, am I glad I to see you. Thanks for bringing dinner. I'll put it on the table. Get two dishes and forks."

"I've thought of you every day, Zoe." And she told Zoe about seeing her father's friend, the psychiatrist in Cambridge. Zoe listened, mesmerized, sat still, and took a tissue out of her pocketbook to wipe her own tears.

"Say, Zoe, did you ever think Zephyr had a heart, absorbing all that happened to you and Zeb aboard, good times, fights?"

"Never, Amy, you're the one who hears music in everything," Zoe said. "She was simply a nice, safe boat. I hear words and phrases. I never felt starry-eyed about Zephyr. And today, I know I'm back where I belong," Zoe said, then telling her about Zeb's sick brother. "We put the boat up in Virgin Gorda. Zeb flew to Sudbury while I came back home. Still, nothing's happened. Not even justice! I see a list of twenty therapists available, and I can't choose one. My dad passed away long ago. My mother's in a retirement home. I've always taken care of my niece, but she's taking care of me. Of course, I don't talk."

Aching deeply, Amy couldn't hold back tears, so apparent the anguish and pain pounded between them. "Go on."

"Zeb's flown back to be with his brother whose sick with lung cancer. I've failed at a relationship with him. Truth is, I didn't want to be on the boat any longer. I'm not sorry Zeb's in Sudbury."

"Since my parents made me see the finest therapist in Cambridge, I must take you. And my dad has a legion of lawyers everywhere. I can't believe you're sitting in front of me, Zoe, because I won't be okay until you're okay. I'm taking you to Cambridge. How soon can we go?"

"To see your doctor?"

"You must! I was able to regurgitate all the shit, all the experiences. We must go. Sessions for you. And being with my parents is what you need," Amy cajoled. "And, please know that you haven't failed if Zeb isn't able to accept you! While I was stunned at how fast Dutch left, I wasn't sad to see him go. I keep rearranging my perception of the people I love."

"Writing your next song?"

"How well you know me," Amy said. "I wish I didn't miss the jerk. I'll always love him. Now, you've a chance to recover. You must come with me to Cambridge."

"How long and when?"

"As long as it takes. You'll stay at my parents' home."

"I'm so tired," Zoe said, sighing. "I'm sad, and I seem to watch everybody else being busy, doing good things. And I sit and mull. But with Zeb in Sudbury and on Manitoulin, distance is stirring up new outlooks. I don't need him; why do love and relationships need to have feelings of shared identity? Zeb and I never shared any identity. I forgot what brought us together."

"Dreams of sailing on a beautiful boat in the Caribbean?" Amy hooted. "That's over!"

"After you and I saved our own lives, I was useless aboard *Zephyr*."

"Has anyone lived happily ever after on a sailboat?"

"Maybe in the movies, or old couples who act like dried turtles."

"Aren't we whiny creeps? Have more wine." Amy hugged her friend, partner in life and death.

"I wish I knew where Beth was."

"Me, too. It's so awful. Not knowing where they are."

The phone rang.

"It's not late," Amy said, "Mind if I answer it?"

Amy took the phone. Gasping, "Thank you!" She put the phone down. "I signed a contract last week, and the first song of my new album made the beginning of some chart this week! I'm drunk!"

Zoe pulled Amy up and they danced around the room. "Yes! Yes! Yes!"

The phone rang again.

"Hello Dutch," Amy said. "You arrived safe. I just got news that one of my songs is on some chart." She stopped, realizing the omen of her announcement. Silence from the other end. "Nels arrived early? This Wednesday? I love you too. Have a safe crossing. What?"

She listened silently. "Of course, I understand. I wish you all the best."

She sat down on the couch and burst into tears.

"What?" Zoe yelled.

"He's officially withdrawn from our relationship. He said 'Congratulations. You must follow through. I will forever love you.' That's what he said. I'm glad you're here tonight."

"Hey, you received a gift!"

"What?"

"To be fully present in your own new life," Zoe said. "I'm staying over with you."

"Good. Open the red wine."

The phone rang again.

"Don't answer that. I can't take any more news," Amy declared, pouring the wine.

"Let me get it. Remember how we joked about depending on the power of three in our lives, our three boats? This could be a good three!"

Zoe picked up the phone. "Amy Sandler's Residence." She listened, stunned. Her face turned ashen. "Please, please, do not joke."

Amy looked up, "What is it?"

"Come right away. This is the address."

"Who is it?"

Chapter Nineteen

Logbook: of *Quadriga*, in Grenada, July, 1981

In Grenada, six days after his final conversation with Amy, Dutch packed the life raft with Nels. The boat seemed empty without Amy, her fragrant smell still in the fore cabin.

Jonesy, the dock master, came down early in the morning to tell Dutch he'd just received a strange phone call. He was asked to deliver an important message to the captain of *Quadriga*: 'He'll be having a visitor.' That's all the information he had.

"Jonesy, should I get my gun? Can you be armed? Anything about the *Yacht Brindisi*?"

"Nope. The conversation was odd. Fast."

Dutch, knowing that nothing was ever what it seemed, had the Walther primed. Not that it would do any good at the busy dock. Was the end to begin now for him? He knew life could, at any second, get worse. The future was unknowable. His beautiful son was aboard. Nels, Dutch's pride, had grown into a competent young fellow. If he got through this day with whatever it was, the Atlantic crossing would be a blessing with his son, especially during calm July.

A tall, gaunt figure, leaning on a cane, walked slowly along the dock, toward Dutch's boat. There was a touch of familiarity in the movement. Was this someone known to him? It was a frail, older woman wearing a straw hat that covered her face. Large sunglasses obscured her identity. Her long cotton dress, to her ankles, billowed in the breeze. The person obviously had been quite ill, or perhaps had a debilitating affliction, yet she moved with steely purpose.

He leapt off the boat and walked toward the figure, stopping directly in front of the woman, careful not to get near or touch her. Wraith-like, she stopped.

Dutch stood with his palms open to her. Shocked doubly that tears rolled from his eyes.

"Sea captains don't blubber," she commanded.

"We thought you were dead."

"I thought so too, but here I am. May I meet Nels?"

"How do you know about Nels?"

"I came from New York. I was with Amy and Zoe."

Dutch shot back "Where's Brad?"

"*Bravo* sank in a storm west of the Galapagos," Beth Turner said softly. "We spent twenty days in the life raft before being picked up by a freighter. We returned with it to Tokyo. Brad died on the freighter. I spent time in the hospital before I could talk. Or walk."

"I'm so sorry. I loved him."

"He loved you too."

Dutch gently took her arm. "You're a miracle. Come, lunch is ready." They walked slowly together, at her pace, and he helped her aboard. Beth moved stiffly into the cockpit and sat under the awning. He couldn't stop his tears from running down his face.

"Nels, come up. I'm honored to introduce you to Captain Beth Turner."

Nels hopped up the companionway. "Captain Turner? A pleasure to meet you. Iced tea?"

She nodded.

How changed she was. She slowly struggled down the companionway to sit in the salon for privacy, with the hatches all open for the constant breeze.

"Hands lifted us aboard the Japanese tanker. Part of our raft had exploded, and the rest sank," she said softly, as Zeb and Nels leaned forward in disbelief. "I told the Captain, 'Please take my gear, it's all I have to give you.' I saw Brad's face for the last time, alive, when we were picked up. *Bravo* was a boat that did not bring us home. I still don't know how he and I had the strength to survive so long in that raft. In Tokyo, I was taken immediately to the hospital, had no memory, and was treated for shock. I couldn't walk for two weeks. Our papers were gone. They were very good to me."

"Shouldn't you be home recuperating with your family?"

"I've done that. I came from Long Island to JFK, and flew here. To see you, Dutch. And Nels."

"Why?"

"I want to finish what Brad and I began..." She stopped and took a sip of her iced tea. "Last week, my brother Curtis drove me to Eighth Street. I'd called Amy's mother to learn Amy and Zoe were both in New York. Brilliant! Together! I surprised them. And they shocked me, telling me everything. All night long, together, the three of us. Crying, laughing. An unbelievable night!"

"She told you how we survived on *Quadriga*?"

"Every bit of it," she said. "How remarkable they both were. We finished three bottles of wine."

The chicken sandwiches, freshly made by Chef Nels, were delicious, enjoyed with more iced tea. Now they chatted about Nels' school. Some memories that had them smiling. Dutch waited. For something. He knew not.

"While Amy misses you, of course, she's thrilled to be working on her album, *Sail to the Morning Sun*" dedicated to you, Dutch."

"She's why I'm alive and *Quadriga's* afloat."

They sat, silently, together, while cheerful vacationing sailors on the dock walked by his boat.

Dutch took a drink, swallowing deeply; "So, why are you here, Beth?"

Beth took a deep breath. Speaking slowly so that he got every nuance, "You and Nels are taking on the Atlantic. I want to, as well. It was part of my dream. With Brad. That we'd sail. Around Europe. I asked Amy. If she'd mind terribly... if I might crew for you. As a friend, of course."

Stunned at this request, he asked, "What did Amy say?"

"First she said no. Then she cried. About me losing Brad. While the night wore on, we three talked, cried, drank, and laughed. Then we all fell into a deep sleep. When she awoke, she woke me. She said she couldn't, wouldn't hold you back, Dutch, from your sailing dreams. Or hold me back from recovery. She said that she had no power to do so. But go, Beth, she said. Yes, go."

As Beth spoke, Dutch looked out beyond and above the harbor to the hills of Grenada that circled The Carenage. This was coming too fast. Her voice pulled him back.

"She understood I need to get back to sea. Dutch, you're almost family. I know you well, respect you. It would be easy for me to crew for you," Beth said.

Dutch's mind whirled, wretched about Brad, stunned having Beth sitting right here on his boat, shocked at her frailty, and ambivalent about Amy's permission. He stood and looked up at the mast. What to do? Maybe *Quadriga* could help him.

Beth's voice again. "Amy gave me her blessings, joking I'd be able to keep you out of trouble."

Taking a long breath, and looking out beyond *Quadriga*, again, Dutch turned to his son. "Nels, we've an important request from Captain Turner."

"Okay, Dad! Yes, Captain Turner?"

"I request permission, Captain and Nels, to make the Atlantic Ocean passage with you. While I hope you'll say yes, I understand if you decline. It's your trip together. You can see I'm not strong, and I'd slowly be building my strength back up. But I can take the helm and navigate, and I can stay in one of the quarter berths in the main cabin. Of course, by the way, I love to play chess."

Nel's eyes brightened; "I always beat Dad!"

Dutch and his son gazed at each other, while she continued. "We had a memorial service for Brad in Oyster Bay. My love and grief for Brad will always be. But, I can't live in a city. Dutch, you understand. When you tire of me, simply say so and I'll get off the boat. When I'm ready to do something new with my life, I'll leave. We sail, it is understood, as friends."

Dutch's mind still tumbled, thinking of consequences, a third person, who they knew and respected. He turned to his son, "Nels, what do you say?"

The boy shouted, "Dad, are you kidding? Welcome aboard, Captain Turner."

"And you, Dutch?"

"Welcome aboard, Beth."

"As I insist on paying my share, I'll contribute ten thousand dollars for expenses aboard *Quadriga*. It's part of the insurance money from *Bravo*'s loss. If we need more, I have it. This money can't sit in a bank, it must float!"

"That's not necessary, unless you make a big sailing mistake!" He grimaced. "Why did I say that, to you? I make mistakes all the time. Shit, I'm thoughtless, as usual."

She smiled. "Its fine, Dutch."

"Beth, I have three questions," Dutch said, "First, are you ready to board? Second, where's your duffel so we can bring it aboard and get you comfortable?"

"Third?"

"How long will you allow me to be Captain of my own ship?"

A ray of laughter shone through her thin, translucent skin. "On this crossing, all I want to be is a rider on the tide. I respect Nels' time with you. I have a driver waiting. The duffel, some stores and books are in the van. He'll bring them down."

"You took a big chance, flying here," Dutch said, rubbing his eyes. Still in disbelief.

"It seemed the only thing to do. Everyone feels sorry for the widow. The one who survived! And you have another navigator. I'm to ride gunshot."

"Don't make that joke," he said. "You do know how to use a Walther and rifle?"

She smiled.

A few days later, *Quadriga* motored out of the harbor bound for the Canary Islands, possibly Candeleria on Tenerife. Dutch was at the helm while Beth and Nels played chess on a magnetic board in the cockpit. "I can see this is going to be quite a crossing. You two seem evenly matched," Dutch declared.

She smiled.

***

Logbook: of the Frumpy, British Fellow on the Dock in Grenada August, 1981

A tired British fellow, just off the plane from London, got out of a taxi and hurriedly walked onto the dock without stopping at the front office. Watching this overly dressed fellow in a heavy suit and a raincoat over one arm, Jonesy, the dock master, followed behind him. The fellow, puffing from his sprint down the dock, stood, perspiring, and pulling out a big white handkerchief.

The dock master shielded his eyes against the sun, looking far to see *Quadriga* recede in the distance.

"Are you, perhaps, the dock master? You seem like the dock master?"

"Yes, sir. I'm Rufus Jones. How may I help you?"

"I'm Constable Thomas McNeil, Scotland Yard, working on a drug case."

"Well," Rufus said, smiling, "You are in the Caribbean, Constable."

"I'm after an American Hinckley yawl. We just received news it was docked here. Red hull. Sailed from the BVI to Montserrat, to Antigua. Down the chain. If you know anything, it's your duty to radio them immediately and call them in."

Jonesy smiled, masking it with his hand, brushing his hair:" Oh, sir that Hinckley you speak of was recently sold to old retired folks from Ithaca, New York, professors in their eighties. They had a paid deckhand. All the lines were fed into the cockpit. They wouldn't be what you're looking for, not worth your trouble. Real greenhorns. They were sailing north. We got red sailboats falling in and out of here all de time."

"We've been chasing a certain cartel for years. Getting closer."

"The persons you might want, I think, may have fled to Belize. Sold the boat to these people and left. Two weeks ago, going to San Pedro," he lied.

"We're looking for two guys, one British, one Caribbean. One named Desmond, the other Hallpike. Part of a big deal. Could be dead, or captured."

"I know nothin' 'bout dat. It's quiet around here. Come on, old chap, I'll buy you the finest Caribbean rum you've ever tasted at the Red Crab. Their seafood stew's the best," Jonesy said. "Come along!"

He took one more look into the horizon, wishing his friend a safe trip across the ocean. *Quadriga* was a boat that would bring them home.

***

In New York, Zoe had carefully stowed the ruby ring in a velvet box, uncertain of its direction. He had not asked her to come up to Manitoulin. She was relieved about that. At least, something.

Zoe traveled to Cambridge with Amy and met the Sandlers, who welcomed her with respect and support. Several sessions with the psychiatrist, and conferences with the lawyer, filled her in on the vast complexity of power, connections and subterfuge that seemed to dominate the Caribbean islands. All an integral part of her visit with the Sandlers.

"How we love you, Zoe," Amy's mother said, hugging her." You belong to us."

"I feel much better, even different," Zoe said. "I can't thank you enough. And I'm ready for a new career.

Glad to be finished with the Caribbean." She told Amy privately, "I don't know what's happening with Zeb in Ontario. It's so hard for someone else to understand what you and I went through. I'm grateful to your mom and dad for all the protection we quietly have…"

"You're my sister, and we have our mom and dad," Amy said, laughing.

***

Logbook: Of landline phone calls from Manitoulin to Manhattan, Late August, 1981

The phone call came from Zeb in his Kagawong farmhouse on Manitoulin. With a few glasses of rum under his belt, he felt expansive.

"Zoe, I hope you remember me, "he joked. "It's been awhile since we talked. How are you?"

One word. "Fine," she said, not coldly, then, "Please tell me about you."

"My brother's doing better. Manitoulin's wonderful in August and September. The nights are beautiful. In clear skies, the Milky Way stars are scattered across the sky over the farmhouse."

"I'm glad to hear your voice. That your brother is better. You sound good. I must tell you the news. While *Bravo* broke up and sank, that stupid leak, they were aboard the raft for twenty days. Miraculously, they were rescued by a Japanese freighter." She stopped. "But Brad was so weak he died aboard the freighter. But Beth's alive.

She recovered in a Tokyo hospital. Her family came to get her and brought her home to New York. She's doing okay."

"Oh my God," Zeb said. She heard Zeb crying. She, too, tears, together mourning the death of their friend.

Zoe said nothing about Beth sailing with Dutch. This was enough.

After a time, she said, "Can you handle more news? Good news?"

"Yes," he said.

"Amy's first professional album has been produced and is doing well. Under the name of Maya. It's called *Sail to the Morning Sun*. Since she's already hitting the charts, and no one knows who she is, which keeps leading to more sales. She has a manager who's working to expand her career.

"Amy deserves a break. I'm glad." Zeb asked again. "And you, Zoe, how're you doing?"

"I went up to Cambridge to meet Amy's parents. Dr. Sandler took me to their family psychiatrist, and I was glad to be able to work with him for ten days, Zeb. It was difficult, of course, this dynamic therapy. I feel better. Lighter. As well, Dr. Sandler has an extraordinary, quietly powerful network of friends and lawyers focused on the Caribbean."

"Zoe, oh my, to hear all this," Zeb sad, his voice sad. "All the things I couldn't do for you."

"Don't do that, Zeb. You did your best," she said. "Basically, that nothing has happened. Except that Amy and I were helped to deal with this."

"We were some lucky, eh? How's rough and tumble New York City?"

"When I returned, those fast moving crowds, waiting for traffic lights, and TV news drove me nuts. I'm no longer writing anything about the Caribbean. No hotels. No sugar-spun beaches. I've been asked to write for a New York music publicity firm. And I can be of help to Amy, although I don't think she needs it. Her manager, Jimmy Bloch, is someone she can lean on. They've been to dinner at my apartment." She asked, "Where is *Zephyr?*"

"She's been sailed up from Virgin Gorda. My friends who own the CYC dock in Gore Bay flew down and brought her up. He laughed. "They loved her so much, they made me an offer to buy her. If I do sell, it'll mean we've sailed free this year. So she's here in Gore Bay."

"Will you sell her?"

"Not yet. I'm busy running our businesses. I called because I wanted to hear your voice."

They said good night. Each to two beds, in two countries.

***

Logbook: On land, Zoe at home in New York City, September, 1981

Iverson Smith, at the British Virgin Islands Tourist Board in New York City, heard Zoe was in town. "Our trip leader's fallen ill. For old times' sake, Zoe, I desperately need you to help us out. Please lead this five-day sales trip for travel agents around the BVI for the Board."

"Must I?"

"You've got to; I need you!"

She actually felt well enough to accept this trip. While it was September, and the beginning hurricane season, she would never be alone, except in her room, and quick to see changes that had occurred in the BVI she knew so well. She'd also calibrate changes within herself. She felt fine getting on the airplane, changing in St. Thomas, taking the ferry to Road Town, where she met her group. She enjoyed every one of them, surprised at how effortless it was. All professionals. Or did she not care?

After her group took the ferry to Virgin Gorda, they settled into the Little Dix Bay Resort, she took them to the yacht harbour to enjoy the sunset and visit The Bath and Turtle Pub, to dance, drink and meet people. Her friend Rose, who owned the Pub, stood on the dock with a tall, good-looking man. Rose introduced Steve Robinson, from Stamford, Connecticut. He told her, "I retired from publishing this year. I bought a boat, *Yellow Cat*. Sailed it down in May. Rose tells me you know these waters."

"Bert Crane's boat?"

"Do you know him?"

"Only of him. Bert Crane owned a publishing company. My friend Amy worked for him."

"Crane sold me *Yellow Cat* and he went to a power boat. Care to see her below?"

She sighed, laughing at herself, knowing her curiosity would never die, unable to resist a sight inspection. She walked along the dock with him to his boat and she took her sandals off to board. *Yellow Cat* looked good. Going below, she looked at the navigation desk. "Is that a fax?"

"Yup, I've got the latest satellite linkups and I handle my investments from the boat," he said. "Surprising what one year in technology does. By the way, I'm a widower, here alone." He looked closely at her. "Would you have dinner with me tonight at the Bath and Turtle? You can tell me all about the Caribbean?"

What? She must have looked pretty good that afternoon. "No, thank you, I'm working with my group. We're together."

"Any single ones? I'll take you all out for dinner," he offered.

Not to be rude, she said, "Thank you. Perhaps another time." She quickly left his boat. Were there any answers to anything? What about the questions? At least, she was happy to be strong and able to ask new questions and find answers about the BVI. It had changed, new buildings up, and she was able to say hello to many old friends. And leave, getting back to New York.

***

Logbook: From the Farmhouse in Kagawong, Manitoulin Island, Mid-September, 1981

"These are second-rate burdens I'm handling these days," Zeb told Zoe, at night, on the phone from his farmhouse. "Life's back to ordinary. It seemed like we had all the time in the world."

"In many ways, we were lucky. Will you sell the boat?"

"No. Sometimes I go sleep on her in the harbor. I miss you there."

***

"I'm using my courage to stand alone again," Zoe told Amy. "While Zeb and I talk regularly, I've realized our failure. My failure. We could never have a fused existence. I'm glad to take that editing job. New field. New writing life. But no new men."

***

Logbook: Of the Sailing Songstress, October, 1981

Time syncopated, and soared to a staccato of life for Amy. *Sail to the Morning Sun* went into distribution. Jimmy worked easily, while MAYA learned how to be on talk shows with their publicity directors. No longer the girl from Cambridge, nor the sailor, veiled, but delighted in developing a new identity.

One afternoon, "I'm sure it seems like, once upon a time, you had a rough go in your life. But whatever it was, has past. You're the boss of your life now, and I support you."

"You're too good to be true, boss," she said, as they sat having coffee at his desk in the office.

"I'm not your boss, I work for you. You've validated yourself on your own terms, as a singer, writer, and musician."

"What do we do next, Jimmy?"

"We get royalties, from the radio and record sales. But the big money, Amy, is from live performances. It you want to do more, do better, you've got to do promotional shows on the radio and TV, and do live dates. It's up to you. But you've got to get there. But I won't push you ahead of yourself." And

"Nor control me," she said.

"Who said anything about that? We're a big company. My staff has me running all day. You are one in our big stable."

"I apologize for being rude," Amy said. The fear was there. She sighed.

"Of course, Amy."

"If I'm not being rude again, Jimmy, what do you personally want next?"

He smiled. "I have basically everything I need, my career and my two sons are doing well. And Amy dear, I mean, MAYA, growing your career is important. There's something about you that touches me, a sadness that I can relate to. My sadness is about my wife, her cancer and her death. Work's the best solution."

"Also friendship and community are most important to me, Amy," he said, gazing at her.

"My kids are asking for you. Would you come and play with us on Saturday afternoon at the park?"

"Oh thanks, but I've made plans. Another time."

***

When Amy and Zoe took a martial arts class together, to maintain and strengthen their physical skills, being attacked 'in class' seemed funny to them.

"When I'm with Jimmy, at work, I feel solid. He is a good manager. I can be my own person."

"You mentioned that he's very attractive! Do you think he's dating these days?"

"That's not what interests me," Amy said. "He validates me on my own terms."

"Getting real technical here, huh, girlie."

"Leave me alone. I'm happy we produce music."

"If you say so," Zoe said.

"Stay in your own lane, my friend," Amy said.

"Ha, your next song. I hear it."

At dinner one evening, Amy handed Zoe an unopened letter that found its way to her at the recording company. Amy was getting letters from fans. From Barbados, a Cora Hallpike. Amy froze; "How did she find me?"

"Your music about the Caribbean travels all through the islands."

Amy held it. "I'm terrified. Zoe, I'm throwing this away…"

"Maybe we need to learn something," Zoe said.

> "Dear Amy, Everett, my husband, disappeared. Some months later, I was able to move to Barbados, where everything felt safe and new. I heard one of your songs on the radio, and I am writing to you at your music company. Meeting you, seeing you sailing with Dutch gave me hope that a woman's life could be as rich and full as that of a man's. You were strong and never seemed afraid. Maybe my life could be like that if I were not so timid a soul. I started my sewing business in Barbados in a shop near a major hotel. I'm doing well. My daughter is growing, a happy child with her aunts and uncles around her. For some reason, I believe my new life has something to do with you, inspiring me to enjoy the new freedom that has emerged in my life.
>
> Sincerely, Cora Hallpike."

"It's well written," Zoe said. "My mind thinks maybe the FBI or DOA put her up to this? Are you going to answer the letter?" "Would you?"

Chapter Twenty

Logbook: of Yacht Odyssey, Long Island Sound, October, 1981

October winds were brisk. Zoe loved sailing as a guest on *Odyssey* with her friends, Barbara and Jay from Port Washington.

Back home in New York City, she opened her door to hear the phone ring.

"Zeb calling. The apple trees are full on Manitoulin. They need picking. I've upgraded our investments. Robbie's holding his own. Listen, Zoe, I've got a new idea for you."

"What?"

"You're curious, imaginative, you like people and have terrific writing skills. There's a fast-growing radio station in Little Current called The Island 100.7. They're looking for a Publicity Director. The owners, Kelly and Craig are terrific. You'd be writing stories, traveling between Sudbury and Manitoulin, around the North Shore, Toronto, and to the music awards. This might be exciting for you, a new country, and a new home and…. your own pick-up truck."

Before she could answer, he said "I put a fax aboard, and a phone. I'm not selling her. She'll charter out next summer. Would you please come up?"

"Thanks, but I don't know…"

"Aboard, you cried in your sleep. My weak point— my daughters are always sore at me for this, is that I run from conflict. I realize how I tried to hold you captive, pretending we were in Paradise."

"What's making you ask me?"

"It's harvest time. My daughters want to meet you. They say I'm an old crank these days."

"You left me."

"I was afraid for my brother, our funds. A man has to provide. Come up!"

"To live in the context of your world, Manitoulin, with your definitions?"

"In the farmhouse, you can decorate it any way you want. You'll have a home, an office, a telephone, a pick-up truck and your own canoe!"

"What's making you offer this to me?"

"Don't you know, Zoe?"

***

On a leisurely Saturday afternoon, Amy and Zoe sat in a restaurant over lunch. Amy's hair was red, and her new makeup and clothes were the latest.

Who can recognize this new singing artist, MAYA?" Amy asked, laughed. But looked at Zoe. "You look so damn sad. Talk to me, pal!"

"I'm busy, with work, friends and safe in my own home. Three locks on the door," Zoe said. "So why am I whining? I'm bored. And still afraid. And, why aren't you getting closer to Jimmy?

"If I get close, and he knows me, he'll hate me."

"Stupid girl, you're now spending Sunday afternoons with him and his sons at the park. Those kids love you."

"We're friends. I need to be safe, and learn how to work this career. Stop bugging me!"

The waitress they knew, as they met there often, came to the table. "Zoe, didn't you, a while back, live on a sailboat in the Caribbean?"

"Why, Maisie?"

"There's a feature on the front page in The New York Times about drugs in the Caribbean. I thought of you two." Maisie handed the newspaper to Zoe.

Zoe took the newspaper, and quickly read that the US DEA and Scotland Yard were tracking down rumours of a big drug shipment, over the past year, that was still in hiding somewhere. She read aloud, "The DEA figured out the cartel was shipping the product from Columbia to Mexico through small personal boats. They had a tip on two major drug lords, who mysteriously disappeared several months ago. It is thought they may have fled to South America. Authorities raided Hallpike's Chicken Farm on the Island of Montserrat to find residues of cocaine among the chicken pens." She stopped reading.

"Stoned chickens, dead us. I almost stopped feeling afraid."

"Did you ever answer Mrs. Hallpike's letter?"

"You know I didn't."

"If Mrs. Desmond is able to contact us, we've got a problem."

"Is this where the nothing stops and something happens, where it gets worse?"

They phoned Amy's father, who talked to his lawyers, and maritime buddies.

"Stay quiet. We're working through this. Live your quiet lives, girls."

***

"You're dragging, Zoe."

"So are you, Amy."

"I'm fine. Have you ever seen me skinnier, busier? I'm dating again. But that's a crap shoot. You know in three minutes." Zoe declared. "And you're in love with Jimmy. Admit it!"

***

Logbook: New York City, November 1981

Amy and Zoe often received postcards from Dutch, sailing from the Galapagos Islands to Sydney, Australia. Postcards came separately from Beth. Amy read the post cards with a small twinge, appreciating that Beth was discreet. Amy had cherished her own time aboard *Quadriga*, the sailboat that had carried her further toward her dreams. And, *Quadriga* was making an odyssey.

Logbook: of Unrequited Love, January, 1982

"Hello Amy," Zeb said "I'm calling from Sudbury. "I bought five dozen of your cassette and albums. Waiting for you to make an LP. Love 'em. I give them to everyone I know."

"That's so nice! How are you doing?"

"Fine, but missing Zoe who aggravated me in all the right ways."

"Spoken like an astute Canadian," Amy said gently. "I'm sure she told you she did well in Cambridge with my therapist. Please call her."

"But she he keeps brushing me off."

"That never stops you, Captain. Keep after her. By the way, you were wonderful with me and Dutch. Thank you for taking care of us. The latest post card from *Quadriga* arrived two weeks ago from Sydney. We can't tell if Dutch and Beth are friends or lovers."

"Do you care?"

"I'm glad for them, if that's so. I have a busy new life," She paused. "Strike, Captain, you don't know hot your iron is!"

***

"Dear Zoe, I'll be in New York City next week for business. I would like to see you. Please come to the restaurant, *one if by Land, Two if by Sea*, on Barrow Street. I have news you'll be quite glad to know on many counts. Please join me at 6 p.m. for dinner next Thursday. Love, Zeb."

***

Logbook: of Amy, phoning her Mother from New York City to Cambridge

"Mom, Zoe was not going to dinner." Amy said. "But with news in *The New York Times*, and possible changes in everything we know, she said what the heck. When she got there, she said Zeb looked so fit, and his blue eyes mesmerized her. She'd forgotten those eyes. That goofy smile. He showed her plans to design a new study for her in the Kagawong farmhouse. Also, he bought an apartment in Sudbury near Laurentian University. It's a lively city where they can go for dinners, concerts, theatre and shopping. He showed a picture of what her new pickup truck would look like. Not used. And a canoe, a kayak, a king-size bed. And Wi-fi."

Her mother chuckled. "Oh, oh, our dear independent Zoe. Was she able to listen?"

"Yes, mom, she was able to let down her guard. She told him all about her extensive therapy in Cambridge, her unresolved feelings toward her submissive mother, mixed with the early death of her dominant father. How Zoe always had to be boss. She had never told us about that. From those moments that she slaughtered Hallpike aboard *Quadriga*, when she began therapy working with the doctor, she began to trigger and free herself in ways she didn't know."

"You girls have such courage. Maybe she'll find new courage to take the step to Zeb."

"I promised I'd never laugh at her denim clothes, work boots, the pickup, or the cows in the back forty."

"What do you mean, 'promised,' Amy?"

"Mom, she's agreed to move up to live with him in Kagawong, redo the farmhouse, meet his daughters and learn how to drive a pick-up. And she has a buyer for her apartment here."

"Pardon me, while I pour a Scotch."

***

Anchored on different islands, countries and harbours of the world.

Beth and Dutch, on *Quadriga*, were in the busy middle of their circumnavigation. While *Bravo,* was sunk in the South Pacific, Beth was still afloat. Parts of her sailing dream were coming true; she and Dutch were evenly matched in the game of chess.

Zephyr was tied at the dock in Gore Bay on Manitoulin Island. The North Shore of Lake Huron and the fascinating inlets and island, the startling pink and dark rocks of the Benjamin Islands, fascinated Zoe. So that no one was Captain in their household, they adopted a huge St. Bernard, who they named Captain. Zoe learned to drive a stick shift. She took a delightful job at the radio station in Little Current, handling sales promotion and publicity in the music business. She began to travel throughout Northern Ontario, Toronto and to the Canadian music shows.

***

In New York City, during the fine reviews of MAYA'S second album, just released and rising on the charts, Amy was having a late dinner with Jimmy, in a restaurant near the studio.

"Amy, you know by now how much I respect and love you," Jimmy said, reaching for her hand. "I want a life with you."

Amy blinked. Here it was. She looked lovingly at him. What could the rest of her life be like? What shards of living were still stolen from her? Her breath at that moment, rose and fell. The way water rose and fell, the way darkness and light rose and fell. The breath was there.

"Jimmy," she said, "I have something to tell you."

Acknowledgments

Even in creative writing and our sailing life, we can do nothing alone. My thanks to:

Darcy Brason-Lediett, for his delightful wit, amazing style and continual wisdom. I cherish his Canadian smarts and brightwork along this voyage.

Roy Eaton, Commodore Emeritus of the Little Current Sailing Club, Manitoulin Island. Dear friend, severest critic and constant inspirer to "Come about and anchor the damn boat!"

Nancy Beckman, Richard Beckman, Susan Blomberg, Myril-Lynn Brason-Lediett, Charlotte Brem, Charlie Brown, Chris Carline, Judi Cartman, Michael Erskine, Treva Farmen, Sandy Fraser, Paul Jenkins, Brenda Fetterly Khan, Marlene and William Jewell, Joe Ann Lewis, Don MacDonald, Chris Phillips, Karin and Larry Rappaport, Jessie Stevens, Ernie and Dave Shineman, Simon Trussler, Leon Tarasenko, Sue Wheatley and Christine White.

Made in United States
Troutdale, OR
06/13/2024

20476703R10217